UNEXPECTED DANGER

UNEXPECTED DANGER

BESTSELLING, AWARD-WINNING AUTHOR
PENNY ZELLER

Dedicated to the Lord, who is our refuge and strength.

I have said these things to you, that in me you may have peace. In the world you will have tribulation. But take heart; I have overcome the world. ~ John 16:33

Chapter 1

The noise jolted her from a sound sleep.

Who could be texting her at this time of night? Her first thought was Brodie. But no, he wouldn't send a text.

Not out of nowhere.

Not after the way she'd broken his heart.

It could be Mom.

But no, she rarely contacted Londyn.

A friend, perhaps?

Was there an emergency?

Londyn Siegler reached an arm across the span of the nightstand to her cell phone. She opened one eye and clicked on the text icon from a number she didn't recognize.

HELLO.

She returned the phone to the nightstand and rolled back over. Likely someone texting the wrong person.

The ping sounded once more. Whoever it was needed to save their communication until morning. She flipped the phone over again.

HELLO, BEAUTIFUL.

Londyn groaned. Most likely some lovelorn weirdo in a different time zone accidentally texting the wrong number at

1:45 a.m. And in all caps?

She was about to replace it on the nightstand again when another text popped up before she could clear her phone.

YOU'RE EVEN BEAUTIFUL WHEN YOU'RE SLEEPING.

Her heart pounded in her chest, and she instinctively peered around her bedroom just to be sure no one was watching her sleep. There would be no easy way for anyone to enter her room, not with the front door and windows locked. Raindrops splattered against the window, and lightning flashed across the sky, lighting up the slim cracks edging the area where the improperly cut blinds didn't reach.

Londyn sat up, slipped out of bed, and padded across the wood floor. Cautiously, she peeked out the window. Tree branches waved in the wind, and a whistling sound from the wind entering the house through the poorly fitted window meshed with the sound of the spitting rain.

It was then that she saw him.

Or at least it looked like a "him". But she couldn't be completely sure.

Londyn rubbed a clear spot on the window where her breath had fogged it up for a better view.

Across the road in front of a nearly identical apartment building, someone lurked in the shadows, a dark-colored hood secured around his head.

He or she looked up, making eye contact with her.

She shivered, and her heart palpitated. Her feet refused to move and remained planted in place.

Seconds ticked by before the person retreated into the darkness of the night.

Londyn gripped the windowsill. Sweat chilled her forehead. Was he the same one sending her the texts? Or was it two different random people with no connection?

Should she call the police? Wait until tomorrow? Londyn left her post at the window. The hairs on the back of her neck stood on end, and she rushed to shut the bedroom door, lock it, and stand with her back to it, willing her heart to stop pounding incessantly in her ears.

Lord, please help me. Please let it have only been a nightmare.

She ignored the niggling voice in her head that reminded her she rarely had nightmares, or at least ones she remembered.

Weak legs carried her to her bed. Staring at her cell phone, she finally worked up the courage to check it for another message. Her hands trembled, and Londyn nearly dropped it as her shaking fingers hit the "block" button.

She'd not delete the texts—that much she knew from Brodie's stint as a sheriff.

Always keep the evidence.

She'd heard him say that more than once, and she'd even heard his dad say it a time or two when the older Mr. Brenneman was the Pronghorn Falls County Sheriff.

Questions swarmed through her mind. If the man on the street and the texts *were* connected, who was he, and why was he contacting her? How had he gotten her number?

The rain continued to pound against the window, and in the upstairs apartment, someone walked across the floor.

Was the man still outside?

Londyn flung off the covers and again strode to the window. She strained to see across the street as raindrops obscured her vision. This time, no one was there.

Had it been her imagination?

She lifted the phone and re-read the texts. While the stranger in the night *could have* been a figment in her mind, the texts were very real. She should probably double-check that the front door was locked. She rubbed her arms from the spring chill in the air and shuddered as she crept to the living room. The glow from the streetlight confirmed the lock was secure.

Londyn froze in place for a second. In her months in a new city, she'd never once felt threatened or fearful. Living in the shabby apartment building with other tenants, she'd never once considered it to be anything but a new phase of starting over.

But now? There'd be no sleeping the remainder of the evening.

She wiped her clammy hands on her oversized t-shirt and tiptoed back to her room. If she were still in Pronghorn Falls, she could call Brodie and tell him. He'd be at her apartment in an instant, reassuring her he'd do all he could to protect her. He'd hunt down whoever it was sending her the texts or enlist the help of the PD if it was in their jurisdiction.

She wasn't in Pronghorn Falls, but instead over three hundred miles away. She opened the nightstand drawer to reveal the pistol Brodie purchased two years ago for her birthday.

A tremor ran through her that she may need to defend herself.

Should she call 911 and report a suspicious person? Years ago, when Brodie's dad was the sheriff, he gave a talk at a self-defense class Londyn attended. *If something isn't right, call law enforcement. It could be that you stop a crime from happening because you reported something.*

Yet, the man was gone, so it was likely the police wouldn't be able to find him. It was the middle of the night, and the rainstorm intensified. She decided to wait until tomorrow morning and visit the police station to report the man and the texts. She didn't have to arrive at work until nine, so there would be time.

Finally, at 6:30, she awoke from a night of tossing and turning, unprepared to face the day. She opened her Bible to the Book of John, which she'd started re-reading two weeks ago. The words of John 16:33 leaped from the page. *"I have said these things to you, that in me you may have peace. In the world you will have tribulation. But take heart; I have overcome the world."*

Brodie removed his cowboy boots and swiped an arm across his forehead. It had been a day.

A good day because two teens had been found alive and rescued.

The Lord had certainly answered the prayers of numerous individuals, not only that the kids would be found, but that those involved in search and rescue would be kept safe as well.

He shrugged off his coat, far too thick and warm now that he was back in Pronghorn Falls and not gallivanting around in a remote area near the summit of Pronghorn Peak. He really should take a shower first since his clothes were covered in caked mud, evidenced by the chips of crusted dirt flaking off his pant legs. But his growling stomach prompted an alternative.

Brodie turned on the bathroom faucet, scraping a plethora of dirt crusted on his calloused hands and under his fingernails. Weariness tugged at every part of him. He caught a glimpse of himself in the medicine cabinet mirror. Dark circles underlined his eyes, splotches of filth covered his cheeks and forehead, and the facial hair he needed to remove from his upper lip and chin was speckled with debris from crawling through brush and hiking up the steep mountainside.

Just another day on the job.

Not actually, for rescuing two teens who'd gotten themselves lost and were unprepared for the spring weather in the rugged Pronghorn Mountains wasn't typically in his job description. But Search and Rescue was short a few volunteers, and Brodie had heard the call come in while he was patrolling the county. Sure, as law enforcement, he made a difference every day, but this was more tangible.

The two teens, frightened and already experiencing the beginnings of hypothermia, clustered in a cave near the peak. No food except for the two granola bars one of the boys brought along with him. No water, no blanket, no jackets except lightweight hoodies, and no boots, only flimsy tennis shoes. The sun had started to set, and one of the fourteen-year-old boys' moms hadn't heard from him in some time. Thankfully, he'd told another friend they were planning to hike up to Pronghorn Peak.

Not the best time of year to climb to higher elevations. While most of the snow had melted, thick, chalky, clay-like sludge covered trails and roads, some of which were still closed. Temps during the day were a pleasant fifty degrees. Temps at night fell to the mid-thirties and below.

Brodie opened the refrigerator door and removed some leftovers from the lasagna Mom had made when he'd joined his family for dinner at her house last night. He removed the tinfoil, scooped a generous portion onto a plate, and popped it into the microwave. With a plate of food and a glass of milk in hand, he shuffled to the kitchen table and prayed. "Lord, You are faithful. Thank You for leading us to the teens and for letting it be a successful rescue attempt. So much could have gone wrong, but You guided our every step and protected all those involved. For that I am grateful."

His prayer concluded with gratitude for the food and requests to keep his family and Londyn safe.

Londyn. The thought of her jolted him from his tired state. How was she? Did she regret moving? Had she texted Mom lately? How did she like living in the city?

None of those questions would be answered tonight. Brodie shoveled a few more bites into his mouth, willing himself not to fall asleep at the table.

Chapter 2

It had been a wearisome day. First, a trip to the police department to report the texts and the suspicious man, then a full day of work.

Londyn hung her jacket on the hook just inside the door when her phone rang. Because the number came up as unavailable, she allowed it to go to voicemail. A few seconds later, her notifications dinged, indicating a message. Likely someone telling her she owed money on her student loans, although she'd never attended college. Or a spam call about a car warranty, which she'd never purchased since her car was over ten years old.

She scrolled to the voicemail icon and clicked it.

Only silence.

Londyn disconnected. It could be just someone with the wrong number. Or someone who had butt-dialed her. Or it could be related to the texts she'd received. Or it could be nothing at all.

Strange.

Could it be related to the man she'd seen outside the apartment yesterday? Or to the texts she'd received?

Perhaps she could call and see if Mom was available to

talk. A stretch, but they hadn't spoken since Mom's most recent wedding. Perhaps a call would alleviate some stress, and maybe Mom would have some advice regarding the texts. Of course, the chances were slim. But still...

Londyn scrolled through her contacts and pressed the number beside Mom's image.

Mom answered on the fifth ring just as Londyn was about to hang up.

"Hello?" Mom was laughing as she said the single word, and there was a male voice in the background. Likely Jason, Mom's newest husband, although Londyn couldn't be positive because she'd only met him twice.

"Hi, Mom."

"Londyn, how are you?" Mom sounded distracted.

"Fine, except for some scary..."

"Londyn, you should see this place. Jason and I are having such a fantastic time. Amelia Island is just gorgeous, and there's *so* much to do here. Yesterday, we visited Fernandina Beach, and let's just say I may have done a little too much shopping!" Mom giggled, and Londyn heard Jason in the background mentioning that she had, in fact, done *a lot* of shopping.

"I was hoping..."

"And here in a few," Mom continued, "we're headed to Amelia Island State Park for some horseback riding. Definitely going to be different horseback riding than what we did in Pronghorn Falls. This will be along the beach, just like in the movies."

"That sounds like a lot of fun. Look, Mom..."

"Oh, it will be. We'll be going birding too. At this rate, we may just pack up all our stuff in Phoenix and move to the beach."

Jason's voice boomed across the line. "I'm all for that."

They'd just moved to Arizona from Pronghorn Falls, and now they wanted to move again?

Londyn was about to attempt to get a word in edgewise again when Mom spoke. "Have you heard from Logan?"

Londyn couldn't remember the last time she'd heard from her younger brother. "No, I haven't."

"Me either. Look, Londyn, I gotta go. Thanks for calling, and we'll chat soon, okay?"

Mom didn't wait for Londyn to respond before clicking off. Londyn held the phone in front of her, discouraged once again that she'd heard all about Mom's life, but Mom hadn't taken the time to even ask about hers. Nothing new there. No wonder Mom had been married five times. There was room in her life only for herself.

She sighed. It wasn't like she could call Dad either. Londyn hadn't seen or heard from him since the divorce. His decision to all but disown her and Logan hurt in a way Londyn wasn't sure she could ever truly overcome. He'd married his much-younger secretary, the one who'd been the catalyst that caused his and Mom's divorce. In short, there was no room in his life for his previous family. When he replaced Mom, he'd also replaced Londyn and Logan as well.

She pushed aside the rejection she'd experienced from both parents. That was another thing she missed about Pronghorn Falls—Aileen Brenneman. Brodie's mom was like the mother she'd always wanted but never had. Brodie and Roarke had no idea how blessed they were to have Aileen for their mom—someone who actually cared. Someone who loved them. Someone who was always there.

Shouldn't a mother be concerned about her daughter? Maybe ask how things were going? Be there when her daughter was struggling with something?

A feeling of loss and homesickness enveloped her. If only she could go back in time.

———

As she always did, Londyn checked the front door before settling into bed. Since receiving the texts and seeing the person across the street last night, she found herself checking the locks several times.

She turned out all of the lights except for the one in the hall, and crept to the front door. The apartment's front yard and adjoining street were empty. Calm, save for the gentle rustling of the oak tree in the front yard. The streetlight flickered, its yellow hue casting an eerie glow.

Dread twisted in her gut. Were last night's events a one-time occurrence, or...

Londyn reminded herself that no one and nothing was out there. That she was safe inside her apartment. Safe behind a locked door.

She inched closer, double-checking that the door was fully locked. Then she checked again.

Londyn pressed on the door, reassuring herself it was completely closed as well, even though such affirmation wasn't necessary. The door wouldn't lock if it wasn't closed.

A car traveled down the street, its lights illuminating the road ahead, and she jumped. When it continued on its route, she pressed a hand to her chest, praying God would calm her erratic pulse.

One final time, Londyn checked the door, then the window, leaning forward and pressing her nose against the glass to peer outside. All was quiet.

She turned around and retreated, satisfied that she'd be safe from whoever lurked outside.

Until she heard it.

The clicking of a door handle. The turning of the doorknob. Was it her imagination? Something else? Or...

She whipped her head around to look out the front door's peephole.

Someone stood there wearing a dark-colored hoodie and a face mask, staring at the door. She screamed, backed up, and tripped over the leg of a small table. Londyn tumbled backward and hit the carpeted floor hard. It jarred her, wrenched her neck, and sent a jolt of pain through her elbow. She grasped the edge of the couch to stabilize herself.

The clicking again caused her heart to stall in her throat.

He was trying to get in.

Whoever it was pounded on the door loudly, as if indicating it was an emergency to get inside.

Begging her limbs to cooperate, she crawled away from the living room and once she reached the hall, stood, and ran on shaky legs to her bedroom. She shut the door, locked it, and shoved the side table against it before snagging her cell phone from the dresser and calling 911.

"911, what is your emergency?"

"Someone is trying to get into my apartment." Her voice sounded breathless and barely audible.

"Someone is trying to get into your apartment?"

"Yes." She put the phone on speaker, tossed it on the bed, opened the nightstand drawer, and retrieved her gun. She may need it.

"What is your address?"

Londyn rattled off the address.

"Police are en route. Where are you at?"

"I'm in my bedroom."

"Is that in the back of the apartment?"

"Yes, to the west side of it."

The operator told her to stay away from the window and to hide in the closet if she could. She did as the operator said, wedging herself among her clothes and shoes.

The pounding on the front door continued.

The operator was keeping tabs, but Londyn barely heard a word she said.

Finally, she noticed lights again coming down the street. She cautiously edged near the window and quickly peeked out before retreating. A police car was parked in front of the apartments. Londyn released the breath she'd been holding and returned her gun to the drawer.

"Officers have arrived," said the operator. "They'll do a perimeter check outside, then come to your door to ask you some questions."

"Thank you." Londyn disconnected, unlocked the bedroom door, and waited until the officers knocked on the front door.

She peeked through the peephole, then opened it, and the officers introduced themselves. "We'd like to get some information," said the burly bald one, who introduced himself as Officer Gann. He asked her some generic questions about her name, age, and the length of time she'd resided in the apartment.

"Can you tell us what happened?" This, from the shorter, squattier officer named Nelson.

Londyn reiterated her story of how she'd seen the man across the street last night, the texts she'd received, and how she'd reported that to the police station earlier that day. Her words tumbling from her mouth as though she were an auctioneer, Londyn told the officers what had just happened.

"Can you give us a physical description?"

"It was dark, but I did notice he or she was wearing a black sweatshirt with a hood and a black mask. Or maybe the hoodie was navy." She clasped her hands so tightly her knuckles turned white. Her stomach clenched. What if the person had gotten in? "He was wearing dark colored clothing and a mask."

"You mentioned it was a he."

"I guess I was just assuming. I think, yes, I think it was a man."

"What about his build?"

"Slim from what I could see. He was taller than me. Maybe six feet?" How could she not have done a better job gathering such critical information?

Officer Gann jotted down notes. "We didn't see anyone outside, so he must have retreated when he heard us coming. Do you know of anyone who would do this?"

"No."

"Any enemies?"

"I haven't lived here very long. Probably not long enough to make enemies. Unless..." The thought hit her suddenly.

"Yes?"

"I work for a company that handles the billing for several doctors and clinics. Maybe someone was unhappy with me because I was attempting to collect payment. Or maybe it's someone who was already turned over to collections."

Officer Nelson tilted his head. "Anyone in particular lately who might be unhappy with you?"

"There is one who comes to mind. He has refused to pay his outstanding debt, although we've done all we can to work with him."

"Do you have a name for us?"

"Yes. BJ Nuss."

"Has Mr. Nuss threatened you in any way?"

Londyn attempted to recall the most recent conversation she had with Mr. Nuss last week. It hadn't been a pleasant one. "We've talked several times, beginning with a plan for him to make payments toward his sizable bill. He has failed to remit any payments since our agreement. After a lengthy discussion where I informed him that we unfortunately had to turn him over to collections, he yelled some obscenities before ending the call by telling me that if I did not find a way to get the bill back from collections, I would pay a steep price." As she said the words, she realized how much of a motive Mr. Nuss, whom she'd never met, had.

"Have you ever seen this Mr. Nuss?"

"I have not."

"Is it common for you or your coworkers to receive threats if you turn someone over to collections?"

Had she ever heard of such an occurrence before? She hadn't, at least not from Jasmine or Dustin, although her boss, Sonja, mentioned some problematic people. "Not that I'm aware of, but I'm sure it does happen. There's probably a reason why this isn't the most coveted job out there. We do our best to work with people and give them several chances, especially since we know times are hard and medical expenses can be steep, but even though my supervisor gives us some leeway, at some point, our hands are tied."

"Have you had any other issues lately with someone trying to break in?"

"No, but I have been receiving some questionable texts. I reported those to the police department this morning."

"Did Mr. Nuss threaten you during the other times you spoke to him?"

Londyn bit her lip. That had been over the course of a few months. She talked to numerous people daily. But she would remember if he'd threatened her. "No, he didn't. He wasn't happy, but I don't remember any threats, not like this most recent time."

"Did you inform your supervisor?"

"After I spoke with him, I did tell her about the incident and filled out a form. I didn't think too much about it as far as danger goes, because some people are just so angry and say things in the heat of the moment. While it rattled me, I attempted to brush it aside the best I could, hoping that would be the end of it."

"Does Mr. Nuss live in Rowland?"

"Yes, I believe he does." Londyn attempted to visualize Mr. Nuss's address, but with the constant flow of accounts she dealt with each day, it was nearly impossible.

"We may need more information if we can't locate Mr. Nuss via the resources we have available to us." Both Officers Gann and Nelson stood. "We will do another perimeter check before we go, as well as patrol the neighborhood for the rest of the evening. In the meantime, if you see the man again, please call 911 immediately." Officer Gann offered his hand, and Londyn shook it.

"Thank you."

They exited into the shadowy night. Londyn locked the door and stood, her back to it for a few brief seconds. *Lord, please allow me to sleep in peace for You alone make me dwell in safety.* She quoted one of her favorite Psalms, calling upon the One who could protect her better than anyone could.

Chapter 3

Despite feeling God's peace overwhelm her, Londyn didn't get much sleep that night. The next morning, she awoke feeling tired and hoping to get through the day.

She tucked her gun inside her purse, intending to leave it in her glove compartment in her SUV. She wished she could take it into work with her, but according to the handbook, that would result in immediate termination.

God had kept her safe last night. He was faithful. And while she was, for the most part, alone in a new city, she was never *truly* alone. Yet, while her heart knew this, sometimes it failed to send the message to her brain.

Hence, the fretting last night before God's peace enveloped her at around two a.m.

She scanned her apartment. It was homey, decorated just the way she liked it, and although she'd never really preferred it as much as her apartment in Pronghorn Falls, it suited her. But it was a peculiar thing when the security of what should be a safe place was threatened. Wasn't someone's home supposed to be their sanctuary? It frightened her to think that anyone determined enough could breach any locked door or window.

Londyn attempted to push aside the paranoid thoughts that

infringed on her morning. Worry would do her no good. She gazed at the up-close view of herself in the bathroom mirror. Tiredness was etched on her face, and dark circles hovered beneath her eyes. Instead of being in her late twenties, she appeared twice as old.

Londyn fashioned her hair into a ponytail, slipped into a sweater and stylish jeans, and attempted to down some breakfast, although she lacked an appetite. The picture on the shelf in the living room drew her attention as it often did. It was one of her favorites with Brodie. They'd borrowed his dad's classic Chevy truck and had gone to the county fair. In the picture, she was holding the oversized stuffed teddy bear Brodie won for her. He had always been thoughtful that way, and she knew the crazy amount of money he'd spent on the tickets for the chance to win the bear would have enabled him to buy three or four. He hadn't given up until he'd won, typical of Brodie Brenneman.

If only things were different. If only things hadn't ended the way they had.

Londyn held the picture in her hands for a few more seconds before replacing it on the shelf. There was no sense in dwelling on things that would never be. She loved him, had broken his heart, and there was no repairing that, no matter the history they shared.

She snagged her purse from the counter and took a deep breath. She would need to be cognizant of her surroundings, keeping in mind all that Mr. Brenneman had taught her about situational awareness.

Londyn walked around the entire apartment and peered out each window, taking an extra few moments to study, in particular, the area outside of the front window. Nothing was out of the ordinary, and she saw no one outside except one of her neighbors backing out of the carport. She slipped out the front door, locked it, then double-checked a second time just to be sure before pivoting and walking to the covered carport hosting the renters' vehicles. The chill in the air and the gray clouds warned of rain. With all the moisture this year, at least there would be fewer wildfires.

Londyn peered inside the vehicle into the back seat, then climbed into her SUV. Rush hour traffic greeted her, something that she had never dealt with in Pronghorn Falls. She tapped her thumb on the steering wheel, silently willing the lengthy line of cars to proceed through the numerous stoplights so she could get to work on time. An occasional glance indicated a red sedan following a little too closely. She squinted, hoping to get a look at the driver. Was it the man who attempted to break in last night?

She didn't have time to take a detour. While Sonja, her boss, was a pleasure to work for, she would not condone lateness for any reason, barring an emergency. Punctuality was of utmost importance to her.

Londyn kept an eye on the car behind her. She'd be surprised if the driver didn't rear-end her before she made it to work. She turned right at the next stoplight, and thankfully, the red sedan didn't follow her. She zipped into the parking garage and again kept her wits about her as she walked through the doors of Zedde and Associates and collapsed into her chair in her cubicle. Her friend and coworker, Jasmine Kurtz, poked her head around the corner.

Jasmine's thick brows furrowed. "Wow, girl, what happened to you?"

"Just tired." She hadn't yet told Jasmine about the texts or the man.

"Are you all right?"

"I think so."

Another friend and coworker, Dustin Haack, stepped beside Jasmine with a box of donuts in his hands.

"Care for a donut, anyone?" He held out the box to Londyn and Jasmine.

Jasmine moistened her lips. "I don't know when I've ever passed up donuts." She reached for an apple fritter.

"You look like you've had a rough morning. Everything all right?"

Londyn appreciated Dustin's concern. "I think so. Just an arduous night."

"Anything I can do to help?" He reached inside the donut box and handed her a glazed, her favorite kind. "Have a donut. They fix everything."

She took the donut from him and set it on a napkin before following Jasmine and Dustin to the small rectangular table with the coffee pot, as she did every morning.

"Are you sure you're okay?" Dustin's brows knitted, his attention remaining on her as he awaited her answer.

"It was just…" The memory of the potential intruder crowded her mind again, and her throat tightened.

Jasmine put her arm around Londyn. "You want to talk about it?"

"I've been told I'm a good listener," offered Dustin.

Londyn supposed there was no harm in telling them what happened. It would probably do her some good to get it off her chest and share with someone besides the police officers. Besides, in her brief tenure at Zedde and Associates, she'd formed a close rapport with Jasmine and Dustin. "It was the weirdest thing. This guy was trying to get into my apartment, or at least I'm fairly sure it was a guy."

"What?" Jasmine held her apple fritter midair. "Have you

ever seen him before?"

"I might have if he's the one who was loitering across the street the night before."

Jasmine's mouth dropped. "He was across the street the night before? How come you didn't tell us this?"

Londyn noticed the hurt in Jasmine's eyes. "I'm sorry I didn't say anything. I do think it's the same one, but I can't be one hundred percent sure. It's intimidating to look out the front door, and there he is, peering back at me after attempting to get in." Fear trundled through her. Would he be back tonight?

Dustin's eyebrows rose into his hairline. "How scary. Did you call the police?"

"I did. They came over and asked me some questions. One of those questions was who had I made an enemy of that would want to try to at the very least stalk me, and at the worst..."

She shuddered. She didn't even want to think of the worst-case scenario.

"I can't think of anybody who doesn't like you."

Jasmine had a point. "The only one who came to mind was BJ Nuss, who was not happy with having to pay his bill, even though we have given him numerous chances."

Dustin poured himself a cup of coffee. "Did the police think the guy had ill intent? Or was he just some homeless dude?"

"I don't know what his intent was. Honestly, I couldn't get any sleep, just wondering."

"So they think it's Mr. Nuss?" Jasmine took another bite of her apple fritter.

Londyn shrugged. "They don't know. I think they were going to talk with him today. I received some texts as well."

"Texts? You think it's from the same guy?" Jasmine dabbed at her mouth with a napkin.

"Probably. Maybe."

"We have to deal with some pretty crazy people," said Jasmine. "But honestly, why would they come to our houses or try to act intimidating?"

Dustin refilled his coffee cup. "Maybe it was revenge."

"But it's not our fault that they owe money on their bills," Jasmine countered.

Dustin leaned his back against the wall. "Do you guys have cameras at the apartment? If so, that could be a big help."

"We don't. I wish my landlord would install some, but it's traditionally been a safe neighborhood. I'm probably the only one ever to have a situation like this."

Jasmine rejoined the conversation. "I'm going to hope that he was just lost and in the wrong place."

Their boss, Sonja, walked toward them. "Are we having our staff meeting early?"

"Londyn had some creep try to break into her house," said Jasmine.

"Oh, how frightening. Did you call the police?"

"I did. They will be talking to one of our clients, BJ Nuss, today to see if it was him. He was the only one I could think of that might be angry enough to do something like that to scare me."

"BJ Nuss. Yes, I do recall that name from when we discussed his spoken threat on the phone to you." Worry etched in Sonja's face. "This is concerning, and I do want you to add this to the paperwork you've already completed about him." She tapped her chin. "I'm not sure how Mr. Nuss would have found out where you live. We don't give out any information about our employees, including their residences, personal phone numbers, or any other private information."

"All he would need was my last name, and he could probably find out where I live by surfing the internet."

Sonja poured herself a cup of coffee. "Well, I'm just glad you're all right. And thankful that the police are looking into it."

"I'm just hoping it was something random and I just over-reacted."

Londyn's boss did not look convinced. "Maybe someone should walk you out tonight."

Dustin raised his hand. "I'd be happy to walk her out."

"Thank you, Dustin. Speaking of staff meetings, we have one in about ten minutes, so I'll meet you three in the conference room." Sonja nodded before returning to her office. Staff meetings were a weekly occurrence, but most of them didn't last more than a few minutes. Sonja trusted her employees, kept an open-door policy, and did her best not to use up valuable work time in a day for the sake of a meeting. However, when there was a staff meeting, it was mandatory.

Londyn ascertained the gathering must be important because when she walked into the conference room, not only was there a fresh pot of coffee and Dustin's donut box—and what remained of the donuts—but also on the table were several balloons tied together attached to a card.

Was it someone's birthday? Ten employees worked in this department at Zedde and Associates, so when there was a birthday, they typically went out for lunch. But usually, Sonja let them know ahead of time in case they wished to attend.

Londyn took a seat in one of the cushioned chairs between Jasmine and Dustin. The rest of the employees filed in, and her boss stood.

"Thank you all for coming to the meeting," Sonja began. "I have a few announcements to make. First off, good job this past month. I have received compliments about the way you have all handled accounts, and our doctors, physicians, and hospital board members are pleased that we have been able to secure more of those outstanding balances. Working with those who owe on their bills in a way that secures payment but also in conjunction with their budgets is paramount, and you have all done stellar jobs attaining that goal. Secondly, we have a new job opening, so if you know of anyone who would be interested, please spread the word. And now, last but not least, we have an award for Employee of the Quarter. It's not typically my habit to choose the same person twice in a row, but this individual has gone above and beyond for the company, so much so that they are fully deserving of again receiving this distinguished award. Dustin, that would be you."

Everyone clapped, and Dustin smiled. "Thank you."

"Your dedication, loyalty, and ability to work with our clients is nothing short of fantastic. Rarely does a week go by without a phone call from a client stating how much they appreciated your patience and understanding. Please accept these balloons and a gift card to one of your favorite places. You'll also receive a bonus."

Everyone clapped again, and Londyn patted Dustin on the back. "Congratulations."

He offered her a broad grin, and she realized perhaps for the second time in as many weeks that he was cute with his short-cropped blond hair and hooded brown eyes.

Dustin opened the card, read it, then held up the gift card. "Looks like I'll be doing some shopping." Everyone clapped again, and after eating doughnuts and drinking more coffee, they were released to their job duties.

Of course, three of the other single women in the office had to approach Dustin and offer some flirtatious congratulatory words. One woman, a rail-thin redhead in her early thirties, gushed and offered numerous light touches and continued eye contact. As one of only two males in the office, Dustin had earned a high ranking of popularity, especially among those hoping he'd ask them out.

The other two single women crowded around him and playfully teased him with hints about them being the ones he'd take shopping.

Dustin flirted right back, giving most of his attention to the redhead. He was a great guy, and any of the women would be fortunate to go out with him.

Londyn appreciated the interruption from the thoughts that permeated through her mind about last night's visitor.

After the meeting, she discovered she had a phone message on her cell. "Hi, Ms. Siegler. This is Detective Rivas. Officers Gann and Nelson apprised me of the situation with the man who paid you a visit last night and the prior episode with him across the street, along with the texts you've received. Do you have time to come down to the police department this afternoon?"

Londyn returned Detective Rivas's call and arranged to meet with him during her lunch hour. Fortunately, Sonja told her that if it took longer, that was fine, but that she would need to make up the time.

She finished making some notes on the computer about the most recent phone call, then logged off, put on her coat, and reached for her purse.

"Do you want to go to lunch with us?" asked Jasmine.

"I'm sorry. I'll have to pass today because I have a meeting with the detective at the police department."

Dustin perched on the corner of her desk. "We can always have lunch tomorrow instead. Do you need anyone to go with you to the police station?"

"I appreciate the offer, but I think I'll be fine. I'm hoping it will just be a quick and painless process."

Jasmine slung her purse over her shoulder. "Hopefully, they'll be able to find out whoever this is. I wonder if they spoke to Mr. Nuss."

Londyn had wondered that herself. If they had, how had the man reacted? Had he admitted it? How had he obtained her personal information?

Dustin offered to accompany her to her car since he and Jasmine were walking to the parking garage anyway. The three of them went their separate ways, and Londyn was grateful she hadn't seen anybody out of the ordinary.

The Rowland Police Department was about three miles from Londyn's employment. It was at least five times the size of the one in Pronghorn Falls, which was combined with the Sheriff's Office.

A man in his late forties, Detective Rivas was a few inches taller than she was, possessed a high forehead and a widow's peak, a broad nose, and a serious demeanor.

Londyn took a seat in the chair across from him in his office.

"According to your file, you have been receiving unwanted texts and have seen a man loitering around your apartment building and attempting to enter."

Londyn shifted uncomfortably in her seat. "Yes, sir." Hearing the law enforcement officer say the words made them all the more real. "Would this be considered stalking?"

"For it to be considered stalking, it has to be a series of events, but I would say this has the potential to reach that point if it is the same person." Detective Rivas rehashed the notes in the file. "We visited BJ Nuss today. You mentioned you had concerns that it may have been him last night at your door."

Could he be the one across the street? The one who texted her? Was it just one individual? Her breath caught in her throat. What if the texter and the visitor were two different people? Finally, she found her voice and answered the detective's question. "Yes, because he's the only one I can think of whom I've ever angered in Rowland."

"Could there be anybody from your former town who could be potentially harassing you?"

She could think of no one. She had no enemies here or there. "No. Not very many people even know I moved here."

Detective Rivas rifled through the papers in the file folder. Had Londyn ever thought she would have an actual file at the police department?

He produced a picture and put it in front of her. "It's my understanding that you have never seen Mr. Nuss and have only spoken to him on the phone."

"That is correct."

"Here is a recent photograph of him."

Londyn stared at the man in the photo. He was thin, red-haired, green-eyed, with a chipped upper tooth, and looked to be in his late thirties. Not at all what she had expected from speaking with him on the phone.

"Could this be the man who attempted to enter your apartment or the one you saw across the street?"

"It's really difficult to say. The man last night wore a ski mask, and the man across the street was too far away for me to determine his facial features."

Londyn squeezed her eyes shut and tried to recall the image from last night before slowly shaking her head. "I am sorry to say that I can't provide any other details about his features. All I saw was that he was on the taller side, skinny, and was wearing a black or navy hoodie and a black ski mask."

"You said that he tried the door. Did you happen to see a weapon?"

Londyn again attempted to think back to yesterday. Her chest tightened. Had the man possessed a weapon? Would he have used it? "I don't know if he had a weapon. If he did, I didn't see it."

Detective Rivas stared at her, his eyes unblinking as if attempting to understand what a poor witness she was.

She was absolutely no help at all.

"All right, then. But you do think there might be a possibility that it is Mr. Nuss?"

"From the photograph you showed me, it could be him. He has the same build as the man at my door and probably a motive since I was unable to satisfactorily assist him with his account before sending it to collections."

"I've spoken with him, and he denies both visiting your apartment and sending any texts. He, didn't, however, have an alibi. Hopefully, my visit will encourage him to keep his distance from you if he is, in fact, the one who has been texting and hanging around your apartment. In the meantime, I would highly recommend you speak with your landlord about the possibility of installing cameras. I will need you to keep a record of each incident and include as many details as possible."

While the landlord was nice enough, Londyn doubted he'd be willing to spend the funds necessary for a camera system, especially since so many things in her apartment needed an upgrade. If he wasn't willing to do that, why would he purchase cameras?

"I assume you have blocked the number from further texts?" Detective Rivas's voice interrupted her thoughts.

"I have."

"Mr. Nuss's phone number didn't match the one the texts originated from. However, burner phones are always an option. Do you have a deadbolt on your apartment door?"

"I do. It's a press-to-lock keypad door lock with an automatic deadbolt."

Detective Rivas nodded. "Good. In the event that this person does contact you again, you will need to keep a log of the texts. You can also screenshot them. While we're hoping this is the end of it, if it's not, keep detailed records."

"Yes, sir." Her voice shook.

"As far as keeping yourself as safe as possible, park in well-lit areas, always carry your phone, be situationally aware, and trust your gut. Attempt to go places with someone else rather than by yourself and alternate your routine if possible. Call us immediately if you see or hear from him again."

"I will. Thank you."

Detective Rivas stood and shook her hand. "Stay safe, Ms. Siegler, and don't hesitate to contact me if necessary." He handed her a business card.

She stumbled from his office, her mind in a haze. What would happen next? Would Mr. Nuss—or whoever it was—return? How long would this continue? She prayed that the detective's visit to the disgruntled client would cause the situation to cease.

Londyn struggled through the remainder of the afternoon, keeping her mind on work. When she entered the office, Jasmine, whose cubicle was directly across from Londyn's, rose and met Londyn at the coffee pot.

"How did it go?"

Dustin sauntered over from his cubicle bordering Londyn's and joined in the conversation.

"Detective Rivas asked me some questions and mentioned he paid BJ Nuss a visit."

Jasmine jutted out her hip and planted her hand on it. "And what did Mr. Nuss have to say?"

"He denied it, although he lacked an alibi."

Dustin refilled his mug. "Don't they always deny it?"

Londyn released a mirthless laugh. "True. The thing that bothers me is that I wasn't paying closer attention to his appearance—if it even was a 'him'."

"You're not sure it was a guy?" asked Jasmine.

"I'm fairly sure, but it could have been a skinny woman. With the hoodie and mask, it concealed all but the person's eyes."

"Don't feel bad about not knowing a lot about the person's appearance. I read somewhere that eyewitness accuracy can be lacking at best."

"I should have paid closer attention so I would know if it was BJ Nuss."

Jasmine drained the coffee in her mug. "BJ Nuss should admit to being the one if it was him."

"And get himself in trouble? Not likely. The guy sounds like a real winner." Dustin set his mug on the coffee cart and cracked his knuckles.

"Thank you for all of your support." Londyn had found strong friendships in Jasmine and Dustin. Something she'd missed since moving from Pronghorn Falls.

Jasmine wrapped an arm around her shoulder. "What are friends for?"

At five o'clock, Dustin escorted Londyn to her SUV in the parking garage. After an uneventful drive home, she changed into a comfortable t-shirt and shorts. Londyn perched on the edge of her bed and opened her Bible to her favorite verse, then prayed.

"Lord, please grant me the peace I so desperately need. Let this all be nothing but someone inadvertently texting the wrong person and a random, homeless drunk attempting to get inside. I pray You would keep me safe. And, Lord, please keep the Brenneman family safe. Please let Brodie forgive me, and if it is Your will, please let us someday reconcile. I miss his friendship. Thank You, Father, for Your faithfulness and for watching over me all these years. In Jesus' Name, Amen."

She put her Bible back on her nightstand and strode into the kitchen to make dinner. Chicken noodle soup, always a comfort food, sounded good on this dreary day.

The three-frame picture collection on the shelf in the living room caught her eye. One was of her and Brodie at the prom. She wore a beautiful purple dress, and he wore a white tux. They'd eaten at a fast-food restaurant, joining with other friends to take a step outside the ordinary. Londyn and Brodie had gone as friends, of course, and visited the local park after dinner and before heading to the prom. It was that event that Brodie had attempted to duplicate the night he'd proposed.

Both times, they'd hopped on the swings, pumped their legs, and leaped out of the swings just as they had when they were younger. She was glad she could still land on her feet over ten years later.

Then they'd climbed onto the old metal merry-go-round. It was a vintage, iconic piece that brought back memories of elementary school. Both times, they'd stepped off, dizzy, staggering, and stumbling to the park bench.

That night, Brodie's hope to recapture the night at the prom had distracted her from Mom's recent choice.

Until Londyn had ruined the evening.

Regret crept into her soul, and she instead peered at the

middle picture of her and Brodie's family at Christmas Eve services at church the year before Mr. Brenneman died at the hands of a drunk driver, and Danny died in a car wreck while moving back to Pronghorn Falls. Everyone was smiling. Happy. Not a care in the world.

The final picture was of her and Brodie hiking up Pronghorn Peak. With their trekking poles, backpacks, and matching ball caps, the selfie reminded her of not only the accomplishment of enduring steep terrain and harsh weather on the hike back, but of a time when Brodie's friendship was paramount in her life. They started dating soon after.

Londyn replaced the picture, grabbed a can of soup from the cupboard, and emptied it into a pan.

She was stirring the soup over the stove when her cell phone rang, causing her to jump.

Londyn didn't recognize the number, so she allowed it to go to voicemail. Within seconds, the ping of a message sounded.

She punched in her password, and the message played.

A message consisting of only breathing.

Londyn instantly set the phone on the counter and walked to the front window. Outside, a few vehicles rumbled by, but there was no man in a hoodie across the street—or even more thankfully—at her door.

Perhaps it was just a wrong number.

She turned off the stove and poured the soup into a bowl when a text notification alerted her.

Londyn clicked on the text icon and scrutinized the words written in all caps:

I SEE YOU.

The phone rang again, and without thinking, she answered it.

"Hello?"

No answer.

"Who is this?"

"I see you."

The distorted voice produced a profound unease. She dropped her phone on the counter as though it were a hot potato and took a step back.

"Who are you?" she repeated to the empty room. "Why are you doing this?"

Londyn rushed again to the front door and each window.

Nothing and no one unusual was outside.

Another notification. She dared a peek at the text.

THAT SHIRT GOES WELL WITH YOUR EYES.

She clutched her arms with icy fingers as the fear seized her. The heavy pounding of her own heartbeat thundered in her ears. With trembling hands, she retrieved her phone.

The number that both texted and called her was unknown to her. She hit the block button. How many burner phones did this guy have?

If anyone could offer her some advice on this crazy stalker, it would be Brodie. Although he'd probably immediately drive to Rowland and offer to find the guy and arrest him himself if jurisdictional laws allowed it.

But calling him wasn't only awkward, it was potentially out of line. How could she not speak to him for months, and then all of a sudden call out of the blue just because she needed help? Sounded like something her mom would do.

As soon as she had dialed the familiar number, she hung up, hoping it hadn't registered as a call.

She documented the disturbing call and texts, then sat at the table, prayed for her meal, and swirled the liquid around in the mug, having lost her appetite.

If her stalker's desire was to frighten her, he'd succeeded.

Chapter 4

Brodie hated high-speed chases. He hated the risks involved. Hated that innocent lives were endangered. Hated that they were put in the path of an idiot. A maniac who thought it was a good idea to do all he could to elude the police, driving speeds far faster than what was safe and prudent. On this occasion, it was a male driver who misinterpreted the speed limit on one of the back county roads. Instead of going forty-five miles an hour, or even a few miles over, he took his speed in excess of a hundred miles an hour. Might work on a straightaway, but not on backcountry roads with curves. The guy illegally passed several innocent drivers on the shoulder of the road. Fortunately, no one else was injured in the chase.

Law enforcement put down spikes, attempting to stop him. Finally, the criminal failed to negotiate one of the curves a mile later. He flipped the car he was driving, and it had come to rest on its roof. The ambulance was en route, and Brodie and one of his deputies pulled the guy from the car before it burst into flames. He was barely breathing and died before the ambulance arrived.

After completing some paperwork, Brodie was ready to be done for the day. He was glad when Roarke called him.

"Hey, Bro, it's Thursday night. You know what that means. You up for a juicy burger over at Jody's?"

Brodie was always up for a juicy burger, especially at his favorite restaurant. However, weariness tugged at him, and he could see himself curling up in his recliner and not making it to the bedroom to sleep. But his rumbling stomach begged otherwise.

"Yeah. A juicy burger sounds good."

Besides, it would take a lot for him to want to miss out on his weekly dinner with his favorite brother.

"All right, I'll meet you over there at six-thirty."

"Six-thirty it is."

Of course, Brodie would do just about anything to get out of having to do paperwork. It was a necessary evil. And if it wasn't done correctly, some overzealous defense attorney would get the criminal off with barely a slap on his wrist. While that wouldn't be the case for this situation, with the man having passed away, Brodie still had to complete the paperwork.

He finished dotting his i's and crossing his t's and climbed into his truck. The drive to Jody's took him about ten minutes from the sheriff's office. He pulled into a parking spot near the back because everywhere else was taken. If there was ever another recession in Pronghorn Falls, Jody's would remain unscathed and probably come back stronger than ever. There was never a day when the place wasn't crazy busy.

The aroma of hamburgers, french fries, and onion rings filled his nose, and he inhaled the savory smell. Roarke found them a booth on the right-hand side of the restaurant.

"Hey, Bro."

Brodie slid into the brown upholstered seat across from his brother. "Hey, Roarke."

"Rough day?"

"Is it that obvious?"

"Looks like you've had a little bit of excitement today."

"Yeah, just a little bit.

"I can only imagine."

"It was a high-speed chase. A guy thought he could get to the next county going a hundred miles an hour. Thankfully, nobody was injured or killed, with him being the exception.

"That's my brother. Always out making the roads in the county safer."

"Glad it's over with. So, what's new with you?"

"Just busy at the ranch today. Mila is ready to have this baby even though it's not nearly time yet. I sure don't blame her."

"Probably not too bad now, but when the summer comes in all that heat...have you settled on a name yet?"

"You're the fifteenth person who's asked me that this week."

"Well, it is the thing to ask when you're about to be a dad, right?" Brodie was happy for Roarke, but secretly, he'd always hoped someday he'd marry and be a dad himself. Londyn's face flitted through his mind.

The waitress came and took their orders and brought them each their tall cups of pop. Brodie guzzled it down within seconds.

"Any word lately from Londyn?" Roarke asked that question each week at their dinners, and each week it was the same answer.

"Just those couple of times and not recently."

"At least she stays in touch with Mom."

"Somewhat. Seems she's enjoying her life in the city." He wanted Londyn to be happy. To live a full life. He only wished that life included him.

The entire Brenneman family cared about Londyn. They had been her surrogate family, and Mom asked about her often as well. Londyn had been a part of their lives for so long that when she had left, she had not only hurt Brodie, but also Mom. Even Xander asked about her on occasion. The thought of Londyn and the heartbreak she caused remained lodged in Brodie's chest.

"I was going to tell you about someone I thought you should date in case you haven't already considered her."

Brodie narrowed his eyes at his brother. "Who?"

"Diana asked about you when I went into the courthouse to renew the tags for my truck."

"Yeah, come to think of it, you told me that last time you visited the courthouse."

"Okay, well, just wanted you to keep your options open. She seems like a nice person."

"I appreciate you trying to be a matchmaker, but I'm not interested."

"Not interested because you're not interested, or not interested because you're not over Londyn?"

Brodie didn't even have to contemplate that question. He'd probably never be over Londyn. He dated a couple of times after she left, but it never transpired into anything. Because how could it? His heart belonged to the woman who rejected his marriage proposal. She was the one who filled his thoughts. Who he kept a picture of on his bedside table. Who meant more to him than she would ever know.

"All right, well, I won't pester you about it."

"Is that a promise?"

A suspicious smirk crossed Roarke's face. "Although maybe I should because you were so annoying about Mila."

"Hey, it turned out well, right?"

"You're right. It did work out. I wouldn't have wanted to miss out on her for anything. Maybe it could work out with you and Diana."

"Yeah…not likely." Not when Brodie couldn't get over Londyn. That wouldn't be fair to Diana, no matter how nice she was.

They talked about the upcoming men's breakfast at church that was held each month, and this time it was Brodie and Roarke's turn to make the breakfast.

"Have you decided what we're going to be serving up for the guys on Saturday?"

Brodie was glad for the change in topic. "Something easy and hopefully palatable."

"How about one of those pancake mixes? We could probably make that and be somewhat successful. You were always good at frying bacon."

Brodie ate a fry. "Yeah, I could probably fry up some bacon again, but if there are going to be twenty guys, I am going to have to fry up more than a few pieces because they're going to want more than one slice each."

Roarke chuckled. "Probably so. They eat like you do."

"I was thinking more like you eating the entire pack of bacon." Brodie steepled his fingers "I say we go ahead and make the pancake mix and see if we can borrow Mom's huge griddle. If we provide enough syrup, the guys won't pay attention to how bad the food tastes."

"I'm really not one to be able to make food, even if it only necessitates adding water."

"You're lucky to be married to Mila. Of course, Mom made sure you were well fed before that, but if you had to fend for yourself on your own, you might become emaciated."

"Very funny." Roarke patted his stomach. "I have a way to

go before I'm emaciated. I think I'm having sympathy belly with Mila's pregnancy."

"You're starting to get a dad bod."

Roarke reached across the table and playfully slugged Brodie. "It's just a case of helping Mila."

"Helping Mila?"

"Yeah. She has cravings all the time, especially for breadsticks from that pizza place. I don't want her to feel bad about having to eat those all by herself."

"You always were a compassionate guy."

Roarke straightened his posture. "That I am."

"Mila is getting *some* of those breadsticks, right?"

They continued chatting and ribbing each other while waiting for their food to arrive. Roarke turned somber after a time. "I sure wish we would hear from Grayson."

"Me too. Hard enough on us, not to mention Mom. At least it would be nice if he would contact her and let her know he's doing all right."

"I guess at least he called that one time and let her know he had taken a job in Denver. But, yeah, it would be good for him to learn how to use the phone on a regular basis."

Grayson was on some type of prodigal journey. Everyone grieved in their own way after Dad died, but Grayson left everyone's lives completely after Dad was killed. Brodie attempted to convince himself that that was just how Grayson handled the situation. But it wasn't right to have left his family when they all needed each other. Especially Mom, who lost the love of her life.

They finished eating and said goodbye before Brodie hopped in his truck and headed home. He took a shower and lifted his phone to find that he had missed a call from a familiar number while he was in the shower. But there was no message.

Why had Londyn called? Should he call her back? And why hadn't she left a message?

Chapter 5

The creaking sounds of the old apartment failed to help her insomnia.

The questions raged through her mind.

How could he have gotten her personal number? Why was he harassing her? Would he take it a step further than texts, visits, and now calls?

How could one man be so upset over a medical bill? Of course, these days, people got upset over far less.

Regardless of BJ Nuss's thoughts about her, he would have had to search to find her phone number *and* her residence.

These days, it was easy to find just about anyone. Londyn tossed and turned as a thought planted itself in her mind. She wasn't sleeping anyway, so she might as well see what she could find out.

She slipped from bed and traipsed into the kitchen. An efficient perusal of the street told her no one lurked outside. She flipped on the light above the kitchen table, opened her laptop, and turned it on. In the search bar, she typed *Londyn Siegler*. There shouldn't be too much about her, seeing as how she'd never been famous, won any awards, or committed any crimes.

Eight results popped up, including variations of the spelling of her name and her first name in conjunction with other surnames. It was easy to narrow down in less than a minute.

Aside from the social media accounts, one of which was hers, Londyn clicked on a result that touted itself as an address and telephone number database. There were four Londyn Sieglers listed. One lived in Maine, one in South Carolina, and two that were her. She clicked on the first of the two, which revealed her name, her Pronghorn Falls address, age, and those affiliated with her, which included her mom, three of her mom's ex-husbands, her dad, Logan, and an unknown person that was probably an error. The second listing provided her name, current address, and cell phone number.

She clicked on the other non-social media result, and it disclosed her phone number on the first line. It also listed a former phone number from over four years ago.

Not too challenging to have ascertained the information her stalker needed.

This must have been how BJ Nuss located her phone number. If he texted the wrong person, it was no big deal, but if he texted the right person, he would have achieved whatever goal he was trying to accomplish.

She cringed. Few things were hidden anymore. If anyone wanted to find someone, they could do so rather easily. She straightened in the chair. After discovering this most recent turn of events, it was doubtful sleep would come, even though she had a busy day tomorrow.

Londyn typed in the name BJ Nuss. Several results flashed on her screen. If the websites were accurate, Mr. Nuss's criminal activity punctuated his background. There was also a notation from the local Rowland newspaper indicating he'd been

arrested for embezzlement, a DUI, driving too fast for conditions, and driving with an expired license. Further searches
showed he typically worked in construction and had been
through a divorce. It stated his age as thirty-eight and also
listed his phone number, which didn't match the numbers that
had been texting and calling her. No surprise there. Burner
phones were easy to purchase.

Desperate to refocus her attention, Londyn needed a diver-
sion. She typed in *Pronghorn Falls Daily Newspaper*.

The tabs along the top of the publication included community news, sports, national, obituaries, and a photo gallery.
Londyn clicked on the news. The first article was one with a
photograph of Brodie and Chief Neeley.

*Local Law Enforcement Sponsors Second Annual
Adoption Fundraiser*

She scanned the article.

*It's nearly that time of year again when
members of Pronghorn Falls Law Enforcement
sponsor an adoption fundraiser at the popular
non-alcoholic establishment, Jimmy's Lounge.
With a goal of raising $20,000 this year, the
event will host a live auction, pizza-eating
contest, line dancing, pool, and music by the
Pronghorns.*

*The money will benefit families seeking to
adopt, whether locally, nationally, or inter-
nationally.*

*"Adoption is near and dear to my heart,
and I encourage us, as a community, to assist*

Brodie smiled for the camera, the dimple in his right cheek prominent. His rugged good looks and kind eyes had drawn Londyn to him as a friend long before she'd begun to have feelings for him.

Feelings she was better off suppressing.

Her text notification sounded. Londyn startled and sat motionless as the second hand on the clock above the mantle ticked by. Part of her wanted to ignore the text, but a larger part of her wanted to know...was it the same person who had previously texted her?

Slowly, cautiously, she slid the phone toward her. On the home screen, it showed the number and the first few words of the text.

Once again, a number she didn't recognize.

Her hand shook as she lifted the phone and entered her password. The text icon showed an unread text. Holding her breath, she clicked on it.

FIND ANYTHING INTERESTING ON THE INTERNET TONIGHT?

Londyn dropped the phone as though it were on fire. She gasped and gripped her forearms with her shaky hands.

He, or she, was out there. But most likely a he. Most likely BJ Nuss.

He was watching her. Knew she was on the computer. *He was that close.*

Did he have that much of a detailed view that he was able to see that she was searching the internet?

She shuddered, the sweat dripping unmercifully down her back. She swept a hand against her cheek. Her heart pounded so loudly in her chest that she heard it in her ears.

Lord, please keep me safe.

Londyn stood, her legs wobbled, and she clutched the table. Steadying herself and praying for protection, she stumbled to the front door.

No one on the street.

Next, she lowered one of the slats of the blinds and peered out the front window.

No one as far as she could see.

Where was he?

Londyn stared, although not really seeing. She blinked, cleared her vision, and inspected the area in front of her apartment from the hopefully safe confines of her living room.

Nothing.

Her leg muscles rebelled, and her knees buckled as she shuffled to the bedroom. She closed the door behind her, locked it, and slid down, her back against the bed frame.

Was it all just a ruse? Or would whomever her stalker was determine that the mere act of texting was only the first step?

Brodie parked his truck in the garage and closed the door. A domestic dispute call resulting in an arrest kicked off the day, and the calls continued at a steady pace. He was still amped up from the high-speed chase yesterday. That was the thing about law enforcement work. It kept your adrenaline hyped long after the fact.

He kicked off his shoes, changed his clothes, and eased into his recliner. He thanked God for keeping him and his deputy and those on the Pronghorn Falls police department safe during the chase, as well as the innocents on the road at the time. He never could understand the thought process behind driving so fast and putting others at risk. The guy hadn't even been chased when he was first discovered driving and clocking in at upwards of eighty miles an hour before increasing his speed.

Of course, after the chase, it was discovered that he had several outstanding warrants. When he flipped the vehicle and succumbed to his injuries, it hadn't been an easy thing to see. But it never was. The suspect's mangled body and loss of life stuck in Brodie's mind as he attempted to wind down for the day. Where was the guy now spending eternity? As mentioned in Second Peter, God wanted none to perish. The suspect's poor decisions cost him his life and could have cost a whole lot of others their lives as well.

It was days like these that reminded Brodie of his dad. A dedicated sheriff, his life had been snuffed out when someone chose to drink and then drive.

Brodie leaned back in his recliner, attempting to halt the thoughts that rammed through his mind. There were times when he fell asleep on the chair, then subsequently attempted to fall asleep in bed with no success. Tonight might be one of those times. Thankfully, crime in Pronghorn Falls was minimal compared to some towns and cities. That was one of the factors for Brodie remaining in his hometown. But the most important reason was that this is where his family was. Where they had settled generations ago and ranched. And while Brodie had chosen a career in law enforcement, he still assisted on the ranch. His family was the most important thing to him after his Savior. He hoped someday to marry and have children of his own and carry on the Brenneman legacy.

Thoughts of Londyn flooded his mind. He withdrew their yearbook from the shelf beside the recliner and flipped it open. They'd been best friends ever since Londyn moved to Pronghorn Falls as a kid. With the exception of his football and soccer pictures, and her volleyball and basketball pictures, they were together in every picture. A picture of them at the prom, a picture of them in the Honor Society sitting beside each other, a photo of them on the tennis team—the team that would have been far better off without the two of them, since neither had ever really grasped the sport. There were pictures of them at games and at the athletic awards ceremony, where they both lettered in their respective sports and went home with various awards. Well, all except tennis awards.

There was a picture of them on the senior trip where the

whole class rode horseback in the mountains. There were pictures of them with other friends sitting in the back of Dad's vintage Chevy. And the list went on.

In short, they were inseparable.

At one point, he thought it would have been her that he would have married and had a family with. In a split second, he was transported back in time.

They'd gone to the park for the prom, she in her purple dress and he in his tux. As far as he was concerned, if he ever wore a tuxedo again, it would be too soon. Others had met them there for part of the time, and they swung on the swings and hitched a ride on the archaic merry-go-round after eating at a fast-food restaurant. Then they'd gone for a walk—everything had been as friends.

Years later, he realized he liked Londyn for more than just friendship. He wasn't getting any younger, and it was time to make his feelings known. After dating for a while, he thought she felt the same—was sure she felt the same.

How wrong he was.

All those years later, he'd attempted to replicate that memorable time after prom at the park. They'd gone out to eat as they often did, then he'd driven to the town park. They'd swung on the swings, gone for a walk, laughed, and reminisced.

He'd put some of their goofy music from when they were in high school on his phone and twirled her around as they danced just like they had at the prom. They were no longer teenagers, but adults. Wiser, more established, and in his mind, ready to take the next step.

The way she'd smile at him, the way she grabbed his hand when they walked, and the way she rested her head on his shoulder on the merry-go-round.

On the merry-go-round, he'd spun it as fast as he could, then leapt on, bemoaning the fact that he wasn't as agile as he'd been a decade ago. They'd sat in the middle, and as she rested her head on his shoulder, he rested his head on hers, and while dizzy and concerned that the food he'd eaten for dinner would be making a reemergence, he'd enjoyed every second of being with her.

They climbed off, teetering and stumbling until they had plopped down on a nearby bench. He reached into his jean jacket pocket. The box was still there. The treasure within tucked safely inside. A month's worth of wages spent on what he hoped would symbolize his commitment to her.

Yes, he'd been so sure she'd felt the same. They shared a history, knew so much about each other, and he wanted a future with her—a future that included marriage.

After their stomachs had settled from the dizzying ride on the merry-go-round, he reached for her hand. Then he worked up the courage. He'd prayed for several days that God would give him wisdom, that he was doing the right thing in asking her. There was no one else for him and no one else he ever wanted to marry, but above all else, he wanted God's will.

God's will strongly differed from what Brodie expected.

Brodie had knelt on one knee in front of Londyn, his hand in his pocket, firmly clasping the green box.

"Londyn..."

She'd already started to shake her head. But he dismissed it.

Surprisingly, he'd been able to speak the words he'd rehearsed, even though his voice and legs shook, sweat trickled down the back of his neck, and his unsteady removal of the box that held the ring was more reminiscent of an elderly man than one not yet thirty. He opened the velvet box, revealing the diamond engagement ring. *"Londyn, I love you. I have for a long time. Will you do me the honor of marrying me?"*

Tears shimmered in her eyes. "I can't."

Had he misheard her?

"What?"

"I can't marry you."

"You can't?"

"I'm sorry, Brodie."

"But..."

She turned from him, and her shoulders shook as she quietly sobbed. He attempted to comfort her, but she broke free of his grasp and walked to his truck without looking back. He followed her and reached for her arm. *"Londyn, wait."*

She turned to face him but didn't meet his eye.

"Help me understand." His words came out more terse and louder than he'd intended.

She flinched, and Brodie removed his hand. *"Please."*

She shook her head and bit her lip.

Brodie needed her to explain. Needed to know the why of her answer.

They stood there beneath the moonlight, the ring tucked haphazardly back into his pocket. *"Londyn, I love you."*

She dipped her head, and he lifted her chin. *"I love you,"* he repeated.

His heart broke into a million pieces when the words he longed to hear were not spoken in return.

It was the only time he'd nearly lost his temper with her, and even then, he'd remained calmer than he ever thought possible. Only by God's grace, because some strange emotion of hurt, anger, fear, and disbelief all rolled into one settled in his stomach.

Somewhere, a car horn beeped, and the streetlight flickered.

"Do you love me?" he'd whispered.

Londyn said nothing.

Just left him there to have his heart torn from his body in one fell swoop.

He drove her home and walked her to her door as he always did. This time, there was no inviting him in for a movie and popcorn. No goodnight kiss. No "see you tomorrow" before he left. Just another muffled apology before she shut the door and walked out of his life forever.

Brodie gave her space, hoping she'd reconsider, but he'd not force her to love him or to marry him. She had to do that on her own.

A week later, Londyn texted him to say she was moving out of town. Just like that. No explanation. No saying she would miss him. Nothing about the enduring friendship they'd shared for nearly two decades or the subsequent dating relationship.

Just, *"I'm moving."*

Mom had grieved as though she'd lost a daughter.

And Brodie as though he'd lost the love of his life.

Because he had.

He'd gone over that day over and over again in his mind at least a million times. Would she still be here if he hadn't proposed? Should he have gone after her? Should he have visited her apartment to say goodbye before she left?

Brodie had wanted to say so much more. In hindsight, it was better that God held his tongue that day. No sense in driving her further away.

If that were even possible.

He had only heard from her a handful of times since. Each time, he'd responded with a lackluster response. He'd pridefully acted as though her decision had little effect on him.

Numerous times, he wrestled with whether to text her more often, but in the end, hadn't. Mom had. She'd heard from Londyn on occasion, although only to say "hi" or "hope everyone is doing well," and one time, an apology. Never an explanation.

And never once to thank Mom for all she'd done and for being the mother Londyn never had.

Even now, when the call came in with no voice message, Brodie had contemplated whether or not to call her back. He stared at his phone and at her number on the screen. His finger hovered over the call button. It was late, but if she needed him—

If that was why she'd called...

Brodie swallowed the bitter taste of indecision, prayed a hasty prayer, hoping God would answer the burning question immediately, then turned off his phone for the night and wandered to his bedroom, all the while knowing sleep would elude him.

Chapter 6

Londyn finished speaking with Detective Rivas the following morning and provided him with the latest details about the phone call and eerie text, before arriving at work.

The phone rang immediately.

"Patient accounts, this is Londyn. Which doctor or provider are you calling about?" She reiterated her memorized spiel.

The woman on the other end set up payment arrangements for the dermatologist, and Londyn returned the phone to its cradle. She rubbed her neck, then stretched it from side to side, hoping to alleviate some of the tension.

Jasmine's head popped above the cubicle wall. "Want to go out for lunch?"

"Sure." Lunch at the Italian restaurant Jasmine was fond of was just the remedy to take Londyn's mind off her stalker.

Dustin joined them, and the three of them walked out of the office building with Dustin in the middle. Thunder sounded, and a steady rain pounded on the sidewalk. This was certainly set to be one of the wettest years on record. Dustin opened his umbrella and shared it with Londyn and Jasmine.

"Surprised you don't have your own umbrella." He tilted his head toward Londyn.

"They weren't really necessary where I'm from."

"Because you had no rain?"

She peered at his face, teasing in his eyes. She appreciated how Dustin's chatty and witty sense of humor lightened the mood.

"No, because we usually made a run for our car. It's a small town, so we didn't spend a lot of time just walking to places."

"Ugh," said Jasmine. "I would *hate* living in a small town. What's there to do?"

"Plenty. You just have to be creative."

They reached the restaurant, and Londyn took a seat in the booth beside Jasmine with Dustin across from them.

"Isn't the server so gorgeous?" Jasmine swooned at the server, the owner's son. "He must be filling in for one of his employees today." She lowered her voice. "Not only is he totally hot, but also incredibly thoughtful with an amazing work ethic."

The server, who obviously spent time at the gym, returned with drinks a few minutes later. He took their order, and Jasmine engaged him in pleasant conversation while twirling a strand of her naturally curly hair.

Jasmine put her elbows on the table and leaned toward Dustin. "How does a girl let a guy know she's interested?"

"Well, for one, she makes eye contact." He sent a probing gaze in Londyn's direction. "Then, she takes an interest in him. Compliments him. Makes pleasant conversation and gets to know him. Maybe smiles or offers some flirtatious gestures." He again made eye contact with Londyn. "Or rests her hand on his arm for some slight physical touch, things like that." He briefly rested his hand on Londyn's.

She waited to feel some sort of zip of electricity up her arm as she had with Brodie. Nothing came. Dustin's warm hand remained on hers for several seconds before he removed it, his attention remaining on her.

"Thank you. It's not like I'm new to this game, and this is far from my first rodeo, but this guy is different. I think he might be the one."

"And you know this how?" asked Londyn.

"When you know, you know," said Dustin. This time, his expression was one of seriousness. Something crossed his gaze that Londyn couldn't quite define.

Perhaps she was placing too much emphasis on "feeling" something. Feelings were untrustworthy. Fleeting.

"You can't do this with the server, but one way I personally let someone know I care about her and would like to get to know her better is to be there for her. Take care of her when she finds herself in frightening situations."

"I do appreciate how you've helped me with dealing with Mr. Nuss's unwanted texts and visits."

"That's because I care about you, Londyn. A lot."

"Wow, so in case you two forgot, I'm here too." Jasmine chewed on a complimentary breadstick.

Dustin laughed. "Aw, Jas, we know you're here."

The remainder of the lunch resulted in delectable food and pleasant conversation. But something niggled at Londyn about Dustin. He obviously had feelings for her and *had* walked her to her car each evening and followed her to her apartment a few times to keep an eye out for Mr. Nuss.

Why then could she only see him as a long-term friend? Because she still and always would have feelings for Brodie? Because she was like her mom in that men were easily disposable?

Dustin was good-looking, kind, and from what he said, a Christian. He attended church with Jasmine, earned a decent income, had an apartment on the east side of the city in a serene neighborhood, and was well-liked due to his charming personality.

"Anyone up for watching a movie tonight?" Dustin asked after they'd eaten their meals.

Jasmine raised her hand. "I am. What about you, Londyn?"

She shrugged. "Sure. It would beat being alone tonight if that creep decides to text me or show up again."

"If he does decide to text you or show up at your door, we'll be there."

Dustin's words comforted her. "My apartment is fine. How about right after work? We can order a pizza."

"Now you're talking," said Dustin, wadding his napkin and setting it on his empty plate.

After work, Jasmine ran to the store on the way for pop and snacks, and Dustin escorted Londyn to her door. It would be comforting to have company if anything nefarious happened.

Jasmine had been to Londyn's apartment several times to watch chick flicks. It would be an interesting dynamic to include Dustin, although he mentioned he was agreeable to watching whatever Londyn and Jasmine chose.

The crisp air smelled like rain, and peeps of sunshine emerged from behind the clouds. True spring might finally be around the corner.

She punched in the code to the door.

"This is a nice place," said Dustin, looking around. Once inside, he stopped at the window and peered out. "I've always appreciated being able to see out the front. When I was a kid, we had a big tree blocking our view. Good for climbing out of the second-floor window and sneaking out. Seeing if someone was at the door, not so much."

"Can I get you a glass of water, milk, orange juice, or

coffee? Sorry, but that's about the extent of the offerings. Hopefully, Jasmine will remember the pop." Jasmine could be absent-minded at times.

"Coffee would be great."

Londyn brewed a cup of fresh coffee while Dustin wandered around her living room. He stopped to look at her few knick-knacks, treasured porcelain dolls, and the photos on the shelf.

"Your family?"

"Yes. They adopted me."

"Who's the guy with you hiking?"

"Brodie. He's a good friend of mine."

Dustin faced her and arced a brow. "Only a friend?"

She didn't have to look in the mirror to know the heat traveling up her face. Dustin regarded her, his eyes remaining steadfast on her while he awaited an answer.

"He is a good friend and was also something more."

"Was?"

Why did she feel like she was being interrogated? "Unfortunately, I broke his heart."

"What does he do for a living?"

"He's in law enforcement—a sheriff."

"Jas told me about that guy."

Londyn sucked in a deep breath. What she'd told Jasmine had been in confidence.

"Are you ever going to get over him?"

"I—" How could she answer that? She handed him his coffee before calling to order a pizza. Jasmine arrived, and they settled into their movie with Dustin sitting between them on the couch. Halfway through the movie, they reached into the snack bowl full of chips at the same time, his fingers brushing hers. He glanced her way before squeezing her hand gently in his.

"You two are so cute," said Jasmine.

Londyn tugged her hand away, but not before noticing a flicker of irritation in Dustin's eyes.

After the movie, her guests left, and Londyn prepared for bed. Thankfully, it had been a quiet night. She turned on the faucet for a glass of water when she noticed something odd.

The three-picture frame collection on the living room shelf had been flopped over facedown.

She righted it, then checked the front door to ensure it was locked, before changing into a comfortable t-shirt. Exhaustion tugged at her. It had been a long day, but a good day.

Although...Dustin revealing his feelings for her and holding her hand on the couch caused a bit of consternation. Yes, she liked him, but only as a friend.

There would never be anyone for her except Brodie.

She flipped open her Bible, read a chapter, then turned off the light and fell fast asleep, forgetting to close the bedroom door.

Sometime in the night, she was awakened by a text notification. She rubbed her eyes and reached for her phone on the nightstand. The words peered up at her.

DID YOU ENJOY THE TIME WITH YOUR FRIENDS?

The characteristic all-caps gave no mystery as to who had sent her the text. He was obviously watching her to know that she'd had friends over. But from where? Fear gnawed at her insides. *Just how close was he?* Londyn immediately blocked the number. How many burner phones had the stalker purchased? Her hands shook as she again set the phone on the nightstand. She'd log it into her records tomorrow and call Detective Rivas. She was curious if there were any updates, anyway.

From somewhere in the apartment, she heard the sound

of footsteps. The hairs on the back of her neck stood on end. Londyn was about to bolt from the bed and shut and lock the door when something caught her attention, and she froze.

There, standing near the bedroom door, was a figure.

She screamed.

A hand waved at her, and she froze. Would whoever it was attempt to shoot her? Or worse?

"Who are you?" Her high-pitched voice sounded foreign in her own ears.

There was no answer, just a swift fleeing from the room.

Londyn's body shook as she stumbled to the door and slammed it shut and locked it. She fumbled for her gun, then the phone, her fingers accidentally entering 611.

A thump sounded somewhere in the apartment.

Would he be back? *Who* was it? She aimed the gun at the closed bedroom door.

When no one attempted to open it, she lowered the gun and lifted the phone, her fingers like jelly, as nausea rose in her throat. Finally, she punched in the number.

"911, what is your emergency?"

"There's a—there's a man in my house."

She fingered the gun while giving the operator her address.

"Officers are en route."

Panic surged through her, and her heart leaped from her throat. Adrenaline coursed through her as she held the phone in one hand and her loaded pistol in the other. She again aimed it at the door.

She readied herself. If he attempted to get in...

But, no, she couldn't shoot someone, could she?

"No one ever wants to shoot someone. No one ever wants to take a life." Mr. Brenneman's words from the situational awareness class rustled through her mind. *"But if your life is in danger and*

you have absolutely no other option, then you might have to do so.”

Her eyes fluttered open. The man was gone, but the fear remained.

The 911 operator informed her the officers had arrived, and Londyn walked through the fog of terror to the front door.

———

The next day at work, Jasmine and Dustin were, of course, supportive, and Detective Rivas said he’d visit BJ Nuss again.

The prints came back inconclusive. It didn’t surprise Londyn. This guy knew what he was doing well enough to know to wear gloves and disposable paper slippers on his shoes.

“I’m here for you, Londyn,” said Dustin, offering her a donut from the box he’d brought to work.

“Thank you. It’s just so scary.”

“This Nuss guy is a lunatic. How did he get into your house?”

“That’s what I’d like to know. The police said there was no forced entry. There’s a padlock button I have to manually press to lock, which I did.”

Dustin patted her on the arm. “Maybe you forgot,” he said quietly.

“No, I know I locked it.” Hadn’t she? Hadn’t she double-checked like she always did?

“If you want, I’ll follow you home tonight and check things out before you go in.”

He was such a sweet guy. “Thank you, but I don’t want you to go through the trouble. One of the officers is going to do a drive-by and a perimeter check.”

“If you’re sure.”

“I am, but thank you.”

Dustin moved closer, his breath tickling her cheek. "I care about you, Londyn. I know this hasn't been easy, but I'm here for you. And if that guy hurts you, he'll have me to deal with."

His protective nature should reassure her, so why did she still feel uneasy?

Brodie was always grateful that at Mom's house, it was all-you-can-eat. He rubbed his stomach after a tasty meal of lasagna, salad, and cookies for dessert.

"Guess what, Uncle Bro?"

"What's that, Xander?"

"The baby in Mom's tummy is going to be a boy."

"Oh, really?" Brodie knew otherwise, but wouldn't dampen the boy's enthusiasm. "How do you know?"

Roarke stood behind Mila, nuzzling her neck, and Brodie shoved aside a twinge of envy. That could have been him and Londyn had she not broken his heart.

"Because I don't want a sister," declared Xander.

"Why not?"

"Because some of my friends at the homeschool co-op have baby sisters and they cry all the time." He folded his arms across his chest. "No one can get any sleep."

"Baby boys can cry all the time, too. Just ask Grammie."

Roarke chuckled. "You don't even have to ask Grammie. I can tell you that your Uncle Brodie cried all the time when he was a baby."

"You were two. How would you know?" Brodie slugged his brother in the arm. "At least I didn't cry all the time over food."

Xander wrinkled his nose. "Over food?"

"Yeah, your dad cried all the time because there was no

more food because he ate it all."

It was Roarke's turn to slug Brodie, and they proceeded to playfully roughhouse. Sure, Roarke was taller and thicker, but Brodie was just as broad-shouldered, muscular, and fit. He overheard Mila ask, "How did you do it with four boys, Aileen?"

Mom laughed. "I sent them outside."

"I'm excited to have a little girl, and now even more so."

Xander, who had joined in the roughhousing, stopped and looked at his mom and grandma. That distracted Roarke and enabled Brodie to get in the last playful jab. "Don't underestimate the little brother," he said.

They were about to continue when Xander tapped on Mila's arm. "I'm not having a brother?"

Mila sat on the couch and gestured for her son to join her. She put an arm around him. "No, sweetie. Mommy and Daddy found out recently that we're having a baby girl."

"Not a brother?" Xander scowled.

"No, not a brother."

Xander's shoulders slumped. "But I put in the request for a brother."

Everyone in the room laughed, and Roarke took a seat beside Mila on the couch. "You're going to be an amazing big brother, Xander."

"And very protective of your baby sister. She'll be blessed to have a big brother who looks after her."

Xander perked up. "I can do that. I can make sure she's safe." He put a finger to his chin and gazed up at the ceiling. "I can make sure no bad bugs come by her, and I can share my bug collections with her. Do you think she'll like bugs? Kit's little sister is boring and only likes babydolls. Kit had to have a tea party with her once." A look of horror crossed Xander's face. "Mommy, am I going to have to have tea parties? Because I don't like tea."

That caused a round of chuckles, and the topic continued until Mom brought up another matter. "I heard from Grayson yesterday."

"How is he doing?" Brodie attempted to shove aside the bad taste in his mouth.

"He's doing well. As I shared previously, he's working on the police force in Denver."

"That must be exciting," said Roarke, although his voice lacked enthusiasm.

"I think he's ready for a change. That's what I needed to speak with you about, Brodie. Didn't you mention there was a vacant spot at the police department?"

"Vacant spot, yes, but it's not for patrol like what Grayson's doing. It's a detective position. Besides, I don't think Grayson is planning to return here. Not after..."

Mom held a finger to her lips, the silent admonishment she'd used since they were kids when she needed to say something important. Brodie stopped talking. "Forgiveness is something we, as Christians, are called to do, and I know Grayson left suddenly after your dad died and hasn't done the best job of staying in touch."

Brodie and Roarke simultaneously snorted.

"Be that as it may, he is your brother and he is my son." Mom's voice shook. "Brodie, can you send him the details about the detective position and put in a good word for him?"

"I don't know anything about his work ethic as a cop, Mom."

"I'm sure it's the same strong work ethic he had working on the ranch all those years."

Brodie could press the issue, but wouldn't. It wasn't worth

upsetting Mom, and she'd suffered enough losing her husband and Danny, and in a way, Grayson. "All right. I'll talk to the chief about it and get you the details so you can forward them to Grayson."

"I'd appreciate it." Mom had that look in her eyes she got when she was covertly demanding a request be obeyed.

"Okay. I'll also reach out to him." He caught Roarke's eye. They shared the same sentiment about their prodigal little brother.

Chapter 7

Unfortunately, the police had nothing concrete to pin on BJ Nuss. The thought of him lurking around every corner or potentially showing up in her house or texting or calling her again caused incredible trepidation.

There was no sign of a break-in. Apparently, Mr. Nuss or whoever it was wandered right through the front door. Detective Rivas, while sympathetic, had doubted her when she insisted she'd locked the door.

Dustin continued to accompany her to the parking garage and home each day. There was only one problem with his repeated offers. She appreciated his thoughtfulness, but it was a little awkward. She knew he liked her, and she wasn't sure she could return his affections. Not that Dustin wasn't nice, because he was, and he was a great catch, as Jasmine pointed out on numerous occasions. But honestly, one of the other single women in the office who had their eye on him should probably make a move because Londyn wouldn't be.

Nothing had happened in the past few days, so Londyn's stress level decreased somewhat. Before they left for work, Jasmine pointed out that Dustin might not wait forever for her when Londyn had declined his offer to take her out tonight.

Londyn had only wanted to go home and snuggle up with a book and relax.

On another note, if she were out with Dustin, she would feel safer than she would even in her own apartment. Even if a patrol officer would occasionally drive through the neighborhood.

Dustin perched near the corner of her cubicle and smiled. "Have you given any thought about tonight?"

How could she deny his request when he had been so thoughtful and dedicated in making sure she was safe?

"Sure," she heard herself say.

"Awesome!"

While she would have preferred to stop at home and freshen up a bit first, it made better sense to go directly from work instead of having him follow her home and wait for her.

Jasmine appeared with a suspicious smirk on her face. "It's about time you said yes, Londyn. You two have fun tonight. I will see you Sunday at church, Dustin."

The partly cloudy skies gave a glimmer of hope that spring was on its way. Dustin walked her to her car, and they stood together briefly in the parking garage. The only other people on this crisp Friday evening were a few people Londyn recognized from the law office in the same building as her employer. Most wanted to exit their work and head home after a busy week.

"Do you want to just hop in my truck and go to dinner? I can drop you off after we eat and follow you home."

"That makes sense, but honestly, I prefer not to come back to the parking garage tonight, especially if it gets too late."

"I understand. How about I follow you over to the restaurant?"

"That sounds good." She anticipated a relaxing evening,

even if her plans had changed.

She pulled out of the parking garage, and Dustin followed her to the Rowland Steakhouse, an upper-end restaurant on the far western side of town. The parking lot was already packed. They might not even get a table.

Dustin parked his maroon diesel truck beside her SUV and exited his vehicle.

"Do you think we'll get a table?"

Dustin grinned at her, a glimmer in his dark eyes. "I'm not worried."

"Oh?"

"Yeah, someone *may* have made reservations."

"But how did you know I would say yes?"

Dustin shrugged. "I didn't. But it's easier to cancel the reservations than to try to make them at the last minute. Besides, now we have a table."

The guy truly thought of everything. Londyn was shocked he wasn't already snapped up and married with three or four kids and living in the suburbs. They wove their way through the crowded parking lot and stepped into the ritzy steakhouse, where the aroma of steak and potatoes greeted them. Dustin informed the hostess that he had reservations, and she led them to a private table on the second floor overlooking the nearby lake.

"Wow, the view is amazing."

"Yes, it is." Dustin kept his focus on Londyn for several seconds before handing the hostess what appeared to be cash, before she went on her way. "I thought you would enjoy this spectacular view. It's the best table in the place." Dustin walked over to her side and pulled out her chair. She appreciated his chivalry. Maybe she should consider dating him.

Brodie's image flashed through her mind. If there was no

chance with him due to her foolishness, maybe Dustin would be a second option.

"You look beautiful tonight," Dustin said, interrupting her thoughts.

Londyn reached up and fiddled with one of her earrings. "Thank you." She appreciated his compliment; however, with the best seat in the restaurant, now she wished she'd been able to go home first and change into something a little classier than jeans and a sweater.

The waiter arrived shortly after to take their drink order. The menu offered multiple palatable options, and Londyn ordered the chicken and broccoli pasta while Dustin ordered a ribeye steak. They carried on a pleasant conversation, first starting with work, and then Dustin asked her a few questions about her family.

"Not much to say. My mom is remarried to her most recent husband, Jason, and they just moved to Arizona. I have a brother named Logan, but I haven't seen him in years."

"That stinks. Jas mentioned you weren't close to your family."

Had Jasmine told him everything?

"Yeah. It doesn't bother me too much." Well, it did on occasion, but most of the time, Londyn didn't give her dysfunctional family a second thought. Especially not since she considered the Brennemans her family.

A niggle of guilt stabbed her in the gut. If someone had treated her like family as the Brennemans had, why had she hurt them so much? Londyn blinked away the emotion. "What about you?" she asked Dustin.

"My family lives in New Mexico."

"That's quite a distance from here. Do you see them often?"

Dustin shrugged but said nothing, leaving her to believe

he was probably not close to his family either. She completely understood. He placed the napkin in his lap. Would he elaborate? Londyn had known him to be a rather private person, even more private than she was.

"What made you decide to move to Rowland?" she asked.

"I saw the job offer, and it paid better than where I was working before."

"Have you lived in Rowland for a while?"

"Yes, several years. And you moved from where?" But before Londyn could answer, the waiter returned with their food. Londyn prayed over her meal and was glad to see that Dustin appeared to be praying over his food as well. She vacillated back and forth once again between giving Dustin a chance and foregoing the possibility.

Thoughts of being just like Mom entered her mind.

But it's different, she argued with herself.

Was it? Could Londyn so easily forget about Brodie, just like Mom forgot about her ex-husbands? She'd initiated every divorce except the one with Dad. If Londyn and Dustin married, would Londyn stay with him until death parted them like Mr. and Mrs. Brenneman, or would she soon replace him?

They finished eating and talked a while longer before Dustin followed Londyn to her apartment in his truck. It had been an enjoyable evening; she would be sure to reiterate to Dustin how much she appreciated a reprieve from the thoughts that permeated her mind over her stalker. And what the stalker's next actions could consist of.

She drove into her carport, and Dustin parked behind her. She grabbed her purse and exited the SUV, making sure she hit the lock button more than once. Dustin leaned against his truck, the slight breeze ruffling his blond hair.

"Thank you for the nice evening," she said.

"My pleasure."

They stood in silence as the seconds ticked by until Dustin spoke. "I can always come in, and maybe we can watch a movie or something?"

Londyn couldn't really put a finger on why she'd decline, other than she didn't want to give Dustin the wrong idea. She had wavered back and forth in her indecision so many times, but something she couldn't determine stopped her from pursuing a relationship with him. If she did choose to date him, she endeavored to take it extremely slow. Her morals and convictions would allow for nothing else. "I'm really tired. But I do appreciate all you have done for me these past few days."

Something akin to irritation flashed across Dustin's face, and then it was gone. Had she even seen it at all? He reached for both of her hands and held them in his.

She waited for that jolt of electricity to rush through as it had with Brodie. But nothing came.

Of course, she couldn't place a huge emphasis on feelings as they were oftentimes untrustworthy and faulty. Just because she didn't experience heart-fluttering moments of being with him didn't mean Dustin wasn't worthy of a relationship.

"Londyn," he said, his voice husky as he inclined slightly toward her. "I really like you and would like to take our friendship to the next level."

Even though Londyn had given this some thought in the past few minutes, his comments still caught her off guard. "I'm not sure."

"Not sure about what? It's obvious we make a great pair."

"We do make a good team, and I do like you."

"Then what's the problem? It might be helpful if we were dating. That might cause that Nuss guy to leave you alone if he knows there's a boyfriend in the picture."

Londyn doubted that anything would dissuade BJ Nuss if he was bent on getting revenge, like she imagined he was. Revenge on her for something she had no control over.

Dustin was so close that she could see what was probably a chickenpox scar on his left cheek.

"What do you say?"

"I don't know."

"Is it because of the guy you still carry a torch for? Jasmine told me how he proposed to you, and you rejected his offer of marriage. Bummer for him."

A ripple of anger rose through Londyn. Jasmine was supposed to have kept that confidential. "I do regret the way things ended between us." She thought of how she'd found the three-frame picture collection facedown after Dustin and Jasmine had come over for a movie. Had that been him or Jasmine?

"His loss, my gain."

Londyn wasn't sure it was Dustin's gain. She hadn't given him the affirmative answer he sought, and she wasn't even sure Brodie would feel like it was his loss. "I need some time to pray and think about it."

Dustin released her hands and raised his eyebrows. "Pray about and think about whether or not you want to date?" His expression of disbelief reminded Londyn that Dustin was still very new in his faith. He didn't understand the need to pray before everything and every decision, whether small or big. The decision to pray constantly, and not just once in a while or before meals. He couldn't possibly understand how she tried to pray about every choice, whether big or small. That she had turned over every area of her life to the one who gave His life for her.

But she hadn't prayed the day she left Pronghorn Falls. That decision had no basis on the Lord's will. She inwardly winced.

"If you like someone and you want to date them, what does God have to do with it?"

"Because I want to be in His will. I need to pray about it, Dustin." She hoped that would keep him from continuing to question it. Something indiscernible flashed in his eyes, and he narrowed them so faintly, she thought she may have imagined it.

Just as quickly, Dustin's smile returned. "Thank you again for the great evening."

"You're welcome."

Dustin again clasped one of her hands and walked with her to the front door of her apartment.

A neighbor turned her way, and Londyn waved, though the greeting was not returned. Unfortunately, it was a sour neighborhood, and she had not had the opportunity to become acquainted with any of her neighbors except the elderly man on the ground floor next to her apartment.

"Good night, Londyn."

"Good night, Dustin."

He brushed a kiss across her lips, veered back, and stared at her expectantly as if waiting for more.

"Good night." She repeated, pivoting and unlocking the door before stepping inside. She watched as Dustin retreated in the direction of his truck.

She locked the door and mentally listed off the pros and cons when it came to a relationship with Dustin. The cons won.

———

Londyn finished her work for the day. She had a decent success rate with chatting with clients and was able to work out several reasonable payment plans. She glanced at the clock and dreaded this time of day. Who knew where her stalker would be? Outside waiting for her? Would he call her or send her more texts? Show up again at her apartment? It seemed like his nefarious actions always occurred after work hours. There had been no breaks in the case, and when pressed by the detective, Mr. Nuss continued to deny any involvement. They had nothing to pin on him.

There was no one else she could think of who would seek revenge due to an outstanding bill. But just because someone didn't express their thoughts didn't mean they weren't resentful.

"Hey, there." Dustin propped himself against her cubicle wall. "Need me to walk you out?"

Londyn would forever be grateful that he cared about her and always appreciated his offers. It did make her feel safer, and she knew he'd come to her defense if her stalker tried anything. But after their date the other night, his unwelcome kiss, and her declining his offer to take their friendship to the next level, Dustin had been standoffish. Now, as he stood beside her desk, a broad grin on his face, she was grateful he wasn't holding a grudge.

"Sure, thank you. I just need to grab my things, and I'll be ready to go."

Dustin accompanied her out of the office building, and they walked to the parking garage. It didn't matter how many lights there were; something about the place always gave her the creeps. That was another thing she missed about Pronghorn Falls. The town was so small that it would probably never have a parking garage. If you wanted to park somewhere, you could park in front of the business or park around the block and walk.

They arrived at her car. "Well, here we are. Thank you, Dustin."

He regarded her for a moment. "Are you doing anything tonight?"

"I have plans to catch up on some household chores."

"All right, well, I was just going to see if you wanted to go to a movie."

"Thank you, but I do need to get some things done." She didn't want to get his hopes up that she had changed her mind about dating him, even if it was something as innocent as going to a movie.

Londyn's back was against her SUV, and she was about to turn around and climb inside when Dustin leaned toward her. In an attempt to put space between them, she reared her head back, nearly smacking it on the window. Dustin inched even closer, bridging the meager distance now between them and entering into her personal space. She flinched, but he continued toward her, leaving her no option but to be face-to-face with him. Before she could say anything or do what she could to avoid him, Dustin brushed his lips against hers. Her arms involuntarily rose, and she pressed hard and firmly on his shoulders and turned her head away from any further contact. "Dustin."

"Sorry, I couldn't resist. You're just so pretty." He smiled at her with what appeared to be a genuine smile.

Anger stirred within her, and Londyn dropped her hands to her sides and clenched her fists. She didn't appreciate him violating her in that way. "I need to go."

He reached for her hand, and she pulled it away. "Whoa. Look, Londyn, I'm sorry. I just—I really like you."

"And I like you too, Dustin, but not in that way."

His shoulders slumped, and he fisted a hand to his chest. "That hurts me here, you know?"

"I'm sorry." What else could she say?

"If we spent more time together, your feelings for me would change. We're meant to be together."

His words caused an involuntary shiver.

"Now more than ever, I'm seeing how much you mean to me. How much I care about you. How much I want to protect you from this crazy guy who shows up at your apartment and texts you. I'm ready to take our friendship to the next level. Won't you reconsider?"

"Sorry, but no. I'm not ready for a relationship at this time."

His eyes narrowed, and his lip curled before his expression immediately changed. Dustin smiled with a nod. "All right, but you can't blame a guy for trying, right? And please don't hold the kisses against me. I promise I won't try anything like that again without your permission."

"All right," she said, her voice wavering slightly. Dustin had been a good friend, and maybe this was just an innocent error on his part.

After parting ways with Dustin, Londyn climbed quickly into her car and, out of habit, clicked the lock button. Dustin slowly walked away from her SUV before shoving his hands into his pockets and meandering toward his own truck.

Her heart pounded, and she exhaled a few short breaths, collecting her thoughts before starting her car and exiting the parking garage. A red flag emerged, one that reminded her that Dustin may not take no for an answer in the future. The thought discouraged her. She could always use more friends.

The twenty-minute drive home gave her time to think about things. That was the only good thing about not living close to your place of employment. In Pronghorn Falls, it took her exactly six minutes to get from her apartment to the clinic where she worked. Gray skies overhead promised more rain, and she stopped at the stoplight and waited behind the expansive line of cars.

Last night, instead of sleeping, she'd weighed the pros and cons of returning to Pronghorn Falls. Pros would be that she wouldn't have to deal with whoever this stalker was. She could return to the town she loved and to her friends. She might even be able to get her old job back. And she could see Brodie again and apologize for what she had done. That was one mess that needed to be corrected.

On the other hand, if she stayed in Rowland, she would continue to work at a job that paid well, she liked her apartment, and she did have friends here, although with the way things were going with Dustin, she wasn't sure how long she could maintain the friendship with him when he wanted something more. She spent a lot of time in prayer seeking God's wisdom, the verse in James never far from her mind: *"If any of you lacks wisdom, let him ask God, who gives generously to all without reproach, and it will be given him."*

Oh, how she lacked wisdom and needed the generous wisdom the Lord provided to those who asked.

Londyn wasn't sure what decision she should make regarding returning to Pronghorn Falls, even though she had surrendered that choice to God. She had learned the importance once again of prayer before action. Especially since she'd failed to pray before leaving Pronghorn Falls.

She debated sending a text to Aileen and seeking her advice. Of course, Aileen would tell her she was welcome back anytime. While Londyn hadn't texted Brodie often, just a few generic texts that he sometimes returned while they exchanged pleasantries, her communication with Aileen had been more frequent and meaningful, although Londyn hadn't shared with the woman about her stalker. She *had* shared about her job, her new apartment, and an apology for leaving like she had. Apologizing to Aileen in person would be much more beneficial than over text.

A car behind her honked, and Londyn realized she'd been sitting at the stoplight for longer than necessary. She pressed on the gas and proceeded. The sign of a pizza place on the corner captured her attention, and her stomach growled. At the last minute, she swerved into the parking lot. Checking her surroundings before exiting her car, she locked the door and hurried inside. There were two other people in front of her—a woman right in front of her, and a man she didn't recognize from the back of his head in front of the woman.

Her phone pinged, signaling a text, and Londyn averted her attention from the people in line to the text that had come through from Jasmine.

Hey, girl! Wanna do something this evening?

She enjoyed spending time with Jasmine, but she was already planning to have a quiet evening at home. Especially since she had a lot to think about if she was going to go through with her plans to leave Rowland. Yet, she didn't want to discourage her friend. Londyn bit her lip. She would have to tell Jasmine about her plans. In person.

Could I get back to you on that? I'm in line at the pizza place.

Sure! I thought maybe we could invite Dustin, too.

Londyn was so not going there. Not right now. Not after Dustin's most recent overtures.

By the time Londyn typed in her response, the woman in front of her was leaving the counter, and it was Londyn's turn to order. She peered up at the menu on the wall, then at the glass cabinet that held the most recently prepared pizzas. Fortunately, they already had thick-crust cheese pizza made, so she was able to take it immediately and not have to wait.

"Can I help you?" the teenage boy at the counter asked. He had such a multitude of fluffy, brown bangs that Londyn was surprised he could see her at all. He reminded her of a sheepdog.

"Yes, I'd like a small thick-crust cheese pizza."

He flipped his head back, causing the pile of hair to temporarily lift from his face. "Yeah, okay. We have one of those right here." He reached inside the glass cabinet and removed the pizza.

As she scurried back to her car, juggling the pizza box, she regretted being forced to park a lengthy distance away instead of close by. Just as she was unlocking the door, a firm hand gripped her shoulder. She startled, then froze, her pulse ticking up at least a thousand notches. In the car window, she saw the reflection of a red-haired man in his late thirties.

BJ Nuss.

Chapter 8

She screamed, but it was doubtful anyone would hear it over the constant flow of traffic on the adjacent busy street and a roar of thunder that sounded above. She needed to immobilize him so she could escape. Londyn dropped the pizza and elbowed him as hard as she could in the nose.

A groan met her actions, and Mr. Nuss clutched his face. She stomped on his foot and threw a kick, her toe connecting with his knee. Londyn flung open her SUV door and slid inside, the pizza forgotten.

"Wait! Please. I'm not here to hurt you." BJ Nuss's muffled voice caught her off guard.

She slammed the door and locked it. Inserting the key into the ignition, she rolled down the window an inch. "Who are you?" she asked, even though she already knew.

He limped a few steps forward. Two people in a nearby car turned to look.

"My name is BJ Nuss. I just need to talk to you."

"How did you find me?" Her finger hovered over the emergency button on her phone. Adrenaline crashed through her. She needed to start the car, leave, and drive directly to the police station. And yet, as bizarre and unconventional as it sounded, Londyn also needed answers. She glanced at the glovebox where she kept her gun.

Blood gushed from BJ Nuss's nose. He swiped at it with his upper arm, leaving a streak of red. He then held up both hands, palms up. "Like I said, I'm not going to hurt you, I just need to talk to you."

"If it's about your bill, you can call me during work hours. You don't sneak up on someone in the parking lot."

BJ Nuss pumped his palms. "I know. I know. Wrong way of going about it. Just hear me out, okay?"

"How did you know I was here?"

"I was two people ahead of you in line."

That must have been the time when her attention was focused on Jasmine's text. While she'd only seen Mr. Nuss once in the photo Detective Rivas showed her, she *would* have recognized him had she been looking up as he passed her.

Londyn craned her neck behind her vehicle. The parking lot not only housed the pizza place, but also a dry cleaner's, salon, Italian restaurant, pharmacy, and a shoe store. There was no way she was leaving anytime soon. Not during rush hour traffic with customers waiting to exit the parking lot. Not when some of them were turning left onto one of the busiest streets in Rowland. Not when the line to exit was a mile long. Not to mention those entering the lot.

"Call me during work hours."

"It's not about my bill." BJ Nuss took a cautious step forward, and she noticed his hunched posture.

"Stay right there," she warned. Her mouth went dry. This crazy lunatic had already been stalking her. What else would he try? She glanced down at her phone, the emergency button begging her to press it. "How do you know who I am?"

"It's not hard. The company you work for has a website

where anyone can see pictures of staff members."

Londyn inwardly groaned. She should have opted out of an online presence when she had the chance. At the time, she hadn't thought it would be an issue.

What else did he know about her? Obviously, he knew where she lived, and he somehow knew her phone number. She allowed her gaze to fall to the pizza box on the ground. Half of the pie had slid out onto the asphalt. Not that it mattered. She'd have cereal for dinner if she needed to. What would BJ Nuss have done if she hadn't fought back? She recoiled at the thought.

She just wanted to get out of there as quickly as possible. She spoke again through the barely rolled-down window. "We have nothing to discuss. I'm leaving." Yes, she wanted—no, needed—answers. But she wasn't willing to jeopardize her life for them.

A man rushed by and took a double-take. His attention veered to BJ Nuss, then back to Londyn. "Is everything okay here?"

She was about to reply when Nuss said, "Yes, it is, we're just having a conversation, but thank you for your concern."

"What is it that you need to say that is so important that it can't be said over the phone?" She sized up the man in front of her. He was thin, and he definitely could have been the man at the door that night and across the street.

"I need you to stop lying about me to the cops."

"I'm not lying about you. You have been texting, calling, and loitering around my apartment. That's called stalking. Grabbing my shoulder today was assault." Londyn was grateful her voice sounded stronger than she felt.

"Texting you, calling you, stalking you, and showing up at your apartment wasn't me."

She wanted to dispute his answer but didn't want to rile him further.

"I haven't done any of those things, just as I told the cops."

She didn't believe him. Londyn turned over the engine. The line to exit the parking lot hadn't budged.

"No, wait. Just a few more minutes to explain myself."

He'd respectfully kept his distance. She'd give him that at least. "Make it quick."

"Look, I was not happy about the hospital bill. It was more than I thought it was going to be for the back surgery, and then with all the additional fees that have accumulated. I was furious when you sent me to collections. But I would never show up at your apartment or send you a text. He ran a hand through his thinning red hair. "The detective even checked my phone. There were no texts to you."

Londyn didn't mention that those could easily be deleted, or in the case of burner phones, discarded. "You mentioned on the phone that you weren't satisfied with the bill."

"I'm not. There's absolutely no way I can pay that. "

"I told you we could talk about payment terms."

"Yes, and I was angry that last time we spoke and said some things I regret. I mishandled that phone call, and I'm sorry about that."

"Those words sounded like a threat." She eyed the increasing line of cars. It would be tomorrow before she was able to exit onto the main road.

Mr. Nuss released a long, slow sigh. "I accumulated a lot of bills while I was out of work after the back surgery. And then you went to the cops, and they showed up on my doorstep and contacted my probation officer. I'm on probation for embezzling some funds from my former employer. Slowly paying that back. But when my probation officer heard that I was potentially stalking someone, it didn't do me any favors. I need you to stop lying to the cops," he repeated.

She couldn't put her finger on it, but there was something that seemed genuine about BJ Nuss's pleas.

"I will pay back all that I owe, along with the interest. I can't do it right away, but I will do it. I just need a little more time."

"This is all stuff that you can tell me over the phone during work hours."

"Not the cop stuff, and not the reassurance that I'm not the one who's stalking you."

"You don't know where I live?"

"I don't. And even if I did, I wouldn't go to your house. I may have made a lot of mistakes, like embezzlement and drinking while driving, losing the only woman I ever loved, and the harsh words I said to you over the phone, but I'm not a stalker. Please believe me."

His eyes searched her face. Eyes that might not have been the eyes of the one who was at her door that day. Eyes that may not have been the ones watching her in her bedroom that night.

"Look. I never meant to scare you."

She peered again at the dilapidated pizza.

"I'll buy you another pizza." Nuss stuck his hand in his pocket and withdrew a wad of cash. "Please take it and get another pizza."

He held it out to her. But no matter what he was promising, Londyn wasn't going to leave the safe confines of her locked vehicle.

"No, thank you. I'm going to go now."

Easier said than done, based on a cursory glance at the line of vehicles still waiting to exit the parking lot. She made a mental note to never again assume "grabbing" a pizza on the way home from work was an efficient idea.

BJ Nuss put the money back in his pocket. "Just please believe me. I'm not the one who's been stalking you. I'm mad about the bill, yeah, but I'm not going to hurt you."

She scrutinized him. Londyn had always figured herself a good judge of character, yet BJ Nuss could be a professional at lying. He hadn't exactly lived a law-abiding life.

Mr. Nuss swiped again at his nose, which had slowed its bleeding. A police car entered the parking lot, and Londyn recognized it as Officer Nelson.

"I will call you tomorrow during normal business hours. Maybe we can get my bill back from collections." He turned on his heel and started toward an older model vehicle that appeared to be held together by duct tape.

Thank You, Lord, she breathed.

Officer Nelson intercepted BJ Nuss. "Please wait a minute, Mr. Nuss." The officer approached Londyn's SUV, and she further rolled down her window.

"We received a call from a concerned citizen."

"Yes, sir. Mr. Nuss needed to talk to me."

"Doesn't look like he went about it the right way."

"No, he grabbed my shoulder, and I defended myself."

"I want you both to come down to the station and give your statements. Nuss?"

BJ Nuss nodded. "Yes, sir. I'll be there."

After another fifteen minutes of waiting in line, Londyn and BJ Nuss followed Officer Nelson to the police station. She thanked the Lord for keeping her safe in what could have been a volatile situation. It was only after she was halfway to the station that her heartbeat finally returned to a normal rhythm.

BJ Nuss was denying his involvement in the past several weeks of texts, calls, and fear. Londyn shook her head. Oddly enough, she believed he was telling the truth.

But if he wasn't the one who'd committed these crimes, who had?

And if BJ Nuss hadn't stalked her, threatened her, scared her, and made her scared to even leave her own apartment, then who was it?

———

Londyn cleaned out her desk the next day. She regretted she hadn't been able to chat with Jasmine beforehand, but she was in Sonja's office. And Dustin was out sick.

Both deserved to know she was leaving. She felt like a heel. Their friendship was important to her.

After the discussion at the police department, she was more assured than ever that BJ Nuss was not her stalker. Detective Rivas informed her that tracing the several burner phones had resulted in mixed results. It had been purchased with cash at an out-of-the-way convenience store located ten miles east of Rowland. The purchaser was dressed in all black, including a hoodie. The images were grainy, but the clerk didn't think it was BJ Nuss. And the purchaser had an erect and upright posture and was a few inches shorter than Mr. Nuss.

BJ Nuss had an alibi for the time the burner phones were purchased.

Which meant it was someone else—someone still out there.

Jasmine poked her head around the corner. "What are you doing?"

"Oh, there you are."

"Yeah, I was in Sonja's office discussing a recalcitrant client. What's going on?"

"I'm quitting."

"What? Are you serious? And you were going to tell me when?"

"I'm sorry, Jasmine. I decided just last night."

Jasmine pinned her thin arms across her chest. "Does this have anything to do with Mr. Nuss cornering you in the pizza place parking lot?"

"That confirmed it even more."

"So, you were thinking of this before that episode?"

"I have been contemplating it for a while." Londyn scooped up some spare change from one of the compartments in her desk drawer.

Irritation edged Jasmine's voice. "What precipitated this?"

"I just think it's time, especially with all that's been happening with this crazed weirdo."

"He's been pestering you for a while now. Why don't the police just arrest Mr. Nuss?"

"I don't think it's him. There are too many inconsistencies."

Jasmine pasted on a hard smile. "But you love this job." She raised her voice. "I truly do not understand you, Londyn."

"I do love this job." Jasmine was a good friend, but she wouldn't understand. Not fully. Londyn stuffed her coffee mug into the box.

"Does Sonja know?"

"She does."

"And you gave her two weeks' notice?"

Jasmine had suddenly become adept at interrogation. "I am unable to give a two-week notice, and yes, Sonja does know, and as I mentioned before, I do enjoy this job, but it's time for me to move on."

"But where will you go? And can we at least throw you a going-away party?" Her narrowed eyes bored into Londyn before she scanned the office. "Dustin is out sick today, but maybe we can take you out tomorrow, and we can invite Sonja and a few of the others."

"That's sweet, but honestly, I'm going to be on the road tomorrow."

"To the road where?"

"I'm heading back to Pronghorn Falls."

Jasmine scowled at her. "Is this some kind of a joke to you?"

"Some kind of joke?" Londyn had seen Jasmine become irritated a time or two if she had to be put on hold or was behind someone slow in traffic, but never as frustrated as she was now.

"Yes, some kind of joke." Jasmine released an exaggerated sigh, and her brow pinched. "Didn't you just leave Pronghorn Falls? Or did you and Brodie get back together?"

A ton of packing awaited her, but Londyn didn't want to be unkind to the woman who had become her friend. It was obvious she'd hurt Jasmine. "I know this is sudden, and I am sorry." Londyn swallowed hard. How could she explain this? "It's just a decision that I needed to make."

"So, you just stay at places for a matter of months and then move on? What about the workload here? It will take Sonja forever to replace you. We're already shorthanded." She took a step closer and tapped her long fingernails on the desk. "And what about Dustin? He really likes you."

She'd told Jasmine more than once that she was not interested in Dustin for more than a friend, but her admonition had fallen on deaf ears. "You have been an awesome friend, Jasmine, and I hope we can maintain our friendship."

Jasmine planted her hands on her hips. "Well, I would hope so too, but if I'm such a good friend, then why didn't you tell me this sooner? You can't just spring it on people like this."

Her friend was correct, and under normal circumstances,

Londyn would have informed her sooner. If she'd arrived at her decision sooner. "After much prayer and with what happened with BJ Nuss yesterday…it cemented my decision of whether or not to return to Pronghorn Falls. I'm sorry I hurt you by telling you at the last minute."

Several other coworkers moseyed by. Likely, they were interested to see what all of the fuss was about. Jasmine lowered her voice to an almost seething tone. "I'm not a psychiatrist or anything, but you have a problem with running away from things and people."

A retort lingered on Londyn's lips, but she refrained from uttering it. Maybe she really did have an issue with running when things became unmanageable. But in her defense, this time it could prove life-threatening. "I need to go chat with Sonja and pick up my last paycheck."

"And that's it, you're just gone? Now I see how Brodie could be so upset with you. And I'm not even as close to you as he was."

At the insertion of Brodie's name, Londyn's heart fell to her stomach. That was something she hoped she could work out when she returned to Pronghorn Falls. "It's just with the stalker and everything, I need to go."

"There hasn't been anything else, has there? I mean, Mr. Nuss's confrontation in the parking lot didn't end badly. Maybe the guy is done with bothering you."

"Or maybe he's not, and the entire thing escalates." Even as she said the words, fear coiled in her belly.

"It's probably another one of our clients. I think you're making too much out of a few texts, and what? Two phone calls?"

"And a man attempting to break in, then succeeding and standing in my room."

Jasmine shrugged off her concerns, and Londyn continued. "There's been no one else as frustrated as Mr. Nuss. I've already talked to Detective Rivas about this. Besides, I need to get back home. I miss my friends. I miss my life I had there. I need to apologize and seek Brodie's forgiveness. Make things right with him and Aileen."

"And yet you chose to leave there." Jasmine's accusatory frown accompanied her tone, which was harsher than normal. "You are so flighty."

Londyn rose and took a step forward to hug her friend. "Thank you for your friendship. I could not have settled into life here in Rowland without you."

Jasmine did not return the hug. Instead, she stiffened, her arms remaining at her sides.

Londyn released her. "I will text you when I get to Pronghorn Falls. Just because I'm moving back doesn't mean I won't return to Rowland, and we can catch a movie or go out to lunch. Or you could even come to Pronghorn Falls for a visit."

"I doubt I'm going to be coming to Pronghorn Falls. I don't care much for small towns. And unlike you," said Jasmine, taking a step back, "I don't run off at the first sign of trouble."

"Stalking is hardly a minor matter. Who knows what this creep is capable of?"

"Maybe. Or maybe you just blew everything out of proportion. Besides, I still think you need to tell Dustin. He's going to be heartbroken."

The continued insistence from her friend that she pursue a relationship with Dustin was getting tiresome, but she was correct in that Londyn needed to tell him she was leaving. While not boyfriend material, Dustin *had* been there for her when she needed him. "Speaking of guys, I forgot to ask you how the second date went with the server."

Jasmine's face fell. "He doesn't seem to think we are compatible."

"I'm so sorry."

"Yeah, well, it is what it is."

"Maybe it's meant to be for you and Dustin to get together."

Something crossed Jasmine's face. A glimpse of hope, perhaps? "I don't know, we'll see. He's in love with you, so that doesn't exactly work too well. So, what time are you leaving?"

"I plan to leave tomorrow, no later than nine. I have to pick up the cargo trailer from the rental place. The forecast is calling for rain again, but from the radar, at this point, I'll miss most of it."

"At least it's all freeway driving."

"That does make it easier and faster."

After a few more minutes of conversing, Londyn was finally able to excuse herself and meet in her boss's office. Sonja, too, attempted to convince her to stay, but Londyn knew she was making the right choice.

Chapter 9

Just another day on the job. Dad had always said that ninety percent of the crimes were committed by ten percent of the population.

Brodie was about to agree with that statement once again.

While Pronghorn Falls was a small town, crime had increased in the past few years. More people had moved in, seeking the slower and more relaxed lifestyle and close proximity to a beautiful mountain range.

Not that it was anything like the larger scale of criminal activity in bigger towns and cities, but it demanded a lot of time and took Brodie away from his main jobs as a sheriff.

A thug named Hyland, a repeat offender who'd previously been arrested for illegal drugs, abusing inhalants, and domestic violence, thought it was a good idea to weave all over the road just south of town on the frontage road adjacent to the freeway.

Brodie called for backup and pulled him over. As predicted, Hyland exhibited all the signs of drug use. The guy was hyper, sweating, and his face was covered in severe acne and sores. He'd retained two lone teeth. Just one look, and Brodie knew the guy was high on something.

He completed the tedious paperwork. It amused, but hadn't surprised him, that Hyland stated he had nothing in his pockets.

K-9 police dog, Radar, had begged to differ.

Hyland said the crystal was planted in his pocket and wasn't his. Same story, different day.

"Brenneman, I'm glad I caught you before you went home. Do you have a minute?" Chief Neeley stood in the doorway.

"I do. What's up?"

"I thought you might want to know that Grayson applied for the open detective position."

"I was wondering if he would follow through with that."

"Well, he did. We received his resume this morning. Seems he may have plans to move back to Pronghorn Falls."

Brodie scrubbed his chin with his hand. "Can't say I'm completely surprised since Mom had me relay the information to him."

"Not my business at all, but kind of interesting that he's choosing to move back, don't you think?"

Brodie stared into the distance, not really seeing what was there. He'd thought about this several times after Mom mentioned Grayson expressed interest in the detective position. Part of Brodie, admittedly a large part, had hoped Grayson wouldn't apply.

A stab right in the center of his gut reminded Brodie that such thoughts weren't exactly Christlike, especially toward his own brother. The niggle of his conscience persisted as the Holy Spirit's conviction pressed. "Yeah, it will be interesting to hear how he's been doing."

"I can imagine."

Chief Neeley knew Grayson had left abruptly after Dad was killed, but that was the extent of it. Rumors had likely abounded. "Have you had many other applicants?"

"We've had four. Of those four, two were immediately weeded out."

"Is Grayson a contender?"

"He is. Grayson is on the young side, but he'll take the national testing next, although with his experience as a patrolman in Denver, I'm sure he'll pass. He will, of course, then take the physical fitness test."

Which Grayson would easily pass if he were still regularly working out like he had when he lived in Pronghorn Falls. The guy loved just about every sport, especially biking and indoor cycling.

"And we'll do the background check," Chief continued. "We'll have him meet before the board for an oral interview."

Chief Neeley was on that board as well as the lieutenant. Brodie studied his friend and fellow LEO. "He has a good chance of cinching the job, then?"

"I think so. He's got the creds, but there are some hoops for him to jump through, and the other candidate is no slouch."

"What time frame are we looking at?"

"Probably within the next couple of months."

A mixture of emotions settled in Brodie's chest. On one hand, it would make Mom happy to have all of her boys back in Pronghorn Falls. On the other hand, Brodie, and likely Roarke as well, would be calling upon the Lord multiple times because forgiving their brother might not be an easy task. Even if that was the right thing to do. "Thank you for telling me."

"You're welcome. Just figured you might want to know."

As Brodie left later that evening, thoughts about Grayson lingered in his mind. Two very important people in his life had left of their own accord, with barely a goodbye. Would Londyn return to Pronghorn Falls at some point as well? Or was it safe to assume she was out of his life forever?

———————

Londyn tucked her gun in the concealed holster and pulled her suitcase from beneath her bed. Unfortunately, she'd accumulated a few items since moving to Rowland, necessitating a small pull-along cargo trailer. Her Rowland apartment was fully furnished, so there were no large appliances to haul except a microwave.

Also, fortunately, Brodie had taught her how to pull a horse trailer the year she won a purple grand prize ribbon for the cow she entered in the fair. Pulling a cargo trailer would be simple.

The man at the rental shop hooked it up to her SUV, and now, Lord willing, Londyn could load it and be ready to leave in two hours. While it would have been advantageous to have Jasmine's help, her friend hadn't offered.

She hadn't heard from Dustin either, despite the fact she'd texted him and told him she was quitting. She'd thanked him again for being a good friend.

Londyn had started typing in Pronghorn Falls in Dustin's text, telling him of her destination. But she stopped just short of sending it. Instead, she hit the delete button. With the way Dustin felt about her, it was best he not know where she was moving.

Freedom beckoned her. In a meager amount of time, she would be free of her stalker.

There had been no more texts or phone calls today, much to her relief. Londyn peered out the window. No one was outside except the elderly woman who always walked her dog about this time, and two moms with their strollers, gabbing in front of the apartment building across the street.

An hour later, she had the suitcase, clothes, Bible, purse, and several water bottles packed in the SUV, and the small, flat-screen TV, microwave, laptop, photo frames, her carefully packed porcelain dolls, and two boxes of dishes stored carefully in the travel trailer. Linens, food from the cupboards, portable exercise equipment, and some miscellaneous items were next. She'd use the linens and pillows to cushion breakable items, although she had no anticipation of anything getting too jostled since ninety-five percent of her drive was on the freeway.

Finally, at 10:00 a.m., an hour behind schedule, she conducted a last-minute recheck of the apartment and added an efficient cleaning of the table, counters, and floor.

She was ready to go.

Just entering the freeway calmed her nerves. The sky was clear, and the spring weather was a pleasant sixty degrees with no sign of anticipated rain. In four hours and twenty-six minutes, she'd be in Pronghorn Falls, including a few pit stops to eat and stretch her legs.

She could do this.

For the first hour, she sang along to her favorite Christian worship songs. It kept her grounded and from thinking about what she'd do if her stalker discovered she'd left Rowland.

An hour later, she spied the exit that boasted four fast-food restaurants. She filled up with gas, then pulled into the parking lot of the restaurant with the most space to park the SUV and cargo trailer, locked the door, and strolled inside. She inhaled a deep breath. Two more hours and she'd be in Pronghorn Falls.

Hamburgers and fries were not her usual go-to, but today it was the fastest she could manage so she could efficiently return to her travel. She was filling her cup with ice water when she felt a tap on her shoulder. Her heart pounded, and she slowly turned to see the clerk behind her with a tray of food. "Your boyfriend said he'd meet you there."

"My boyfriend?"

The woman, barely out of her teens, smiled, exposing a mouthful of braces. "Yes, he came in when you were in the restroom and said he'd meet you wherever it is you're going. He said the town, but I don't remember it right off."

Londyn took the tray from her. "Thank you, but I think you might have the wrong person."

"Pronghorn Falls! That was the place. Yes, he said he'd meet you there."

Her stomach clenched, and Londyn nearly dropped the tray. "He said that?"

"Yeah, he did. Is everything okay?"

She scanned the restaurant and what she could see of the parking lot from the window. "What did he look like?"

"Your boyfriend?" The woman's painted-on black eyebrows rose into her forehead.

"Uh, yes, just making sure it was my boyfriend."

The woman wrinkled her nose. "Well, he was slim, taller than me, blond hair, a nice smile... Like, way charming."

A peculiar panic rose in her throat. She set the tray on the counter, reached for her phone, and brought up Dustin's image. "Was this him?"

"Yeah, that was him."

"And he was here?"

The clerk offered an incredulous stare as if Londyn were missing a few brain cells. "Yes. He was here. Like I said, he told me to tell you he'd meet you in Pronghorn Falls."

"Can I get a to-go bag, please?"

"Sure."

Londyn hurried to the window. No sign of Dustin, but obviously, he was somewhere watching her.

There was no reason for him to follow her to Pronghorn Falls. No reason for him to meet her there. No reason for him to become obsessed. Because that's what it was—obsession—if he was planning to follow her from Rowland.

Something was off. Dustin was her friend. Yes, he'd been pushy about dating, but he *was* her friend. Why was he stopping at the fast-food restaurant and giving an update to an anonymous clerk? Why hadn't he texted her back and told her he would like to see her before she left Rowland?

If he had, she probably would have rejected the idea due to time constraints and not wanting to lead him on.

Surely it wasn't anything dire. Just a friend wanting to say goodbye. Right? Yet...

The woman handed her the bag. "Here you go. Anything else?"

She shook her head. Should she call the local police? And say what? That she thought a friend was following her and had been since Rowland? That a man lied and said he was her boyfriend? That he was her friend, but was acting bizarrely?

No, it was best to get back on the road. Perhaps the clerk misunderstood. But even as Londyn attempted to convince herself of that, she knew that wasn't the case. Had Jasmine told him Londyn was returning to Pronghorn Falls? She was the only one who knew. Not even Sonja knew.

Something wasn't right. She spied a tall, chubby male employee wiping off the tables. Perhaps he would walk her to her SUV. "Sir?"

"Yes?" Irritation settled into a frown.

"There may be a problem in the parking lot. Could I ask you

to accompany me to my vehicle?"

"What kind of problem?" He threw the rag on the table.

"A strange man has been following me."

"Shouldn't you call the police?"

Yes, she should. But again, what would she say as she hadn't *actually* seen Dustin, and he'd never given her any reason to doubt he was anything but a concerned friend in the past. Why should it bother her that he was accompanying her to Pronghorn Falls? Maybe he worried the stalker would discover her plans. "I just need to get back on the road. Even if you just walk out there to take the trash out or something…" She didn't have time to argue with the kid.

"Weird, but yeah, okay. Sure. I could use a vape break."

Londyn stepped outside and abruptly stopped to once again peruse the parking lot. The boy ran into the back of her. "Whoa, lady."

"Sorry," she muttered.

Good. No sign of Dustin. "I'm right over there." She pointed to her SUV, but the teen had stopped, his back against the brick building, and pulled out a vape pen.

"You go ahead. I'll watch from here."

But he clearly wasn't watching as his focus was on preparing to vape. Londyn clicked the unlock button, looked both ways, and ran to her car just as the swirl of vanilla bean ice cream vape filled the air.

Once safe inside her vehicle, she set the food on the seat, locked the doors, inserted the key into the ignition, plugged in her phone so it would have a full charge, and exited the parking lot, her appetite forgotten.

If Dustin was following her, she hadn't seen him in the past few minutes on the freeway. Nothing in her rearview mirror, no one that she could see waiting alongside the road, and no four-door, maroon-colored, diesel truck.

Still, her hands shook, and her stomach clenched. If he did find her on the freeway, she'd have little place to go to escape him. Every car that passed and every vehicle that merged from the on-ramps caught her eye. A wide green rectangular sign loomed in the distance, indicating Pronghorn Falls was now seventy-four miles away.

Not much farther now.

The smell of the hamburger and french fries reminded her she hadn't eaten since breakfast. It likely wasn't safe now to eat the contents of the bag, but Londyn doubted she'd be able to do so anyhow, not with the way her stomach was in constant upheaval.

The gray sky ahead forecasted a storm, normal for this time of year. Brodie's dad was always fond of saying that it was the plentiful rain God sent that provided for lush green ranchland to feed the cattle.

She still wasn't breathing easily when a sign indicating fifty more miles caught her attention. Then twenty-seven more miles, and finally eight miles to Pronghorn Falls. Rain had begun to fall, round pea-sized balls of hail intermixed with the rain. She flipped on her windshield wipers full force and leaned forward in her heated seat to see better.

After taking Exit Thirty-Two, she took a turn onto Highway Three, a shortcut to the ranch. Regret competed with fear that she hadn't kept in better touch with Aileen. But since they were close, Londyn hoped showing up on her doorstep in the early evening hours would be all right.

The rain and hail pelted her car, and a wind gust caused the cargo trailer to fishtail, and Londyn nearly lost control. She slowed her speed and checked her mirrors. A vehicle was a few car lengths behind her. Maybe they'd pass and she'd be able to follow their lights.

A collection of hail formed on the hood, and her breath fogged the windshield. She squinted. Thankfully, she knew the constant curves of the highway, or she'd never be able to ascertain where the shoulder started and the road ended.

Carefully reaching down without removing her eyes from the road, she pressed the defrost button, allowing a gush of air to emerge from the dash vents. A glance in the mirror again showed the vehicle behind her gaining.

Quickly.

Londyn gripped the steering wheel, the knuckles in her fingers aching due to the firm hold. Another gust jolted the SUV, and the wind whistled through the window. She had to be close to the turnoff. And why was the driver behind her going so fast—too fast for the conditions?

She couldn't make out the type or the color, just that it was a pickup truck.

Despite the cold, sweat slicked her forehead. *Lord, please get me there safely.*

The vehicle was now just a few feet behind her, its bright and higher lights further indicative of a truck. "Pass me," she said aloud.

But the truck remained on her tail.

Please, Lord, don't let there be any deer on the road today. But even as she said it, Londyn knew this was a common area for herds of both deer and antelope to congregate. Didn't help that ample vegetation provided ample food for them, especially in the spring when they traveled from the mountains to the valley below.

A nudge on the cargo trailer bumper thrust her forward, and her head hit the seat. She struggled to maintain control of the SUV. Was the driver texting or otherwise being inattentive? Or was it the wind? There was no way to know for sure with the poor visibility.

Another nudge. Was it intentional? Her speedometer showed forty mph, far from being considered too slow for the forty-five mph limit.

Thank goodness it hadn't happened on the freeway with faster speeds.

When the truck began to pass her, she released the breath she'd been holding. "Good, get ahead of me."

But the driver didn't pull in front of her. He instead stayed beside her.

A car coming from the opposite direction flashed its lights, and the truck again pulled in behind her. It was then she noticed something disturbing.

It was Dustin.

Or maybe it just looked like Dustin's truck. Dizziness clouded her mind. If it was him... *Lord, please let it be anyone else. Just not him.*

If it was him—why would he do this?

Surely not deliberate. Surely.

The truck pulled beside her again. The hail increased to the size of a quarter, the thump-thumping on the roof likely causing dents.

Londyn hazarded a glance out her side window. Raindrops and her rapid breathing obstructed her vision.

She cranked up the defroster and tore her eyes away from him and back to the road just as he sideswiped her SUV. The trailer swung to the side, causing her to nearly lose control.

He repeated the hit, and Londyn veered off onto the shoulder before reacting with an overcorrection that slammed her back into Dustin's truck. She slowed the SUV, hoping he'd get far enough ahead of her.

But he decelerated as well. The front end of his truck swerved into her front fender so hard that it shook her car. She lost control and drove off the road and into the borrow pit.

Everything went black.

Chapter 10

Brodie turned onto the shortcut on Highway Three on his way to the ranch for an early dinner. After a hectic day, it would be good to connect with his family and eat a delicious meal. Just when he thought the day's craziness was over, a call came in over his radio.

"Accident on Highway Three, milepost nineteen."

Brodie's windshield wipers failed to keep up with the heavy rain that alternated with bouts of hail, but he knew from driving this stretch so many times that he was near that milepost. He reached for the radio. "Brodie here. I'm in the vicinity and can take it."

"Thank you, Sheriff. An ambulance and fire truck are on the way."

Brodie continued down the highway, the lights of an occasional oncoming vehicle making it even harder to see on the rainy afternoon.

A truck had pulled over with lights flashing. Brodie did the same, ensuring he was far enough over to avoid causing a traffic obstruction. He backed up and reparked so his truck's bright lights were angled perfectly on the vehicle in the borrow pit. From what he could see, it was an SUV pulling a small cargo trailer. He put the hood of his coat on his head, grabbed a flashlight from the glove compartment, and exited the truck.

The rain pummeled him the second he left the shelter of the truck.

"Can't tell if the driver is okay or not," said an older man who emerged from the other truck and shuffled Brodie's way.

"Are you the one who called it in?"

"Yes, sir. Was driving along and thought I saw something in the borrow pit. Turns out I was right. I've been up here praying for the driver."

From the man's appearance, it was clear he would be physically unable to traverse the rough terrain down the side of the embankment and into the borrow pit without great difficulty. "Thank you for calling it in and for praying. I'll check on the driver. The ambulance and firetruck should be here soon."

"Want me to stay here?"

"Yes, I'd appreciate the extra set of lights."

The man rubbed his hands together. "All right. I'll do that. Gonna climb back in my truck."

Without waiting any longer, Brodie hurried off the asphalt and into the tall weeds. The vegetation hampered his efficient movements and slapped against his pant legs. He'd be drenched before he even reached the vehicle. The light from his flashlight bobbed along the uneven ground as Brodie moved as swiftly as possible while remaining vigilant. The poor visibility made it a struggle to be watchful for rock chuck or snake holes. It wouldn't do to twist an ankle.

He detested car accidents, detested what he might find inside the cab of a vehicle that had lost control on the winding roads. Detested the heartache of the family when he had to deliver the news about their loved one perishing in a wreck.

Or being on the opposite side of things and hearing from

a fellow law enforcement officer that his dad had died in a head-on collision when a drunk driver crossed the center line.

Keep your wits, Brodie. This was no time for him to regress into the horrible memory of losing Dad.

Seconds later, he neared the SUV, which had come to rest on all four tires, despite having rolled. A perusal told him it was as stable as could be given the circumstances. The sight rattled him, and he forced a lung-filling inhale. Brodie raised the flashlight to get a better look, and his heart froze mid-beat.

The pale-colored SUV was not just anyone's vehicle.

It was Londyn's.

He tore through the remaining distance, his heart pounding in his ears and his chest heaving with the exertion. "Londyn!" His cries echoed in the night and competed only with the thrum of the trucks' engines and the occasional semi's thundering roar on the freeway several miles away.

Brodie shone the light inside. Londyn's head rested against the airbag—unmoving. *Lord, please let her be okay. Please.* Brodie prided himself on reacting calmly in desperate and at times, volatile situations. It was one of the things that made him an effective sheriff.

But there was no calmness in him today. He pivoted and peered up at the road. Where was the ambulance? Where was the firetruck? How long had she been trapped inside the SUV? Returning his attention to Londyn, he knew he'd need to remove her from the vehicle as soon as possible. The dented door would not make it easy to open. "Hang on, Londyn. I'm right here." Panic surged through him. Spring weather in Pronghorn Falls varied greatly. It could be seventy one day and fifty degrees the next, with nighttime temps hedging in the freezing range. The last time he'd looked at the temperature indicator in the truck, it was forty-two. With the wind, that was cold enough to cause hypothermia.

Where is the ambulance? He craned an ear for the wailing sounds indicative of its pending arrival.

Nothing.

Rain splattered him in the face, followed by an abrupt onslaught of hail. Lightning flashed across the dark sky, and the sound of thunder boomed. Dodging the hail and mindful of the uneven ground, Brodie dashed again to the truck to retrieve a crowbar.

"Everything okay?" The man rolled down his window just inches.

"Can you call 911 again? Tell them we need an ambulance as soon as possible."

"Will do, Sheriff."

Brodie pulled the crowbar from the toolbox in the back of the truck and bolted to the SUV once again. He shone his light inside and noticed she hadn't changed her position. Was she alive?

Lord, please, please...

So much he needed to tell her. So much he needed to say.

So much love for her.

Brodie stuck the crowbar into the crack of the door and used it as a lever. In one swift movement, he tossed the tool aside and leaned into the SUV. He felt for a pulse.

She was still breathing.

Thank You, God!

Indecision weighed briefly on him. If she had spinal injuries, it was best not to move her. But he couldn't leave her here. He waited a few more minutes for the ambulance to arrive before offering another quick prayer for wisdom and direction, before unhooking Londyn's seat belt. Brodie removed his coat and wrapped it around her as best as he could. "It's gonna be okay," he said.

It *had* to be okay.

The hail stopped, and a steady pitter-patter of rain replaced it. Another crash of thunder sounded, but no sirens.

Had the man gotten through to 911?

Gently, Brodie extracted Londyn from the SUV and held her close to his chest, hoping to temporarily warm her somewhat during the trek to his truck.

The elderly man exited his truck. "Want me to get the door?"

"Yes, please."

The man opened the passenger side and Brodie rested Londyn inside, then turned on the heated seat.

"I called 911 again. They said the ambulance was on its way."

Brodie clapped the man on the shoulder. "Thank you. I appreciate all your help."

"Is she gonna be okay?"

"Keep praying."

"I'll do that."

Brodie needed to increase the heat in the truck and make his own call to dispatch. He collected the man's contact information before adding, "Sir, you can go ahead and go home now. Please drive safely, and thank you again."

"You bet."

Brodie climbed back into the truck and cranked the heater. He grabbed the emergency blanket from the back seat, removed his wet jacket, and draped the blanket across her.

Bruises and scratches marred her face. Long lashes fringed her closed eyes, and her breathing was shallow.

Lord, I've loved her for so long. Please don't take her from me.

A thought popped into his head about why she had returned to Pronghorn Falls. Obviously, she was moving back if she had a cargo trailer. But why? Dare he hope it was to reestablish their relationship?

He couldn't think of all that now, but later, after he ensured she was all right, he'd ponder it.

"Dispatch, this is Sheriff Brenneman. I am on Highway Three, milepost nineteen, at the scene of the rollover. What is the ETA of the ambulance?"

"This is dispatch. Sheriff, there was a four-car pileup on the interstate, so there is a brief delay."

"Is everyone all right?"

"I do believe there was a fatality."

Brodie closed his eyes and leaned his head on the headrest. That was never news he wanted to hear. "I'm going to take the victim of the crash at milepost nineteen to the hospital. She's breathing, but I'm not sure of other injuries."

"I'll let EMS know."

Brodie didn't hesitate a moment longer. He ensured Londyn was belted in, then fastened his own seat belt and started to Pronghorn Falls Memorial.

He'd driven this route through town and up the hill to Pronghorn Falls Memorial so many times, yet this evening it took twice as long as usual.

Londyn groaned, agony written on her face. "We're almost there." He wanted to take her into his arms and erase any of the pain she was undoubtedly feeling from the wreck. Driving the distance from the accident to the hospital offered him time to think.

About Londyn. About why she was here. About how close

he'd come to losing her. About all the years he'd loved her. And still did.

When she'd left, he'd been broken. Yet through it all, he knew there would never be anyone else for him. His family and law enforcement coworkers had attempted to set him up with women over the past months, but Brodie hadn't been interested. Roarke would tell him he was a romantic softie at heart—and maybe he was.

He'd prayed mightily prior to the night he'd proposed, asking that if it was God's will, that Londyn become his wife. Loving someone since sixth grade and planning to love her for at least another eighty years was the main plan on the agenda he'd laid out for his life.

Just as he had the night of the prom, Brodie twirled her around. This time, she wasn't wearing some frilly purple dress, but jeans and a pink t-shirt. This time, her hair wasn't fixed all fancy by a hairstylist at a salon, but was pulled into a ponytail. She wasn't wearing some uncomfortable-looking pointy-toed girlie shoes, but her regular tennis shoes—the ones she wore when they playfully raced to the truck earlier that evening. The race she'd won.

Yet on that night, beneath the stars in the crisp evening, she'd looked more beautiful to him than ever.

Mom, Roarke, and, of course, the jewelry store clerk had known of his plans. But even though he and Londyn had been dating for several months and had been friends for years before that, she seemed taken aback by his declaration and the question that followed.

In the sappy movies he watched with her on occasion, the woman always agreed to the proposal before flinging her arms around the man. He'd lift her off her feet and swing her around. They'd plan their lives together.

But Londyn hadn't reacted that way.

In the well-lit park, he could see the fear in her eyes. Fear mixed with something else he couldn't ascertain. Not even after years of practice in reading her expressions. She rejected his marriage proposal and sobbed afterward. What should have been a happy occasion resulted in a dismal one. How had he somehow misread her plans for the future—their future?

That night, he was both shattered inside and angry at the same time. He drove her home in an awkward ten minutes of silence with nothing explained and nothing resolved.

Thankfully, the jewelry store offered refunds.

Brodie zipped into the circular ER drop-off at Pronghorn Falls Memorial. He parked, put on his flashers, then removed Londyn from the passenger side and rushed through the automatic doors.

He knew the intake nurse and gave her the details about the car accident, as much as he knew, anyway. "I think she might have a concussion and possibly some internal injuries."

"We'll take good care of her, Sheriff. I will need to get some information from you." Another nurse wheeled Londyn back into the emergency room.

"Date of birth?" the intake nurse asked.

Brodie rattled it off.

"Address?" Brodie wasn't sure how to answer that question. Was Londyn planning to stay in Pronghorn Falls, or would she be moving on? The thought tore at his heart, but he was just thankful that she'd survived the accident. He pondered his answer and shrugged. He'd just give the ranch address. If nothing else, it would take Londyn some time to heal before she moved on, and if Londyn was amenable, Mom would enjoy having her stay while she recuperated. He provided Mom's address.

"Go ahead and have a seat," the nurse told him after he had given the information. "We'll let you go back with her in a few minutes."

Next, Brodie dialed Mom's number.

"Hi, I was just about to get worried. I don't know the last time you were late to dinner, especially when we're having spaghetti."

Mom knew him well. "Sorry, but there's been an emergency."

"Are you all right?"

"I'm fine, but it was Londyn."

"Londyn? She's in town?"

"I'm surprised she didn't text you. Apparently, she was driving on the highway and lost control of her SUV. She was pulling a trailer and ended up in the borrow pit."

Mom gasped. "Oh no, is she all right?"

"I think she will be. We've had quite a few accidents this evening with the hail, pounding rain, and strong winds." He winced when he thought of the fatality. That could have been Londyn.

"We will be praying for her."

"Thanks, I'm sure she'll appreciate that. Would it be all right if she stayed with you? I'm not sure for how long because I don't know her plans, but she'll need somewhere for a few days after she's released from the hospital."

"Absolutely. She knows my door is open anytime."

"Thanks, Mom."

"You are welcome. Did you get the call on the radio about the accident?"

"I did. The EMTs were tending to other car accidents, so I took Londyn to the ER." He regretted the way his voice broke.

"That must have been a shock to see her."

"Yeah, especially in that condition. She probably has a concussion. I'm hoping they'll call me back soon and apprise me of her injuries." He took a deep breath. "I'm just grateful that guy had called it in and was there to help. The sight of her vehicle and then not knowing whether..." he cleared his throat. "Anyway, God is good, and she'll be all right, so I will be there as soon as they get her settled. I'm going to assume they'll keep her overnight."

"That sounds fine. You get here when you can, and if not, I will save the spaghetti for you for tomorrow."

"Depending on Londyn's prognosis, I may just head home or even spend the night in the hospital."

We'll be praying," said Mom. "Oh, Roarke would like to say something to you before we hang up."

"Hey, Bro, I overheard what happened. Do you need me to come to the hospital?"

"No, I think I'm good. The roads are pretty bad, and there's talk of some flash flooding, but thank you for the offer."

"Anytime. Any idea why she's in town?"

"No idea at all. Her texts have been pretty vague since she left. I was surprised she hadn't mentioned something to Mom."

"Maybe the choice was sudden."

"Could be."

"Well, let me know if you need me."

"Thanks, Roarke. Will do." Brodie disconnected and attempted to distract his myriad of thoughts by watching a game show rerun from the 1980s on the flat-screen TV in front of him.

An hour later, Londyn was moved to a private room. Seeing Kayla Dwyer, one of his deputies' wives, offered an extra layer of reassurance.

Chapter 11

Londyn awoke with a startle. Where was she? And why did her head ache and her entire body feel as though she'd been run over?

She had a dream that Brodie was carrying her through the rain. Her head rested against his chest, and he'd stumbled and nearly fallen as he tramped through tall weeds. The downpour pelted her, and whatever she was wearing was not enough to keep out the chill of the brisk winds. She recognized the familiar scent of his cologne and the safe, reassuring feel of his arms.

Brodie.

Would he ever speak to her again after what she'd done?

She kept her eyes closed and took a deep breath. The odor of antiseptic flooded her nostrils, and the sound of something beeping, muffled voices, and obnoxious snoring at extremely high decibels garnered her attention. Londyn strained her eyes open and stared at the ceiling before allowing her gaze to wander to the thin white blanket covering her. A glance to the right revealed a man sleeping in a chair near the window.

Brodie?

Londyn attempted to sit up and winced with pain when a

pinch surged from her hand up her arm. She reflexively jerked, causing even more of the stinging sensation to again shoot through her hand from the IV. "Brodie?" she croaked.

Londyn recognized the snoring. When they rode in the church van during a mission trip in high school, Brodie had fallen asleep on the return ride home. He'd never lived down the teasing from the other passengers about his thundering snores. Snores that lived in perpetuity and had been recorded more than once.

She blinked as her vision cleared. Brodie's head lolled to one side, his mouth was open, and his shoulders far too broad for the narrow chair. A surge in her chest reminded her of the reality that she still loved him.

And always would.

He wore his sheriff's uniform—a tan shirt and brown pants. The poor guy was folded so awkwardly in the chair that he'd likely be unable to move once he awakened. It was just like him to sacrifice whatever was needed to care for another. In this case, that must have had something to do with her being in a hospital bed. But why?

The door creaked open, and Kayla Dwyer, her friend since junior high, entered. "How are you doing, Londyn?" Kayla asked, her voice low, likely to avoid awakening Brodie.

"I think I'm fine. What happened?"

Kayla took her vitals. "You were in a car wreck. Brodie found you, rescued you, and brought you to the ER."

"A car accident? He brought me here?" The latter question shouldn't surprise her. Brodie had always been her hero.

"The doctor will likely release you today after he stops by on his morning rounds. He wanted to keep you overnight for observation, especially with the bad concussion and severe bruising you experienced. Praise God, it wasn't worse. From what Brodie said…" Kayla's voice trailed.

Memories came flooding back. "I was run off the road," she muttered.

"Are you serious?" Kayla's brows knitted. "Does Brodie know?"

"I don't think so. I had a dream that he was carrying me through the rain, but now I'm thinking that wasn't a dream."

Kayla rested a hand on Londyn's arm. "I just assumed you lost control of the vehicle because the storm caused so many accidents, but if someone ran you off the road, you need to tell Brodie."

"I will. It was…" She thought again of Dustin's truck ramming the side of her SUV. Of how he'd known she was coming to Pronghorn Falls. Of how his feelings toward her had gone from friendship, to more, to obvious hate if he wished her harm.

The questions that pummeled through her mind caused her head to ache worse. "I will tell him," she promised Kayla, who was still standing beside her bed, concern in her pale blue eyes.

"Well, I'm off my shift," said Kayla. "It's good to see you. We've missed you." The nurse's attention veered in Brodie's direction. "Especially some of us."

"I'm not sure he missed me after what I did."

"You two go so far back and have known each other forever. It's not my business what happened, but I do hope you'll reconcile. Text me and let me know how you're doing in the coming days."

"Thank you, Kayla. I will. It's good to see you, too."

Brodie released an especially thunderous snore, and both Londyn and Kayla muffled their amusement.

"Remember the incident in the church van on the way back from the mission trip?"

"I do. I was just thinking about that."

"Brodie's a good man," said Kayla, her eye meeting Londyn's and holding it.

"I know."

Kayla said nothing more, but her probing gaze confirmed what Londyn already knew—that she'd made a grave error the day she walked away from Brodie Brenneman.

Ten minutes later, Londyn heard Brodie shift in the chair. He groaned and reached a hand to his neck.

The man was handsome on any random day, but he was downright cute when he just woke up. Dark brown hair stuck out at odd ends, and his bleary blue eyes and the crease on his cheek made him appear younger than his twenty-nine years. He moaned again and sat up and stretched his long legs before easing out of the chair. "That is the most uncomfortable place I've ever slept." He stood, shook out a leg, arched his back, rubbed his eyes, cracked his neck, then tugged on his rumpled shirt before limping over to her.

"How are you feeling?"

A crusty drool mark edging just below his lower lip on the left-hand side lent to his charm. "Thank you for saving me. When Kayla said I was in a car accident, bits and pieces of what happened started coming back to me. Some of it's still a blur." Her head throbbed, and she realized there wasn't anywhere on her that *didn't* ache. She needed to inform him about Dustin and how he'd run her off the road. There was so much to tell.

"I'm just glad you're all right." He extended a hand toward her, then pulled it back and instead rubbed the back of his neck.

She needed to tell him she was sorry. But the word seemed so pithy in light of what she'd done.

The IV machine's constant beeps filled the silence between

them. Brodie cleared his throat and finally spoke. "I'm going to run home and get a shower. Then I'll be back. Do you have somewhere to stay, or are you just passing through?" There was no condemnation in his voice, but his clipped tone edged with a mixture of curiosity and something else she couldn't quite ascertain.

"I'm hoping to stay in Pronghorn Falls."

He stared at the railing on the hospital bed. Was he glad she was staying?

"Do you have a place or—?"

"Do you think I could stay with your mom at the ranch? Temporarily, of course, until I find a place to rent."

Wariness captured his expression. "Mom already offered, so yeah, sure. The tow truck has towed your SUV and the cargo trailer to the ranch so we can unload them."

"Thank you. And, Brodie, thank you for rescuing me. I don't even want to think about what would have happened if someone hadn't seen me in that borrow pit, especially with the weather conditions the way they were."

"There were a couple of intense moments there. But, yeah, you're welcome." He fidgeted with a button on his sleeve. "I'm going to leave, but I'll be back."

She was about to mention that she needed to tell him about what transpired, but Brodie didn't wait for her reply. He grabbed his coat from the lone hook on the otherwise bleak wall, waved, and left.

The new nurse entered several minutes later and opened the blinds to reveal a beautiful sunny day. Londyn could see the meandering sidewalk outside where a few people nonchalantly moseyed. The cloudless weather was a welcome change from the storm the day before.

"I'm Dorena, the nurse on this shift." The auburn-haired

woman took her vitals. "The doctor will be here as soon as he's able to see about releasing you. Breakfast will arrive soon. In the meantime, is there anything else you need?"

"No, thank you."

After breakfast, Londyn closed her eyes for a few minutes while she awaited Brodie's return and the doctor's visit. A tap on the door interrupted her attempt to rest.

"Miss Siegler?"

"Yes?"

An older man carrying a bouquet strode toward her. "I'm from Pronghorn Falls Florist and Gifts. This was ordered for you."

"Oh, how pretty!" The spring flowers boasted daisies, baby's breath, and two carnations in a stubby plastic purple vase. A card stuck out from a plastic forked card holder.

The man set it on the movable table beside her, told her to get better, then left.

Londyn's first guess was that the flowers might be from Brodie. He'd never admit it, but he was romantic. If they weren't from him, her second guess would be Aileen.

But when she opened the card, neither of her guesses was accurate. Her heartbeat stalled when she read the words.

Hello, Beautiful.

Where had she heard that before? A glance upwards and out the window confirmed the dread that engulfed her.

Dustin stood at the window, peering in at her.

It had been him all along. The one who'd texted and called her. The slim, tall man who'd attempted to break into her apartment. The one who'd been in her bedroom that night. He must've watched her enter the code the night of the movie.

Why hadn't she realized it before?

Gooseflesh prickled on her skin, and dread twisted her gut.

What was he doing here? And how had he found her *again*? Not that it would be too difficult to discern she'd be at the hospital after the accident he'd caused. But how would he know she'd been rescued?

How, unless he'd been watching the rescue as well.

Londyn pressed the call button.

"Is everything all right?" Dorena walked through the door.

"Yes, a man was at the window." Londyn pointed in the direction of where Dustin had stood just seconds before. As quickly as he'd appeared, he'd vanished.

Dorena walked to the window and looked right, then left. "There's no one at the window." She pivoted toward Londyn, frown lines grooving the corners of her mouth. "You have a serious concussion, and it's not uncommon to be confused."

She hadn't imagined it, had she? "I saw him there." But even as she said the words, Londyn doubted herself. One thing she didn't doubt was that Dustin had sent the flowers on the table beside her. Flowers that would be donated to someone else in the hospital once she told Brodie.

"Dr. Goley was unavoidably delayed, but he should be here soon. In the meantime, do you need anything else?"

"No, I think I'm fine. Thank you."

"All right. Try to get some rest."

The nurse left the room and closed the door three-quarters of the way behind her.

Londyn glanced again at the window. No sign of Dustin. At least she was safe inside the hospital.

Hopefully, Brodie would return soon. Should she call him? But what if he had to work? She couldn't expect him to tend to her when he had other things to do.

The notecard from Dustin lay on the table beside the flowers. It wasn't in his handwriting, which she'd only seen once at her former job. Had he called in the order? If so, would the florist be able to identify him?

Londyn reached for the remote on the table and clicked on the TV. Forty channels ranging from home improvement to game shows, from news channels to soap operas, were at her fingertips. Nothing sounded appealing, but she needed to distract herself from the flowers and possibly seeing Dustin at the window.

She closed her eyes and attempted to calm herself. She called to mind Isaiah 41:10: *"Fear not, for I am with you; be not dismayed, for I am your God; I will strengthen you, I will help you, I will uphold you with my righteous right hand."*

In the verse, the Lord offered reassurance that one needn't worry. That He would provide strength, help, and the ability to forge ahead. He would uphold her.

Why then did her heartbeat fail to return to a normal rhythm, and why did the monitor indicate her normally low blood pressure at elevated levels?

She must have fallen asleep at some point because she startled when the sound of the door latch clicked. Londyn kept her eyes closed. It was likely Dorena arriving to take her vitals.

How Londyn had been able to sleep at all due to the circumstances was beyond her.

Likely exhaustion.

She rolled her head to one side, wincing at the pain. When he spoke, a chill barreled through her. Londyn's eyes fluttered open.

"Hello, Beautiful. Well, maybe not so beautiful with the head bandage and bruising." His familiar laugh caused her stomach to roil, and her heart to pound in her ears.

Dustin stood near the chair Brodie vacated, arms folded across his chest. But even so, she could see the disposable gloves on his hands.

What was he planning to do?

Her gaze drifted to the closed door. She was trapped.

Lord, please help me.

Dustin's unblinking gaze settled on her. "Did you like the flowers?"

"You need to leave."

"Is that any way to talk to a friend?" He offered a grin she'd once found charming.

Fear crept up Londyn's spine. Dustin had already attempted to kill her. Would he try again? She perused the immediate area. If he did, she had nothing to protect herself, except a call button.

Which she pressed.

"You need to leave," she repeated, hating how her voice quivered.

"Nah. I think I'll stay."

"Why are you doing this?"

And why wasn't someone answering the call button? She pressed it again.

"Come on, Londyn, you know why."

Was her rejection enough to cause him to stalk her and threaten her life?

For Dustin Haack, it apparently was.

He stomped toward her and ran a gloved hand down her arm, the latex cool against her skin. "Need me to remove the IV for you?" He plucked at it, and the jiggling motion tugged at her tender skin. She pushed him back with her other hand.

"No, it's just fine."

He studied her, his hardened eyes never blinking. Londyn held his stare while simultaneously recalling something Mr. Brenneman had told her and the others in the women's self-defense class. *"When your life is in danger, remember many things can be weapons."*

Not much to defend herself in a barren hospital room. A pen lay next to a thin three-by-five-inch notebook on the table beside the landline phone and the bouquet of flowers.

He towered over her bed, this time his eyes roving over her. Bile lodged in her throat, and she pressed the call button again.

"The hospital is really busy today, so you might as well give up on that."

Londyn's gaze rested briefly on the landline phone.

"Don't even think about that either." Dustin shoved her cell phone further from her reach, then lifted the landline, yanked the cord from both the handset and the jack, and straightened it between his hands, released it, then flipped it again so it was pulled taut. "You weren't thinking of calling someone, were you, Londyn?"

Her head swirled with dizziness. "You won't get away with this."

"What? You'll tell your boyfriend on me? Oh, wait. He's not your boyfriend anymore. Not after you broke his heart."

Jasmine had shared far too much.

"But you don't need him anyway. You have me, and we were meant to be together."

How had Londyn ever considered Dustin a friend? How had she ever considered dating him?

She was such a fool.

It took him all of three seconds to confirm he still loved her.

Which really wasn't a surprise.

Brodie climbed into his service vehicle and drove first to

the sheriff's office. He'd check in, head home for a shower, then return to the hospital. Hopefully, by then, the doctor would have released Londyn.

Sleeping in the avocado-green chair in the hospital hadn't been conducive to a good night's rest. The crick in his neck wouldn't be going away anytime soon. But it had been worth it to ensure Londyn would be all right.

Brodie couldn't stop thinking about her. Their past and the present.

He was a guy, for crying out loud, and men didn't think about broken hearts, or at least they usually didn't. Why then couldn't he get Londyn off his mind? Why then had he been glad and disappointed at the same time to hear she was going to be staying in Pronghorn Falls?

A call came over the radio just as he was about to turn into the sheriff's office parking lot.

Chapter 12

This time, Londyn pressed and held the call button. There was no way Dorena could be the only nurse on duty today. And where was Brodie?

Dustin stood so close she could smell his cologne mixed with a hint of body odor. He snapped the phone cord again before pushing the button that lowered the rail on the right-hand side of the bed.

Her pulse surged, and she felt the thundering rhythm of her heartbeat in her throat.

"If only you had agreed to date me," he hissed. "You know I love you." Dustin planted one knee on the bed beside her and folded himself forward. He pressed the cord against her neck.

Londyn attempted to push him away, inadvertently jerking the arm with the IV, causing her to wince in pain as it pinched the skin at the access point. But she was no match for him, especially given her weakened state.

He pushed harder on her throat. She choked and gasped for breath. *Lord, please help me!*

Mr. Brenneman's words again came to mind. *"When your life is in danger, remember many things can be weapons."*

Londyn wriggled and attempted to put a hand between the

cord and her neck. She kicked her legs and writhed. With her other hand, she felt around on the table, the tips of her fingers grasping for the pen while she attempted to retain consciousness. She rolled it toward her, but it flipped from her fingers. Londyn strained and tried again while attempting to squirm from Dustin's grasp. He pressed harder.

Finally, she wrapped her fingers around the pen, and in a burst of adrenaline, she aimed for his eye.

"Nice try," he growled, turning his head.

She aimed a second time for his neck, but he lowered his head to avoid her attack, causing her to jab him as hard as she could in the cartilage of his upper ear.

"Ah!" He screamed and released the cord. He clutched his ear while uttering a stream of profanities.

Londyn gasped, attempting to inhale full breaths. With effort, she seized the flower vase and whacked him in the side of the head. He bowed over as water and flowers spilled everywhere.

"Knock, knock."

Dorena entered, a smile pasted on her face. "Oh! Are you all right?" She rushed in Dustin's direction.

"I'm fine," Dustin said, still gripping his ear.

"Good. I heard all of the commotion in here. Due to her concussion, we need to let Londyn rest." Dorena patted Dustin on the shoulder. "You two sure made a mess in here. What's with the flowers and water everywhere? We'll have to change your bedding, Londyn." Dorena shook her head. "Sir, are you sure you're all right? It looks like your ear might be bleeding." Dorena scrutinized Dustin at close range.

"I'm fine." Something unspoken passed between them before Dustin backed toward the door. "Until we meet again, Londyn," he said, then disappeared so quickly it was almost as if he'd never been there.

Except that Londyn's throat ached and her pulse refused to return to normal.

"Can you please plug in the phone?" she rasped. "I need to call the police."

Dorena's thick black brows knitted. "Sure. But why do you need to call the police?"

"He just attempted to kill me."

Dorena plugged in the phone. "Do remember that sometimes people with concussions experience memory loss."

"This was not memory loss. It just happened!" She pointed at her throat. "Do you see a mark here?"

"Not really." Dorena inspected the area on Londyn's neck. "All I see is a small scratch, but you had that after your accident." She reconnected the phone cord to both the phone and the jack.

"Why didn't you answer the call button?" Her throat hurt to talk.

Dorena narrowed her eyes as though she might be offended by Londyn's question. Her mouth barely moved as she voiced the words. "We are shorthanded, and I was busy with a patient in room 201 who reacted badly to his medicine."

Londyn cleared her throat, coughed, then took a deep breath before continuing. "I kept pressing it, and no one came. Are you on duty alone today?"

"Like I said. We are shorthanded. We do our best, but we can't be everywhere at once." A flash of irritation flickered in her brown eyes. "You mentioned you'd like to call the police. Would you like me to call for you?" Dorena's condescending tone reeked of disdain. Or maybe Londyn imagined it?

"If you could just please hand me either my cell phone or the hospital phone."

Dorena did as requested, but she moved at a snail's pace. She handed Londyn the hospital phone, the presence of the stretched cord reminding her of how close she'd again come to losing her life at the hands of Dustin Haack. Her arm shook as she moved the handset to her ear.

Slowly and methodically, Dorena pressed 911. "I'll leave you to call." With a wave of her hand, she left the room. Londyn thought she noticed Dorena's shadow hovering near the partially closed door.

Londyn spoke with the dispatcher, who informed her that Officer Robinson would arrive soon. She struggled to her side to replace the phone in its cradle and reach for her cell phone, which was still charging. The railing hit a sore area, and she winced, returned to a resting position on the pillow, then tried again. Finally, she dialed Brodie's number. It went to voicemail.

She had just placed her cell back on the side table when a plump man in scrubs entered. His hair was styled with a bald spot in the front and stringy shoulder-length hair in the back. He wore thick, black-rimmed glasses and introduced himself as the environmental services aide. He tugged behind him a mop in a portable bucket and carried a canister of antibacterial wipes.

"You want to keep these?" he asked, lifting the heap of flowers from the floor.

"No, thank you."

He shrugged and tossed them into a trash can on wheels. While at first glance he may seem lethargic, the man was expedient and efficient. He'd wiped off everything, including the phone and its cord, the door handle, bed railing, and the chair in the corner, before mopping the floor and removing the garbage, all before Officer Robinson arrived.

It was then that Londyn realized something disturbing.

There would be no fingerprints to prove Dustin had even been there.

Officer Robinson took Londyn's statement. "We are short a detective right now, but I want to reassure you that we will check out the camera footage and we will catch this guy."

"Thank you, I appreciate that."

"Have you told Brodie about any of this?"

"No, I haven't seen him since he left early this morning. I expect him back anytime."

"All right. I'll brief him. How's your throat?"

"Still sore." Londyn gently massaged it with her hand.

The door opened, and Dorena walked in. Her eyes flitted between Londyn and Officer Robinson. "Oh, I'm sorry, I didn't mean to interrupt." She slowly backed toward the door.

"You have perfect timing," said Officer Robinson. "I was just about to come find you and ask you a few questions."

"Me?" Dorena's voice rose several octaves, and she fiddled with her lanyard. "Why would you need to ask me questions? What's going on?" Either Dorena was a gifted actress, or she truly did not know why Officer Robinson was there.

"I need to mention that I will be recording this conversation."

Dorena nodded and fidgeted with the stethoscope around her neck. After securing Dorena's full name and information about where she lived and how long she had been an employee at Pronghorn Falls Memorial, Officer Robinson began her formal questioning. "Ms. Siegler mentioned that a man attempted to strangle her with the phone cord earlier today."

"That is awful!" Dorena held a hand to her mouth. "Officer, I just figured that she was having confusion because she suffered a serious concussion in the car accident she was involved in."

"Did you notice the mark on her neck when you examined her after the occurrence?"

Dorena took several steps forward and squinted in Londyn's direction. "No, I didn't notice."

"Do you know a man by the name of Dustin Haack?"

"I don't."

"Did you see the man who was in the room with Ms. Siegler?"

Dorena nodded. "I think so. He's a sheriff, isn't he?"

"Not him. The one who was in here about forty-five minutes ago."

Several seconds ticked by before the dawn of realization occurred. "Oh, him. No, I haven't ever seen him before. I just—uh—assumed he was Londyn's boyfriend."

Officer Robinson continued her line of questioning. "Ms. Siegler mentioned that she pressed the call button numerous times to get your attention, but no one arrived."

Dorena pressed her thin lips into a fine line, causing them to nearly disappear. Finally, she spoke. "We are short-staffed today, so if she did press the button multiple times, I do apologize. In addition, we had a patient with a severe allergic reaction to their medicine. Please accept my apology."

Officer Robinson scribbled something in her notebook. "Explain to me the protocol for cleaning up a patient's room."

"Sure. We do have some guidelines for that, and since Ms. Siegler does have a few open wounds from her car accident, she is vulnerable to infection. Whenever someone is vulnerable to infection, that necessitates us cleaning the room more often. For whatever reason, the vase with flowers in it was on the floor, the water spilled, and the plastic vase was broken with pieces everywhere. This necessitated us to call housekeeping and have them come and clean. We have a strict policy here to maintain cleanliness."

Officer Robinson finished the interrogation, and another officer was on their way to sit guard outside Londyn's room until Brodie arrived. Even so, every time the door opened, Londyn flinched. Fortunately, it was only Dorena taking her vitals, and one time the cafeteria brought her a meal. Londyn sat up with some difficulty and reached for her phone to see if it had finished charging. Thankfully, she'd had that in her pocket when she was rescued. As for her gun, which she'd tucked into the glove compartment in its holster, and the rest of her possessions, she had no way of knowing what condition the accident left them in. Although after the real possibility of losing her life, none of her belongings meant much to her, besides her Bible, the framed pictures, and maybe her porcelain dolls.

Her phone was seventy percent charged when it rang. At first, she hesitated, but then realized it could be someone important like Brodie or Aileen. When she flipped over her phone, Aileen's number flashed across the screen. The tension in her shoulders eased.

"Hi, Londyn. I'm just checking in and making sure you're all right."

Tears stung her eyes, and Londyn spent the next several minutes speaking with Aileen. It was amazing how much more relaxed and reassured she felt after the call concluded. Londyn had just hung up when the phone rang again, and this time, Jasmine's image flashed on the screen.

"Hello?"

"Hi, Londyn. Just checking in to see if you made it to Pronghorn Falls since I didn't hear from you."

"I did."

"Good to know." Jasmine sounded miffed, and Londyn was about to explain the delay when she continued. "We already miss you here. Sonja just placed the ad to find your replacement, but I know it's going to be a lot of extra work for us for the next few weeks until she hires someone else."

"I'm sorry about that."

"Yeah, well, it's also not helping because Dustin is out for several weeks."

Even though she already knew the answer, Londyn asked, "Where is he?"

"It's his grandma. She's not well. She lives in Washington, and Dustin has gone to take care of her in her last days. Hospice is there keeping her comfortable. It's been a devastating blow to him. You know how close he is to his grandma."

Londyn had no idea Dustin even had a grandma, let alone one he was close to. When she said nothing, Jasmine continued. "I took to heart the words you said about maybe Dustin and me going out. We talked for a few minutes before he left to go to Washington and decided to go on a date when he returns. I hadn't realized how much we connected."

Londyn cringed at Jasmine's revelation. How long before her friend was in danger? "Jasmine, there's something you should know about Dustin."

"Are you having second thoughts about dating him?"

"No, not at all. How do I say this?"

"Say what?"

"Did you happen to tell Dustin that I was moving back to Pronghorn Falls?"

"I did. Why? Was it some big secret?"

Londyn tempered her comment. "No, not a secret at all. Dustin and I were friends."

"Were? Why not now? He was upset that you didn't tell him where you were moving."

"He was out sick that day, and I didn't have the chance to tell him, but I did text him."

It sounded like Jasmine was rearranging things on her desk, a trait she often did while on the phone. "He cares about you a lot, and when he came into work and realized you were gone and weren't coming back, it devastated him. I didn't think where you went was confidential." Her tone as she said "confidential" bordered on sarcastic.

"It wasn't confidential." Before all this had happened, Londyn wouldn't have minded if Dustin knew she was moving to Pronghorn Falls, but now... "Jasmine, I hate to have to say this, but Dustin followed me to Pronghorn Falls and ran me off the road."

"Now I know you've really lost it," she sneered.

"No, seriously. And then he attempted to strangle me with a phone cord in the hospital, which is where I still am. That's why I didn't call you sooner to let you know I had arrived. I was rushed to the ER after the accident."

"I'm not sure why you're trying to paint Dustin as a monster, but he is not. He's on a plane to Washington as we speak. I just received a text from him a few minutes ago. I know you have a lot of issues, Londyn, but pinning weird made-up things on Dustin is taking it too far. He is the nicest guy and would never do anything like what you're saying."

A sickening feeling washed over Londyn. "I'm fairly confident he's the one who's been stalking me as well."

"That's BJ Nuss."

"No, it's not Mr. Nuss."

"All right, Londyn, now you're taking it too far. Honestly, girl, you need help. I hope you get it." Jasmine hung up, and Londyn held her cell phone in her hand. Tears stung her eyes.

How could it be that someone she'd considered a close friend didn't believe her?

Brodie finished assisting highway patrol with a semi-truck accident that occurred on the highway leading to the Pronghorn Mountains. The driver, who'd failed to negotiate a 25-mile-per-hour curve, overcorrected and caused the truck to crash through the guardrail and slide over the edge of the mountain.

The man was fortunate to be alive.

Brodie completed his report and glanced at the clock on the wall. He should have agreed to Mom picking up Londyn at the hospital. As it was, she'd been there far longer than he'd planned.

His fingers flew as he sent the text message.

Hey, Londyn. I'm sorry about the delay. I was called out on an accident. Are you okay?

There was no answer. Either she was asleep, in the bathroom, or her phone was off. It'd had a dead battery when he'd plugged it in this morning.

Officer Robinson stood in his doorway. "Can I come in?" she asked.

"Sure. What's up?" One of the things he appreciated about working at the Pronghorn Falls Law Enforcement Center was the exceptional way both the Sheriff's Office and the PD worked so well together. While some agencies experienced rivalry or even disregard for each other, that wasn't the case in Pronghorn Falls. Both offices made it their goal to join together for the benefit of the community.

Robinson briefed him regarding a man who'd attempted to strangle Londyn. Brodie tensed. Who was this guy, and what was his motive?

Brodie should have been there. Should have already picked her up at the hospital. Then none of this would have happened. "Thanks, Robinson. Let's get an APB out on this guy."

"Sure thing, Sheriff."

He typed in the name Dustin Haack into his database. No criminal activity. He searched the internet and found Haack's mug on a social media account. The thirty-one-year-old man with blond hair stared back at him.

To the average person, Dustin Haack may seem like a decent-looking guy with a lot going for him. To the trained eye, such was not the case. The man's overly dark irises and vapid stare, even though he was smiling, told a different story. Who was Dustin Haack really, and why was he terrorizing Londyn?

Minutes later, Brodie drove to the hospital to take Londyn home. After the nurse gave Londyn her discharge papers, Brodie pushed her to the truck in a wheelchair and assisted her into the passenger side. "I wanted to let you know that I had a tow truck tow your SUV and the cargo trailer to the ranch."

"Thank you. I appreciate that."

It was the least he could do. "Did you have your gun with you?"

"Yes, it's in the glove compartment."

"Good. I'll get that for you, and maybe I can secure Roarke's assistance in unloading your belongings from the cargo trailer."

It would be beneficial to have Londyn settled in at the

ranch, where he and Roarke could keep an eye out for Haack. The sooner they caught this guy the better.

Chapter 13

Gorgeous scenery greeted her for the seven miles to the ranch. Scenery she'd memorized. The ranchland, the rise of the Pronghorn Mountains in the distance, and the homes set on generous parcels of land brought back vivid memories.

Had it only been a matter of months since she'd left?

"I think he's the one who's been harassing me in Rowland."

"Someone's been harassing you in Rowland? Is that why you came back?"

His words, not meant to be terse, came across that way. Londyn stared out the window, unsure how to respond.

"Why didn't you tell me?"

She reached up and rubbed her temples. "I'm sorry. I just now figured out it was him after he ran me off the road and attempted to strangle me."

Londyn knew Brodie well enough to know he was angry with her. Not because he was prone to temper, but because he cared.

The guilt suffocated her. If she had never left Pronghorn Falls in the first place...

"I need to know all you know about him and everything that happened." The sharp edge of his voice remained.

She attempted to blink back the tears to no avail.

Brodie pulled to the side of the road. "Londyn."

She tore her gaze from several cattle grazing in a nearby pasture and faced him. The words wouldn't come.

"I'm sorry that came out harsher than I intended. I'm just glad you're okay." His voice croaked the last couple of words.

"I know," she whispered. "There's so much...Brodie, I'm so sorry for..." The words stuck in her throat, threatening to choke her.

He gently wiped a tear with his calloused thumb. "We can talk about that later. For now, I need to know everything about this Dustin Haack. Everything that happened while you were in Rowland, and how he came to follow you here."

She could have told Dustin where she was going, and he would have followed her that way, too. She couldn't completely blame Jasmine. Londyn formerly had no real reason to withhold her new whereabouts from Dustin until he'd made two attempts on her life.

Thoughts of Jasmine entered her thoughts. Londyn didn't trust easily, but she *had* trusted Jasmine. With her secrets. With her plans. With her background. With the pain she'd experienced at the hands of her parents and the pain she'd caused Brodie and Aileen. Yet, the woman had taken that information and thrown it in Londyn's face.

Brodie veered the truck back onto the highway, and Londyn shared about all that had happened in Rowland, from start to finish. Dustin's visits, the creepy texts and phone calls, and the way he'd befriended her and wanted to date her. She omitted how he'd kissed her against her wishes.

Occasionally, Brodie would take his eyes from the road and look at Londyn as she spoke. He waited patiently until she was finished before interjecting.

"This guy is dangerous. And we *will* catch him."

While nothing was guaranteed, Londyn knew Brodie well enough to know she could trust that he would do all he could to capture Dustin.

When they arrived at the ranch, a slew of emotions stirred within Londyn. She had spent so much time here over the years. Brodie assisted her out of the truck, and Aileen opened the door, her arms outstretched.

Londyn allowed Aileen's warm embrace to comfort her as the tears streamed down her face. "I'm so sorry," she whispered.

"There now, there will be plenty of time to discuss that." Aileen held her at arm's length then brushed Londyn's hair from her face, just as a mom would do. "Praise God you are all right."

Fresh lines edged Aileen's eyes, and her face looked more drawn than Londyn remembered. In her fifties, Aileen had suffered for years from chronic health issues, but that never stopped her from caring for those she loved. "Why don't you come inside? Roarke, Mila, and Xander are here. We'll get you settled into your room."

Her room. Yes, it had been her temporary sanctuary when she'd visited the Brennemans, especially the night before they would go camping or on another special trip. They had always treated her like another member of the family.

"Aileen, I need to apologize."

Their conversation was interrupted when Xander skipped through the doorway. "I think I might have met you before," he said, stopping just in front of Londyn and tilting his head to one side. "I'm Xander Brenneman, bug collector ex-tror-naire."

Londyn laughed, thankful for the reprieve from more serious topics. Xander had always been a smart little fellow. One who had been through so much when his parents died in a car accident. She'd heard from Aileen that he was subsequently adopted by Roarke and his wife. "I am Londyn. Pleasure to re-meet you, Xander." She extended a hand, and Xander shook it.

"That's right. Aunt Londyn. I remember you now."

Aileen ushered them into the house. Xander tapped on her arm. "What happened to you?" he asked.

"I was in an accident."

"What kind of accident?"

Londyn didn't want to say too much and scare him. "An accident where I got a few owies," she said.

"I was in an accident once when I was first learning to ride my bike without training wheels. I was all wobbly and going from side to side, and then I crashed." Xander gestured with his hands as he spoke in an animated voice.

"Oh, no, I'm sorry to hear that."

"It's all right. It was when I was younger. But I did have a couple of confusions."

"You mean contusions," said Roarke.

"Yeah, those too."

Roarke nodded at her. "Good to see you, Londyn." While Roarke's words were cordial, she knew him well enough to know there was a hidden layer of disappointment in his features. He and Brodie were not only brothers but best friends with an unbreakable bond of loyalty. It would stand to reason he was irritated at her for breaking his brother's heart, and rightfully so. She'd need to apologize to him as well. "Thank you. You, too."

"I'd like to introduce you to my wife, Mila."

Aileen had invited Londyn to Roarke and Mila's wedding,

but she'd been unable to take time off work, and back then, she couldn't face Brodie yet.

"Nice to meet you. I'm Londyn."

They chatted for a few minutes, and Londyn liked Mila immediately. She complimented Roarke well and was the perfect mom for Xander.

Yukon licked her hand. "It's good to see you too, Yukon," she said to the friendly dog she'd thought of as her own pet.

"Hey, guess what, Aunt Londyn?"

"What's that?"

"I had show and tell at the homeschool co-op yesterday."

"How fun. I used to love show and tell. What did you share with the other students?"

"I think it's time for Xander to go play," said Brodie.

Xander's brow crinkled. "Uncle Brodie, can I tell my story first?"

"Yeah, Uncle Brodie, can he tell his story first?" teased Roarke.

Brodie shook his head. "I suppose."

Xander returned his attention to Londyn. "I shared about Uncle Brodie."

"You mean that he's the sheriff?"

"No. That he's the loudest snorer in the whole wide world!" Xander opened his arms to illustrate his point.

Londyn laughed. "That he is."

"Remember that one time on the mission trip?" asked Roarke.

"I don't think anyone will forget that time," added Aileen.

Brodie coughed. "Excuse me, but do we have to bring this up right now?"

"Why not?" asked Roarke.

Xander ran from the room and returned with a hand-held

tape recorder. "Wanna listen to it, Aunt Londyn? I recorded it when he was on the couch last Sunday after church. Mom said he was snoring loudly enough for the neighbors to hear him."

Brodie patted Xander on the head. "Considering the closest neighbors are you guys and then some about a mile away."

"Uh-huh." Xander pressed play, and an obnoxious sound, reminiscent of a booming chainsaw, infiltrated the room. The inhale was nearly as blustering as the exhale, and the predictable pattern was just as it had been that time on the mission trip.

"Good thing you were checked for sleep apnea," offered Mila.

"Yeah, yeah. I don't have sleep apnea."

Xander pressed the stop button after torturing his listeners. "I have an idea, Uncle Bro."

"What's that, Xander?"

"When bad guys steal and hurt people and are put in jail, you could make them listen to this. They would promise never to be bad guys again."

Everyone laughed except for Brodie, who looked slightly offended. "Very funny." But Londyn could see he struggled to withhold a grin even as red dotted his cheeks. Brodie Brenneman was handsome all the time, even when he was embarrassed.

"How about we let Londyn go downstairs and rest?" suggested Aileen.

"Roarke, would you mind helping me unload her belongings from the SUV and the cargo trailer?"

"Sure."

Londyn watched as the two men walked toward her vehicle, which was parked at the far end of the circular drive.

"Make yourself at home, sweetie. And let me know if you

need anything."

Aileen had always been so kind and comforting. "Thank you, I will."

The guest room where Londyn had always stayed was the same as she remembered it. Homey, pale blue, with a queen-sized bed and an oak dresser. She allowed herself to recline on the bed as she struggled to stay awake.

Thank you, Lord, for the Brenneman family.

―――――

"What is it about you guys razzing me about my snoring?" Brodie and Roarke headed outside.

Roarke chuckled. "Paybacks."

"For what?"

"That time you thought it would be funny to stick that rooster in my room after Mom said the only pets allowed in the house were the dog and the frogs in the aquarium. I was grounded for a month."

"Holding grudges, much? That was like a hundred years ago."

"What? Were you embarrassed in front of Londyn?"

"No, she knows of my..."

"Condition?"

"You make it sound so detrimental."

"It could be if you use it for what Xander suggested." Roarke smirked. "Just think. Having to listen to that rumbling freight train twenty-four seven. That would set me on the right path for sure."

Brodie slugged Roarke. "Thanks a lot. I just happen to have good lungs."

Brodie unlocked the back door of the five-by-ten enclosed

cargo trailer after he and Roarke unloaded Londyn's suitcase from the SUV. He expected to find some of the items damaged when the trailer rolled. Sure enough, the microwave suffered dents and scratches and came to a rest on the floor of the trailer. But beyond that, everything else seemed to be in acceptable condition.

"Did you find the guy who ran her off the road?" asked Roarke.

"Not yet. And not only did he try to run her off the road, but he also assaulted her in the hospital." How many times, just in the last couple of hours, had Brodie thanked the Lord for keeping Londyn safe? What if Haack had been successful in strangling her? Or when he ran her off the road?

"Are you okay with her being back?"

Brodie hefted one of the boxes. "Yes."

"I'm sure you still have feelings for her." Only with Roarke could Brodie talk about such intimate topics.

"I do. When I saw her in the vehicle after the accident, I thought I'd lost her for sure." He heard the emotion in his voice and cleared his throat. No sense in having Roarke think he was going soft.

Brodie peered in the direction of the house. He could hear Xander laughing and Yukon's intermittent barks. "This guy is relentless. Londyn told me the entire story on the way home. He wanted to date her, and apparently, she refused to be anything beyond friends.

"Sounds like he's manipulative."

"To say the least." Brodie pushed aside the thoughts that maybe she had rejected Haack's advancements because she still cared for him.

Roarke gripped his shoulder. "We'll catch him."

That was one thing Brodie appreciated about his brother.

While not in law enforcement, he knew no matter the stakes, Roarke had his back.

"She's where she needs to be, even if I am irritated with her for what she did to you."

Brodie valued Roarke's loyalty. "I just hope I can keep her safe. Not sure if I could handle losing her again."

"I understand," said Roarke. And Brodie knew Roarke *did* understand because he'd nearly lost Mila to nefarious individuals set on punishing her for witnessing a crime.

Brodie and Mom sat at the table that evening. Brodie drained his decaf coffee and stood to put the mug in the sink when Londyn hobbled up the stairs. Her glossy brown hair stuck at odd angles, partly due to the bandage on her head. Deep bruising enhanced the exhaustion that lined her features.

The accident could have been so much worse. At least Londyn would be at the ranch where she would be under Mom's care, and if necessary, Mila's. It helped that Mila was a trained nurse.

Brodie pulled out a chair, and Londyn took a seat at the table. Mom reached over and squeezed Londyn's hand. "I'm going to go ahead and go to bed now, but if you need anything, please let me know, and as always, help yourself to anything you need."

Emotion stirred in Londyn's eyes. "Thank you Aileen, I will. And thank you for allowing me to stay here."

"Stay as long as you need. We're glad you're back."

Londyn whispered, "I'm sorry," before the glint of tears shone on her lashes.

Mom slung an arm around Londyn's shoulder. "No worries at all. I'll see you in the morning."

Brodie and Londyn sat at the table in silence for a few

minutes. Did she feel the magnitude of the thickness of the unspoken words between them just as he did?

"Care to go out on the porch? It's a nice evening."

"Sure."

At some point, they would need to tackle the elephant in the room. Brodie figured tonight wasn't that night. They stepped outside in the cool, crisp evening air. The wide covered porch had always been one of Brodie's favorite places at the ranch. He offered his arm, and Londyn stuck her hand through it and hobbled outside with him, where they took a seat on the porch bench.

Stars glittered overhead in the clear night, such a change from the previous night's storm. The porch light cast a soft glow on Londyn's face. Even with the bandage and the bruising, she was beautiful. But the injuries broke his heart. Why would anyone want to hurt her?

During their dating days, she would rest her head on his shoulder, and he would tug her close, brushing a kiss across her forehead, her nose, and finally her full lips. Brodie instinctively reached for her hand, then pulled away. She'd made her feelings clear the day she left. There was no sense in tormenting himself with another round of rejection. So instead, he clasped his hands in his lap and stared out over the immediate driveway and front yard. To the right was the bench that he, Roarke, and Grayson had constructed on a piece of concrete in honor of Danny's memory. Mom had planted several pots of flowers to stick on either side.

"I think often about Danny," said Londyn.

"Yeah, me too. There are days when I can't believe he's gone. It was always the four of us."

Londyn nodded. She would know exactly what he was talking about because she'd been there for much of those growing-up days. He turned to face her. The wind had blown some of her hair across her cheek, and he instinctively reached over and gently tucked it behind her ear. Her nearness brought about a copious amount of thoughts and emotions. He wanted to lace his fingers through hers, tell her they could get through whatever it was that had come between them. That if she only wanted friendship for the rest of their lives, he'd be okay with that.

Only he wasn't.

Pain squeezed his heart, even as it pounded heavily in his chest as he sat beside her, their upper arms touching.

He held her gaze for a moment, searching her face, searching her heart, searching her thoughts. Yeah, Roarke would tell him he was a romantic sap, but what he wouldn't give to know why she left the way she had.

But he may never know, and for now, he'd be content spending time with her, even in silence.

Chapter 14

Londyn's follow-up appointment with her primary care doctor at the Pronghorn Falls Clinic the following week couldn't come quickly enough. She couldn't wait for the go-ahead to be able to drive and, hopefully, begin looking for a job, even if that employment was working from the ranch until Dustin had been arrested.

Which she knew would happen at some point. The man wasn't invincible—although he might think he was.

"I wish I could take you, but I have to be in Lyleville this morning," said Brodie.

"I don't anticipate anything happening. Dustin doesn't know I have a follow-up appointment."

Her statement seemed to appease Brodie. "Roarke and Mila are out of town and won't be back until tomorrow."

"I can take her," said Aileen. "I have an eye appointment, and it's in the medical complex just a few doors down from the clinic."

Brodie vacillated his attention from Aileen to Londyn, then back to Aileen. "All right."

While she appreciated Aileen's offer to take her, Londyn wanted to do nothing to put the woman who'd become like a mom to her in jeopardy. "I'll reschedule."

Aileen shook her head. "It'll be fine, and you need to be checked out for the concussion."

Three hours later, Londyn and Aileen drove in the rain to what would soon be a cluster of one-story buildings that resembled a cleaner and larger strip mall. A lot had changed even in the time Londyn had been away. The clinic was formerly housed in the hospital, and the eye doctor, dentist's office, and chiropractor, who now had offices in the complex, were formerly disbursed throughout town.

More trees had been planted in a common park area, and the town had removed a dilapidated structure and added more parking. Stationary heavy equipment, including a skid steer and backhoe, remained parked on the site, temporarily stalled due to the weather.

Aileen zipped into the closest parking spot, down and around the corner of the L-shaped complex.

"Since your appointment is a half hour after mine, I'll just meet you there," suggested Londyn.

"Sounds good. If anything changes, let me know." Aileen put an arm around her. "So glad you're back in Pronghorn Falls."

"Me too."

They dodged mud puddles and went their separate ways. The spitting rain dampened and humidified Londyn's hair, and she wondered why she'd even bothered to fix it. But the smell of fresh rain was glorious, and the vividness of the plush green grass recently planted in and around the buildings sharply contrasted the gloomy gray sky.

The primary care clinic boasted a spacious waiting room and a counter extending the length of the front office. After checking in, Londyn met with the nurse, then waited for Dr.

Murnane.

The older male doctor, who still looked the same as he had when Londyn was a teen, with his snowy-white hair, mustache, tiny eyes behind glasses, and thickset build, entered ten minutes later. "Haven't seen you in a while, Londyn." He shook her hand, then took a seat across from her on a cushioned stool with wheels.

"It's good to be back."

"Staying long?"

"I hope so." So many factors would affect that decision.

"I see in your records you were in a car accident a couple of days ago and suffered a concussion, several lacerations, rib contusions, and whiplash. They performed a non-contrast CT scan to rule out more extensive intracranial bleeding and monitored you for signs of internal and peritoneal bleeding. That's quite the laundry list. How are you feeling overall?"

"I feel much better. Still sore, and I do have headaches and some difficulty concentrating from time to time, but improving every day."

Dr. Murnane asked her to sit on the exam table, where he inspected the bruising on her face, torso, and ribs and checked to see how the lacerations on multiple parts of her body were healing. "Good. There are no signs of infection." He then shone the light into her eyes and subsequently tested her balance. "Any problems with vision?"

"No."

"Are you more sensitive to light or even sounds?"

"No."

"Good. What about fatigue? Or sleeping. Any concerns there?"

Londyn surmised any difficulties with obtaining a restful night of sleep weren't due to the injuries, but rather to the fear that Dustin would find her again. "Not really."

Dr. Murnane arced a fuzzy gray eyebrow. "I've known you since you were a teen, Londyn. Honesty helps me evaluate you more thoroughly."

"Yes, Doctor, I know. It's just that I don't believe my insomnia has as much to do with the injuries as it does with all of the changes and concerns for the future."

"Understood. Sometimes even though we know the Lord is in control, it's still a challenge to thoroughly comprehend that."

One of the things Londyn always appreciated about Dr. Murnane was his strong faith. He served as an elder at the church she'd attended in Pronghorn Falls and filled in a time or two for the youth pastor. "That's true, and I do try."

"Anything I need to add to my prayer list?"

"Just safety. There's a man from my former place of employment who has been a little challenging." *To say the least.* But Dr. Murnane needn't know all the details.

The doctor nodded. "I assume if there's anything concerning, you've told Brodie?"

"Yes, sir."

"Good." He asked a few more questions before completing the appointment. "I do want to see you again in a couple of weeks for a final follow-up."

"Can I drive?"

"I want you to rest as much as possible, as fatigue can linger, and your body heals best when it's not stressed with activity. As far as driving, let's give it another couple of days, and if your symptoms continue to lessen, you can drive."

The relief flooded her. "Thank you."

Ten minutes later, she exited the clinic and walked in the direction of the optometrist's office. Just knowing God was healing her and that soon her life would return mostly to normal—as normal as it could be with the exception of a crazy stalker—caused her to feel lighter than she had in months.

The rain was intermittent now, and a mild breeze blew. Spring in Pronghorn Falls was her favorite season—when it wasn't snowing or hailing. She rounded the corner and entered the vacant alleyway a short distance from where she'd meet Aileen.

As she stepped out of the alley, she eyed Aileen's SUV just steps away in the front row, where only two other vehicles were parked, one beside two vacant spots. One would think it was a holiday with the lack of people out and about. As far as she could tell, she was the only person in the parking lot.

The realization caused her pulse to quicken and hairs on the nape of her neck to stand on end. She sped up her pace.

Londyn heard the gunning of an engine and smelled the diesel fumes first.

Then she saw him.

A familiar maroon-colored truck with a dent in the right fender swerved into one of the vacant parking spots. Londyn peered behind her and to the sides. No one was around. She sped up her pace to cross the street and dash inside Pronghorn Falls Eye Center.

But Dustin was quicker.

He'd bolted from the truck and flung open the back door of the truck all in one fell swoop. He grabbed her arm. "Not so fast, Londyn."

Bile rose in her throat. "Let me go."

"Unfortunately for you, the two buildings on this part of the complex are vacant."

"Not true. The eye doctor up ahead..." Did Dustin detect the tremor in her voice?

She could reach that office if she were able to tug out of his grip. She screamed, a piercing and shrill shriek. Would anyone hear her?

"That is enough of that!" Dustin squeezed her arm tightly, directly on the wound from her accident. The pain nearly brought her to her knees, as her legs attempted to fold beneath her. She winced as he dug his fingernails into her flesh. Dustin gritted his teeth. "You're coming with me."

Londyn would *not* go anywhere with him. She spun and kicked him as hard as she could in the kneecap.

Dustin grunted, but held fast to her arm. She squirmed, bemoaning the fact that her injuries made her less capable.

How had Dustin known about her appointment? She'd process that question later.

"Do as I say, Londyn, or I will see to it that that older woman you arrived with seeks medical care from more than just the eye doctor."

His words stunned her, and she simmered with rage. "You will *not* hurt Aileen."

"Aileen. Oh, yes, that's her name." He snarled a distorted smile that made him appear like a depraved villain in the worst of nightmares. She regretted instantly mentioning Aileen's name. Loyalty, love, and fondness for the woman would cause Londyn to do whatever was necessary to protect Brodie's mom.

Dustin dragged her toward the truck, and she fought him, clawing his face with her free hand. A brief perusal indicated no one walked about on such a dismal day, and inside the occupied buildings were other noises that would compete with her screams. No one else was in the immediate vicinity save elderly Mrs. Rumberger, who inched their way.

"Londyn, is that you?" Mrs. Rumberger adjusted her cat-eye glasses with their jeweled strings as she drew near with an oversized pink-and-purple umbrella.

"Do anything foolish and the old lady dies," Dustin hissed in her ear.

A rush of panic flooded her, but she'd do her best to hide it. "Yes, it's me. What are you doing out on such a bleak day?"

"I had to gather a few things from the corner store. My car wouldn't start, so I figured God gave me two good legs, so why not use them?"

Mrs. Rumberger looked the same as she always had, with her thinning gray hair wound into a sparse bun, brightly-colored moo-moo, knee-high stockings that had begun to roll down her calves, and plain white tennis shoes. As was her trademark, she'd tucked a silk flower behind her ear. "I'm so glad to see you, dear."

Londyn held a special place in her heart for the woman who'd once been her family's neighbor and whom she'd known most of her life. "It's nice to see you too." *Please, Lord, please don't let Dustin hurt her.*

Mrs. Rumberger shifted her floral needlepoint purse on her forearm and squinted. "Is this your boyfriend?"

"Yes, I am. It's a pleasure to meet you, ma'am," said Dustin, his countenance suddenly changing from a threatening demeanor to the charming man Londyn had once thought him to be. He released his hold on her, and Londyn debated running.

But she couldn't. Not with Mrs. Rumberger at risk. Londyn had no doubt Dustin would make good on his word to harm her.

Dustin smiled broadly at Mrs. Rumberger, his piercing eyes temporarily lighting.

"Well, that's nice." Mrs. Rumberger directed her gaze to Londyn. "I'm happy for you with your new boyfriend, but I always wished you'd marry Brodie. You two make such an attractive couple. Whatever happened?”

Londyn wanted to dispute Dustin’s comment about him being her boyfriend and to assure Mrs. Rumberger she and Brodie were still somewhat friends—or at least she hoped Brodie thought of their relationship in that way after she’d broken his heart—but the narrowing of Dustin’s eyes and a sharp pinch on the underside of her bicep prompted her to refrain. So she said nothing.

“Well, I best be on my way. Do come over for dinner sometime. I’d love to catch up.”

“I will. Thank you, Mrs. Rumberger.”

The woman shuffled away with her cane and umbrella, again leaving Londyn and Dustin alone. His eyes darkened, and his malevolent demeanor returned. “It would be so easy to run her over.” He shrugged. “At her age, she’s a drain on society anyway.”

His words caused Londyn’s temper to flare. All life was precious from womb to grave.

“Would you like the old woman to die because of you, Londyn?”

Unfortunately, Mrs. Rumberger was such a slow walker that Dustin could hop in his truck and mow her over before she reached the other side of the buildings.

“Leave us alone.” She attempted to wrangle from his grasp, and he tightened his hold on her arm.

“Just think. If you scream, Mrs. Rumberger will come back and attempt to help you. Would be a shame for her to die for being so heroic. And no one else will hear you.” The hiss of Dustin’s words pricked the back of her neck, and she shivered. He was right. Mrs. Rumberger would turn around and do what she could to assist Londyn. He was also right that it wouldn’t take much for him to harm her.

"I have my trusty knife and will use it if I need to. Now get in the truck!"

With his free hand, he gripped the side of the cab, and with the other, yanked her closer to the vehicle.

Lord, please help me.

She knew if he succeeded in getting her into the truck, her chances of survival were slim.

Dustin was perceptive and astute, making any scheme more challenging. Additionally, she lacked sufficient time for a well-thought-out plan.

Lord, please give me wisdom!

Dustin sized her up, his gaze roving over her, lingering before settling on her face. It was a game of cat and mouse, as the saying went, and from his devious expression, Dustin enjoyed every second of his malevolent plan.

She caught a glimpse of his hand on the inside of the truck doorframe. He clutched the area near the foam insulation strip, likely for leverage as he attempted to shove her inside.

Dustin tugged on her, Londyn's feet stuttering along the pavement. A feral flash of teeth reminded her of the seriousness of the situation.

As if she needed a reminder.

Her chest tightened as worry snaked through her. She struggled to breathe normally, to think clearly. To react efficiently.

Hooking two fingers on the door, Londyn slammed it as hard as she could, directly onto his hand.

"Ah!" he thundered, his immediate response followed by a string of the vilest profanities Londyn had ever heard.

She didn't wait to see what would happen next. Launching into a run, she scrambled to the optometrist's office, her sore body begging for mercy.

Londyn flung open the door to the Pronghorn Falls Eye Center. She heard the sound of squealing tires and saw the flash of maroon as Dustin barreled out of the parking lot. A plume of thick black smoke lingered in the air, the only evidence he'd been there.

Except for the claw marks on her tricep and the nonstop pounding of her heart.

"Londyn?"

Aileen pivoted from her place at the front counter. Londyn's shoulders slumped with the overwhelming release of tension. She stumbled forward, her toe nearly catching on the gray vinyl flooring.

"I need to call Brodie." The urgency in her tone belied her slow movements.

Aileen clutched her elbow and guided her to one of the chairs in the waiting area. "What happened?"

"Dustin was outside." With trembling fingers, she fidgeted with the zipper on her purse until finally, she disengaged it and removed her phone. After calling 911, she dialed another familiar number.

———

Brodie was on his way back from Lyleville when he received Londyn's call three miles outside of Pronghorn Falls. There was no sign of Dustin Haack by the time he arrived. Two officers joined him at the parking lot of the Pronghorn Falls Eye Center. The fear in Londyn's eyes shook him.

It wasn't the first time he'd seen it, but he prayed it would be the last.

Of course, until they caught Haack, such wouldn't be the case.

"I want someone at the ER monitoring whether or not he shows up there," Brodie commanded.

Officer Robinson, while not his employee, eagerly obliged. "I'd like to catch this scumbag."

The other officer took Londyn's statement. Her voice quivered as she spoke.

"Why don't we take you back to the clinic and have you checked out?" Brodie suggested.

"No, I'm fine. Just rattled is all." She rubbed the underside of her right arm.

"Did he hurt you?"

"Just a pinch. Can we just go home?"

The fact that she referred to the ranch as her home always warmed his heart. She was as comfortable there as he was.

"Mom?"

"I'm fine. Just worried."

He knew Mom feared for Londyn's safety, as did he. "All right, then, I'll check your SUV and then follow you back."

"How did Dustin know about my follow-up appointment?" Londyn's eyes drooped, dark, half-moon circles beneath them. She'd been unable to rest much after the car accident and attempted strangulation before having to deal with Haack again. The sooner Brodie caught this guy, the better.

"I'm not sure, but I aim to find out."

Normally, Brodie would say he loved a good mystery, but this one was far too personal.

He stood and offered his hand to Londyn. She accepted his offer, and he held her hand a few seconds longer, wishing the closeness was due to something other than helping to ease the fear that rippled through her.

Mom returned to the counter to make her subsequent appointment. "Brodie?" Londyn asked, her face only a few feet from his.

"Yes?"

"I—" tears welled in her gray-hazel eyes. "I can't put your mom and your family at risk."

He knew what she was saying. Knew her heart. Knew her compassion for others. And knew the close bond she shared with Mom. "Everything will be okay." But even as he said the words, statistics drummed through his mind. Yes, Mila had nearly lost her life to crazed gang members who were bent on destroying her. Yes, Pronghorn Falls experienced an explosive growth of fentanyl and meth in recent years. Yes, it was no longer the town he'd grown up in, due to the infiltration of new people moving in every day.

But that didn't mean the Lord wouldn't still keep those Brodie loved safe. That the Lord wouldn't guide him with wisdom and discernment as he sought to seek justice. Although if he were honest, this entire turn of events with Londyn and a man named Dustin Haack unnerved Brodie and left him with an unfamiliar, unsettled feeling of distress and frustration.

Brodie followed Mom and Londyn home, his situational awareness skills on overdrive. At least Haack had no idea where Londyn was temporarily residing.

Chapter 15

Londyn threw the load of clothes into the dryer, then headed upstairs to the kitchen. Aileen was in town today, and Londyn hoped to have the kitchen and living room cleaned for her before she returned. It was the least she could do in gratitude for being allowed to temporarily stay at the ranch.

She opened the dishwasher, loaded the breakfast dishes, then swiped the counters with a wet rag. She took a deep breath. It was so nice to be somewhere safe away from Dustin's threats. She hadn't seen or heard from him in three days. Not since the incident in the parking lot. Londyn had attended church with the Brennemans, just like old times, and her injuries were beginning to heal.

Was Dustin still in Pronghorn Falls? Had he returned to Rowland? Would he give up chasing and stalking her?

Would the authorities catch up with him at some point?

Londyn paused a moment and stared out the large windows that faced the majestic Pronghorn Mountains. The Brennemans couldn't have chosen a better location for a home. Snow capped the tallest peaks, and timber and plentiful aspens dotted the mountainside that led to Indian paintbrush-covered meadows, which gave way to abundant ranch land.

A thump startled her and drew her from her appreciation of God's creation. She scanned the living room and kitchen, peered again outside to the driveway, and rechecked the doors—all of which were locked.

Only her battered SUV remained in the driveway, the damaged cargo trailer having been returned to the moving company, and an insurance claim filed. She tiptoed to each of the upstairs rooms and bathrooms. Nothing. It was times like these she wished Yukon, the friendly dog the Brennemans had owned since forever, still resided at the ranch, instead of with Xander.

Satisfied no one lurked in the house and that her imagination was only getting the best of her, Londyn cleaned off the table, straightened the placemats, and pushed in the chairs. The dryer timer buzzed, indicating the clothes were dry, and Londyn proceeded down the stairs to the basement. She opened the dryer, removed the clothes, folded them, and walked to her room to put them away. Just as Londyn opened the top dresser drawer, her attention was fixated on the torn window screen.

"Hello, Beautiful."

She gripped the drawer handle so hard her knuckles turned white, and her heartbeat jammed into her throat. She knew that voice without even seeing him.

"You locked the doors, but left the window open? Thanks for that." Dustin appeared from behind the door. He turned the doorknob, shut the door, leaned against it, and folded his arms. One of his hands—the one that had been slammed in the truck door—was wrapped in beige-colored dressing. A white pad with medical tape wound over the top of the cartilage of his ear where she'd stabbed him with a pen.

Blind terror coursed through her veins, and her legs wobbled, threatening to collapse beneath her. How had he found her? "What are you doing here?"

"Is that any way to greet me?"

Dustin had chosen an opportune time to execute any plans he may have, since Londyn was the only one home, and running to Roarke and Mila's house—if they were home—was not an option if she couldn't escape the bedroom.

She mentally reviewed her options, refusing to believe she was trapped. Her gun was in the bedside dresser drawer. Could she make it there before he realized her plan? The screen, a large hole cut out of it, would enable her to escape—if she could climb out of it before he grabbed her. His back against the bedroom door prevented her from fleeing that way.

"I chose the clothes for you to wear on our date." Dustin nodded at a shirt and pants on the bed.

Their date?

She froze, even as the sweat trickled down her back and her hands grew clammy. *Think, Londyn, think!* But the only thought in her mind was Dustin's psychotic belief she'd date him, especially after all that had happened.

"The green shirt will really bring out the hazel in your eyes."

The creep factor ratcheted up several notches, and Londyn involuntarily shivered.

"I thought maybe a movie, dinner, and then who knows?" Dustin raised his eyebrows and winked at her.

The man was delusional if he thought she'd go anywhere with him.

"The ones I chose are my favorite pants on you."

Fear clawed at her throat, but she'd not let him win. She prayed for God to help her voice not to waver as she conjured up a plan. "The clothing choice is perfect." She wiped her hands on her leggings. "But what about shoes? What shoes should I wear?"

"Hadn't thought about shoes." Dustin relocated from his place at the door and entered the small walk-in closet.

"Boots? Sandals? Tennis shoes?" Londyn trembled inside as she calculated the steps to the door and the speed with which she could make it there.

Dustin remained in the closet, inspecting her shoes. Londyn edged, then full-out ran the few feet to the door, threw it open, and dashed through it. She heard him release a stream of profanities.

She scurried up the stairs, but tripped on the fourth one. Her shin bashed hard into the carpeted step. With effort, she righted herself.

He was directly behind her, and she could feel his warm breath on her neck. She could smell the fetid odor of his breath—a smell reminding her of sweaty feet. He yanked her arm, and she pulled it loose and continued up the stairs to the main level.

Dustin wrested her ankle, squeezing it hard with his uninjured hand. Londyn whipped her head around and noted the positioning of her foot, and with all the strength she could muster, kicked him in the chest. He released his hold and gasped for breath. Londyn reached the top of the stairs and sprinted to the front door. A familiar truck was coming up the driveway.

"Brodie!" she screamed his name, even knowing there was no way he could hear her, as she threw open the front door and ran outside in her socked feet.

Help had arrived.

Brodie turned onto Esther Lane and proceeded up the driveway to the spot where he always parked when he visited the ranch. For the first time since he could remember, he'd been able to leisurely wake up, sit with a cup of coffee on his front porch, and plan his day.

Not that thoughts of Londyn didn't interfere. So many questions lingered in his mind about where he'd gone wrong in asking her to marry him. Hadn't she felt the same about him? Wasn't it the logical next step after dating to make things permanent?

He crested the hill when he noticed Londyn emerging from the house, shoeless and waving her arms.

Something wasn't right. Was Mom all right? Roarke? Mila or Xander?

Barely leaving time to fully stop the truck, Brodie jerked the gear into park, killed the engine, opened the door, and exited as quickly as he'd been trained to do in an emergency. "Londyn?"

"It's Dustin. He's here."

Brodie briefly rested his hand on his gun. "Are you all right?"

"I'm fine."

"Is he in the house?"

"Yes—or he was."

"Get in the truck, lock the door, and call 911. My phone is on the seat. Tell them I need backup. Do not get out of the truck."

"All right."

"Londyn. Do *not* get out of the truck."

"I won't."

He handed her the keys. "After you call 911, call Roarke and let him know to keep everyone inside." Without awaiting her response, Brodie then charged inside the house. How had Dustin discovered where Londyn was staying? Had he hurt her? His shoulders tensed as he ran through the house, looking in each room on the main level before heading upstairs, then finally downstairs.

His head on a swivel, he exited the house. How could someone disappear so quickly?

"Brodie!"

Londyn rolled down the truck window. "I just saw him going the back way, running through the trees." She pointed in the direction, and Brodie sprinted across the front lawn in pursuit. The unexpected physical activity jolted him for a brief second before his lungs acclimated, and his speed increased. He lost sight of Dustin as he rounded the area near Mom's garden.

Out of nowhere, an older model tan car veered toward him. Brodie jumped out of the way and rolled to the ground, hitting his elbow hard on the gravel. The car spun around and came for him again. His brain computed, but his body refused to obey the command to stand and seek shelter from the out-of-control vehicle careening toward him.

"Brodie!"

Her voice competed with the gunning of the car's engine.

"No, Londyn. Get in the truck!" Brodie jumped up, ignoring his sore ankle, and leaped over the fence and into the pasture, seeking temporary shelter behind a tree as he unholstered his gun. The car's tires squealed in the driveway, and Brodie peered around the tree and took aim.

Londyn was running to the truck, and Dustin spun another

donut in the dirt and aimed his car in her direction.

"Londyn!" Brodie increased his speed, and Londyn flung open his truck door, jumped inside, and closed the door just as Dustin's car narrowly missed the truck and sped down the driveway.

Brodie climbed in his truck, started the engine, and contacted dispatch regarding the pursuit of an older model tan four-door car with county plate number 8765. Dustin had already entered the highway and swerved carelessly around the corners.

"He won't make it far or fast on these roads," muttered Brodie.

A tractor ahead promised to stall them, and Dustin veered around it just as an oncoming car emerged. Dustin clipped the side of it, causing the other vehicle to spin into the borrow pit as Dustin continued toward town. The tractor temporarily blocked Brodie's view, and two trucks coming in the opposite direction hindered traffic. He slammed on the brakes near where the car went into the borrow pit and again contacted dispatch. "This is Brenneman. We have possible injuries due to a car off the road." He gave detailed directions, then reiterated Dustin's last known location.

Haack had escaped. Again. Brodie clenched his teeth, making his jaw sore in response. He needed details. Needed a game plan.

Needed to catch this guy.

Failure was not an option, and something Brodie didn't handle well. "How did he know you were at the ranch?"

"I have no idea."

"Have you received any further texts or calls?"

Londyn shook her head.

"How then?" He drummed his fingers on the steering wheel as they drove. "There's got to be some way he's figuring out your whereabouts. He's not omniscient." Brodie thought for a minute. "Has Haack ever had access to your vehicle?"

"Yes. He could have accessed it in the parking garage in Rowland at any time, although there are cameras. He knew where I lived and accompanied me home often before I knew he was the stalker. My SUV was parked in an open carport." Londyn paused. "Where was the vehicle before it was towed here?"

"At the crash site."

Their gazes met, and Brodie wagered they were thinking the same thing.

"He had access to it there," Londyn said.

"Bingo. I'd bet my truck there's a tracker on it."

And Brodie never bet his truck on anything unless he was ninety-nine percent sure of it.

After they returned to Mom's house, Brodie tested his theory. He pulled his gloves on and slid beneath the SUV. Sure enough, attached to the frame was the magnetic tracker. "Just as I suspected," he muttered to himself. Dustin Haack was using cell phone technology to track everywhere Londyn's SUV traveled or was parked. It was time to store it elsewhere.

The backyard was warm and inviting, and encompassed by a tall cedar fence surrounding the immediate yard. Londyn looked forward to spending some time with Mila and Xander and taking in some of the beautiful sunshine.

Xander was hyper, as was his friend, Kit, who was having a playdate. "Mommy, can we swim yet?"

"Soon, sweetie, soon." Mila ruffled her son's hair. "Go get your swim trunks on, and I'll make some sandwiches."

Xander didn't need to be asked twice. He returned in seconds with a pair of blue swim trunks and a towel. Yukon ran around in circles and barked in anticipation.

Londyn hadn't been around children much—being the oldest and with only a brother a few years younger than her. No cousins lived nearby, and she had never taken a job babysitting, although she had volunteered in the church nursery a time or two.

She assisted Mila with carrying out some snacks, a pitcher of water, and two lawn chairs, which she placed just beyond the plastic blue swimming pool that had been set up for Xander and Kit.

"This is such a nice place."

"Thanks. We were finally able to get some sod in and plant a few trees. The fence is an added bonus to keep Xander somewhat corralled."

"It's good to see it finished. I remember when Roarke first built it." She didn't add that it remained unfinished for some time after the girl Roarke was to marry decided she would rather spend the rest of her life with his former best friend. Londyn was thrilled that in Mila, Roarke had found the love of his life.

Now, the homey abode was the perfect place for them to raise their children.

"Mom, can we swim now?" asked Xander.

"In just a few minutes. Let's have some lunch first." Mila opened a plastic container and withdrew several sandwiches. Xander and his friend flopped down at a kiddie-sized picnic table.

Xander brought out his live ant farm habitat and set it on a chair near the pool. "It's so that the ants can watch us in the pool," he told Londyn.

He was such a cute little kid, and Londyn was so grateful that Roarke and Mila had adopted him after he lost his parents. She had known both Danny and Drea well. She still couldn't believe they were gone.

Xander scrunched up his nose. "Can I ask you a question, Aunt Londyn?"

"Sure."

"Do you have any children?"

"No, I don't."

"Well, then, do you at least have grandchildren?"

"No, none of those either. I'm not married."

That seemed to satisfy Xander, and in response to his mother's asking, Xander led the prayer before lunch. Londyn closed her eyes and bowed her head.

"Dear Lord. Thank you for bugs, my parents, Grammie, Yukon, Spider, and my friend, Kit. Oh, and thank You for Aunt Londyn. Please help her not to be too lonely because she has no husband, children, or grandchildren. And, Lord, please bless this food and let it help us to grow big and strong. We love You, Jesus. Amen."

Xander's prayer touched Londyn's heart. He was such a thoughtful and sweet little guy.

They ate the sandwiches, slices of cantaloupe, and some cookies before Xander sprang from his seat. "Is that a new friend I see?"

Kit leaped off his seat as well and joined Xander on the right-hand side of the patio, where two pill bugs crept along. Xander reached down and allowed the pill bug to climb onto his hand. He giggled. "That tickles," he said. He held up his hand as the bug traveled up his arm. "I love pill bugs."

"You love all bugs," said Kit.

"Not all bugs," said Xander. "I don't love mosquitoes, or wasps, or ticks, or pincher bugs."

Kit shook his head. "Me either."

"And once upon a time, I found a pincher bug in the house by my room." Xander scowled. "They're mean and they climb into your ears and pinch the insides of them."

"Ouch." Kit shook his head. "No pincher bugs for me."

Xander grabbed the hose a few minutes later, and Kit turned on the water. They started filling up the swimming pool, and Yukon yipped, his tail wagging before he leaped into the pool. The dog jumped out just as quickly and shook his fur, causing drops of water to reach as far as Londyn and Mila.

Yukon then dashed over to Londyn and rested his wet face on her leg. She patted him on the head. "Yukon, you're a goofball."

Xander zipped over as well with goggles stretched across his round face and the strap bending over his left ear. "Did you know I'm taking swimming lessons?"

"That's wonderful. It's always a good thing to know how to swim."

"Yes, and some of my friends were in the water at our last lesson too."

Xander had become even more talkative since she last saw him. "That's good. Friends are great to swim with."

Xander tilted his head to one side. "Yes, but really, caterpillars and box elder bugs don't like the water a whole lot." He bounded off and took a flying leap into the pool, splashing Kit, who giggled.

Londyn laughed. "So that's what he meant by friends."

"I've never seen a little guy who loves bugs as much as he does." Mila leaned back in the chair and rested her hands on her baby bump.

"Do you guys have names picked out yet?"

"We do. While we still have lots of time, I think I just about have Roarke convinced regarding a first name. The middle name was easy; it will be Nan-Aileen, hyphenated."

"Oh, that's pretty."

"Thank you. It's of course after Roarke's mom, but also my grandma, Nan."

"And for the first name?"

"Zoey, so Zoey Nan-Aileen Brenneman."

"I like that."

"It will be a mouthful if both kids are being naughty at the same time. Xander and Zoey."

Londyn took a sip of her lemonade. "I'm really happy for you and Roarke."

"Thank you. God is good."

Xander, Kit, and Yukon splashed in the pool, the cold water not deterring them at all.

Mila propped her sandaled feet on an overturned bucket. "Roarke mentioned you were practically like family."

If only Londyn could turn back time. If she could, so much wouldn't have happened. She wouldn't have broken Brodie's heart, and she wouldn't have disappointed the woman who was more like a mother to her than her own mother.

"Yes. They were my surrogate family. My mom is too busy marrying and divorcing, and my dad has no room in his life for us. The last time we heard from him was because he was attempting to convince Mom to reduce his child support."

"Wow. Sounds like father of the year."

"Yeah, pretty much. I lost track of him years ago. The

Brennemans became the family I never had. Whenever they would go on vacation during my junior high and high school years, they would take me along with them. I joined the church youth group upon Brodie's suggestion, and it was there that I surrendered my life to Christ."

"They really did have a lot of influence on you."

"They did." Londyn stared out across the yard. What would she have done without the Brennemans?

"When I was going through some tough stuff, Aileen opened her house to me. She is a wonderful woman. My heart breaks for her that she struggles with ongoing chronic pain."

"Aileen definitely has the gift of hospitality. I'm thankful the Lord made her strong, as she's dealt with a lot over the years." Londyn turned to face Mila. Allowing a new friend into her life wasn't easy. Not after Jasmine and Dustin, but there was something different about Mila. Not only because she married Roarke, but because she was genuine. "I heard about you witnessing a murder. I'm so sorry about that."

"Thank you." She shivered, even in the heat of the day. "Were it not for the Lord's protection, we wouldn't be having this conversation."

They sat and watched the boys splash around in the water, and Yukon's continual standing in the pool and shaking out his fur before Mila spoke again. "I understand about not having parents who are positive role models. My mom was a drug addict, and I never knew who my dad was. My grandma raised me."

"I'm sorry. That's tough."

"It was. But my Grandma Nan was such a godly influence in my life. Had my mom raised me, I would not be the woman I am today."

Londyn had never known her grandparents. She had spoken to her maternal grandmother once, but had never met her.

Mila crossed her legs at the ankles and reclined further in the chair. "So, you and Brodie have just always been good friends and had just recently dated?"

"Right. We'd recently begun dating before he proposed." She'd fallen for him so easily, but fear, trepidation, and concerns allowed Londyn to be content with the role of being girlfriend and boyfriend, even though marriage was the next natural progression.

For a moment, Londyn was back at the park that night. It was the same park they'd gone to for the prom all those years ago. Perhaps that's why Brodie had chosen it to pop the question. A man who savored tradition, he was also predictable, which was why it still shocked her that she didn't realize what he was planning to do.

"Brodie popped the question ten years after our prom date. I broke his heart that day."

There was no judgment in Mila's gaze as she asked her next question. "You left after he asked you to marry him?"

"I did. Much to my regret. I broke up with him and left town." Should she share more with Mila? Confide in her? It did feel good to get some of it off her chest. "Just between us..."

"Of course."

Londyn had no reason to doubt Mila's sincerity. Unless she was like Jasmine. Which, Londyn doubted. Mila was different, and they'd connected immediately. "I think a big part of it was fear. Fear that I would be like my mom and someday break his heart. The ironic thing is, I did break his heart."

"Like your mom?"

"She can't stay married for anything. As a matter of fact, it's probably only a matter of time before she tires of her current husband."

That day was cemented in Londyn's mind, not only with what happened with Brodie, but also what happened earlier that day. Mom had called her to say she was divorcing her fourth husband, Lance, after seven years, the longest she'd been married to any man. While most of Mom's husbands entered and exited through a revolving door without much notice of Londyn, Lance had been different. She was already an adult by the time Mom married him, yet she was the closest to him and second only to Mr. Brenneman, considering him somewhat of a father figure. He had grown children of his own, but he always included her in any of their family activities.

That was until Mom decided she'd found someone else. Then Lance walked out of Londyn's life as well.

"But you're not your mom." Mila's words interrupted Londyn's recollections.

"Thank you. I know, but it's just…" How could she explain it? That she was wary of deep emotional attachment, although she and Brodie had always shared that through their friendship and later their relationship? Londyn had freaked out that day, to the detriment of losing Brodie's friendship, his respect, and his family's respect. But Londyn knew—she just knew—that someday she'd probably be just like Mom. Tiring of the men she'd welcomed into her life. Casting them aside as if discarded clothes. Initiating divorce and moving on. Never caring how it impacted her kids.

If Londyn had agreed to marry Brodie, she wouldn't have been the wife he needed.

"Do you think there's a chance you two would maybe someday be more than friends?"

"I don't know. I don't think so." If Londyn were honest, she longed for that. She wanted to be close to Brodie again. And she prayed that if it was God's will to be more than a friend to him, that it would happen.

Xander and Kit hopped out of the pool and ate another cookie that Aileen had made before they continued running around playing cops and robbers to get dry. Yukon ran along behind them, barking.

"And then you pretend like you can't see me," suggested Xander. Kit did as he requested and looked from left to right and all around, even though Xander was right in front of him.

"And then I go and stand by the fence, which is the police station," said Kit, a little blond boy with numerous freckles sprinkling over his nose and cheeks.

"And then you catch me and put me in jail."

Kit did as Xander suggested, and Xander pretended to be arrested with his hands behind his back. "But I didn't do it," he said.

Londyn and Mila laughed at the excuse so often heard by law enforcement.

Kit placed Xander against the cedar fence. Xander leaned forward and peered through one of the knots that had become a hole. "Mom, who's that guy?"

"What guy?" asked Mila. "Maybe one of our ranch hands?"

"No. It's not a ranch hand. I don't know who it is."

Would Xander joke about something like this? "Xander, are you sure you see someone?" Londyn asked.

"Yes. He's out in the field, and he's not a ranch hand. I don't know who he is. Why is he there, Mommy? Why does he have a glove thing on his hand? And why is he carrying a black backpack?"

Londyn's heart raced. Surely it was just Xander's vivid imagination.

"That guy out there walking in the yard outside the fence is coming this way, Mommy."

"That guy out there walking…" Mila's gaze connected with Londyn's.

Lord, please don't let it be Dustin.

She couldn't forgive herself if she placed Mila and the boys in danger because of her association with the man who'd made it a game to stalk her.

Yukon growled.

"We've got to get the boys inside." Londyn sprang from the chair, but her feet remained planted as the fear shimmied through her. Finally, she took one step and then the other before launching into a full-out run toward the boys.

Mila opened the sliding glass door and motioned at the boys. "We need to go inside."

"Aww, do we hafta?" Xander turned and peeked a third time through the knot. "That guy is fast. He's almost to the fence."

Londyn grabbed each of the boys' hands and nearly dragged them across the yard and onto the patio just as the latch to the gate clicked.

Chapter 16

Yukon barked, his piercing yips directed at Dustin, who entered the yard and bolted toward the back door. Mila slammed it and flicked up the lock seconds before Dustin reached it. She shut the curtain. "The windows in the kitchen and bedrooms are open. Can you close those? I'll check the other doors. Boys, please go to Mommy and Daddy's room."

Londyn didn't need any further prompting.

"Why did we have to come in? We were having fun out there," said Kit.

Xander held both palms up, and his eyebrows knitted. "Can we stay outside?"

"To Mommy and Daddy's room now, please."

Londyn slammed the kitchen window above the sink closed as Mila issued her order to the boys. Fear flickered in Xander's eyes, and he pulled his friend down the hall and to Mila and Roarke's bedroom. Londyn sprinted first to Xander's room, which overlooked the backyard, and slammed the window shut.

Panic settled in her chest, and her rapid-fire heartbeats pounded loudly in her ears. She forced her unsteady legs to run next to Roarke's home office, where another window was open. Fortunately, this one faced the front of the house.

Dustin pounded on the glass door leading to the patio. Londyn checked the remainder of the windows in the laundry room and the living room. Her foot connected with a toy dump truck, and she stumbled, losing her balance and landing in a heap on the floor.

"Londyn. Oh, Londyn...I know you're in there. Why are you hiding from me?"

Would he be able to get inside? How had he found Roarke and Mila's house?

Her hands shook as she rose to her feet and staggered to the lone bedroom on the left-hand side. She turned the knob and entered the safety of Roarke and Mila's bedroom. Londyn locked the door, then leaned her back against the door, her chest rose and fell with the gasping of her breath.

"Why are you breathing so hard?" asked Kit.

"I was—I was running."

Xander's brow crinkled. "From that man?"

Londyn dragged one of the nightstands against the door. It would only deter Dustin from getting in, but it was something.

Mila crouched on the floor against the bed. Londyn prayed she wouldn't go into premature labor. The baby still needed four more months in the protection of the womb before being born. Londyn yanked her phone from her back pocket and dialed 911.

Mila scooted to the side and motioned to the boys. "Let's go into the closet and play a game of hiding."

Kit shrugged. "The closet?"

While Londyn told the dispatcher their location, all four of them and Yukon, who scratched at the bedroom door, ducked into Mila's sizable walk-in closet, and Londyn shut the door behind them. She flicked on the light.

"We'll play a game of hiding," said Mila, who rubbed her stomach and heaved a deep breath.

"Can I be the seeker?" asked Xander.

"For this game, we're all going to be hiders."

Xander's shoulders fell.

They hunkered against the clothes and shoes. The dispatcher notified Londyn that law enforcement was on its way and to stay on the line.

"Why did that man wear a weird glove?" asked Xander.

Obviously, Dustin still wore the wrap on his hand from Londyn slamming it in the truck door. Had he sought medical attention? Brodie mentioned there had been no record of Dustin visiting the ER or the clinic here or in surrounding towns.

"Why did we have to come in?" asked Kit.

Mila was on her cell with Roarke and pulled it briefly from her ear. "It's only for a short time," she promised.

The doorbell rang repeatedly. If law enforcement had already arrived, which was doubtful this quickly, they wouldn't incessantly ring the bell.

"Someone is ringing the doorbell," Londyn told the dispatcher.

"Do not answer the door. The sheriff's office has not yet arrived."

Just as she'd thought.

"This place is too small to hide in. Mommy, can we please play the hider game outside?"

Mila shook her head at her son's request. "Daddy would like to talk to you." She handed the cell phone to her son.

"Hi, Daddy. Yeah, we had to come in, even though we didn't want to. Now we're in the closet playing the hider game, but no one is seeking." Xander pouted and folded his free hand across his chest.

Londyn could barely hear Roarke's voice above Yukon's barks, which had become more constant. "I'll be there soon, Xander, and then you and Kit can go back outside and play. Did you know that sometimes bugs hide in closets?"

"Yes."

"Why don't you and Kit try to find some bugs?"

"What kind of bugs, Daddy?"

There was a pause, and it sounded as if Roarke had gunned the engine. "Any kind of bugs. Maybe box elders."

"Pill bugs?"

"Sure. Do you remember the other name for pill bugs?"

"Yeah. Roly polies."

"Yep. You and Kit try to find some bugs hiding in Mom's shoes or maybe along the molding."

"And what if we find some?"

Mila handed Xander a plastic container. "You can put them in here."

"And here's a flashlight," said Londyn, withdrawing one from a corner of the closet.

"All right. Love you, Daddy."

"Love you too, son. I'll be home soon."

"Hey, Dad?"

"Yes?"

"Who was that guy outside in the field? He wasn't a ranch hand, and he wasn't Uncle Brodie. Who was he?"

Londyn's gaze connected with Mila's.

"I'm not sure, Xander. Maybe the guy from the electrical company or something."

"Yeah. Probably so. They come to our house and see if we left the lights or the heater on, huh?"

"They do. All right. I'm gonna go now, but I'm almost home.

Uncle Brodie will be stopping by, too."

"Oh, good. I want to tell him all about my swimming lessons."

Xander handed the phone back to his mom. Londyn strained to hear if Dustin had gotten inside the house.

Where were the police?

What was taking so long?

Had Aileen returned from town? "We need to text Aileen."

Mila did so while Londyn remained on the line with the dispatcher.

"The sheriff and a deputy have arrived. They will check the perimeter for the suspect first before coming to the door."

Londyn thanked the dispatcher. Would law enforcement find Dustin? The man up to now had been elusive. Where was he even staying? Why hadn't the BOLO law enforcement shared produce any results?

Why had no one found him, even though he always seemed to find Londyn?

***

Brodie entered the sheriff's side of the law enforcement center in Pronghorn Falls. It had been an uncharacteristically busy morning. Aiding the police department with an issue, assisting a motorist on Antelope Road, answering a domestic, followed by a report of someone driving without an interlock device, and finally rounding up some loose livestock monopolized his morning. He glanced down at his boots, still caked with mud. Most of it, he'd been able to scuff off outside in the grass. He immediately headed to the staff room and poured himself a much-needed cup of coffee, which he doctored with a generous amount of creamer and two sugar packets.

Some people required strong black coffee when under stress. Brodie? He preferred extra condiments when that occasion arose.

He nodded at two employees in the staff room, the newest deputy, Tanya Overton, who had taken the place of Deputy Garriot when he was fired after deciding to side with criminals in the murder that Mila had witnessed. Overton was chatting with the temporary dispatcher, Juanita Andrade, who was filling in for the regular dispatcher on maternity leave.

"I do believe I have found the one." Juanita clapped her hands together and beamed. A smile lit her chubby face, and her thin eyes had disappeared into her abundant cheeks.

A woman in her twenties, Juanita had not been Brodie's first choice for the temporary position. Not that she was incompetent, but her overzealous excitement made her more suitable for a position that didn't require, at most times, a serious demeanor, and at all times a firm head on one's shoulders. Juanita, however, did possess the necessary characteristics of communication, decision-making, multitasking ability, and compassion. That was why the majority of the hiring board agreed to recruit her. That and she had a clean record with not even so much as a parking ticket.

Perhaps Brodie was just biased in favor of their permanent dispatcher, who'd been with them since his dad was sheriff.

"That's awesome." Overton, a self-proclaimed health freak, munched on a bowl of fresh fruit.

"I know. Who would have thought? I've only lived here for two years, and in that time, there has been no one. Zilch. Nada. But I went to the bar with friends and there he was—the man of my dreams." Juanita paused, closed her eyes, and swooned. She reopened her eyes and held a hand to her heart. "Not only is he hot, but he is so sweet. He's already sent me flowers."

Overton nodded. "Sounds like a winner."

"Oh, he is. We just had our fifth date. Can you believe it?" Her voice rose several octaves. "Five dates in a matter of less than two weeks. I don't even remember the last time I had that many dates in a span of six months."

"Congratulations." Overton forked a piece of cantaloupe. "Is he from here?"

"Thanks, and yes, he is. Grew up here as a matter of fact."

Brodie wondered who it could be who had taken such an interest in the temporary dispatcher. He was about to ask his name, but Juanita's droning on and on allowed for zero interruptions.

She finally noticed Brodie for what was probably the first time. As though a deer in the headlights, her eyes enlarged, and her mouth fell open. "Oops! I guess I really didn't notice the time. Suppose my break is over, and I should return for duty." Without another word, she rushed from the break room, a glazed doughnut in each hand.

"How is she working out?" Brodie asked.

Overton shrugged. "Fine, I think. She's enthusiastic, and I haven't heard any complaints. Yesterday, she walked someone through CPR."

"That's good to hear. I'll be sure to let her know we appreciate her hard work. You off for the day?"

"Yes, sir. Just have to finish a report."

Overton was turning out to be a good choice. She was committed, knowledgeable, and a leader. A transfer from a neighboring county, she'd moved to Pronghorn Falls when her husband relocated for his job.

"Thank you for your diligence. Have a good afternoon."

Brodie believed in awarding his staff with praise, and when the governing body allowed it, periodic raises or bonuses.

Somewhere along the way, he'd missed things with Garriot, much to his irritation and a generous slice of guilt. Could he have been more observant? Paid closer attention to his deputy? Watched for signs? Hindsight, as they said, was twenty-twenty, but at least the entire situation grew Brodie in his own career.

Roarke always said Brodie was too trusting. Maybe so. But while he'd never be a micromanager or opted to look for the worst in others—that wasn't his M.O., he *was* wiser about who he chose to work for the department he'd been elected for. He kept an open-door policy, attempted to be an effective communicator, and endeavored to be fair in his assessments. Most of all, he wanted to do what would have made Dad proud.

Brodie left the staff room and entered his office. He settled into his chair and took a deep breath, hoping for even ten minutes of downtime. He reached for the blue stress ball and squeezed it several times in rapid succession. While he did so, he pressed the voicemail button on his phone to listen to his messages.

The first was Mom inviting him for dinner tomorrow night. The second was from the local homeschool co-op asking if he would be willing to come to their career day. That was one of his favorite parts of his job, encouraging young people. Who knew if his words could make an impact on someone desiring a future in law enforcement? Not to mention, he wanted kids to feel comfortable approaching law enforcement if they ever needed to. It was all part of cultivating a culture where citizens and law enforcement worked together for the betterment of the community.

He listened to the remaining three messages when he received the call.

Suspicious person on Esther Lane.

It took exactly one point five seconds for the address to register. It was Roarke and Mila's house.

Deputy Dwyer was on the other side of the county, but said he was en route.

Some suspicious person calls resulted in a hiker or someone lost who'd wandered inadvertently onto someone's land. Or maybe a trespasser or poacher.

But with Dustin Haack determined to stalk Londyn, the term *suspicious person* took on a whole new meaning.

Brodie answered the call in the affirmative, and minutes later, he was on his way to the ranch.

Calls came in all the time, and Brodie answered many of them if he was able to do so. But never had he answered so many that pertained to probable danger involving Londyn. And this time, Mila and Xander.

He pressed his foot on the gas and maneuvered his service truck as fast as safely possible along the country road to Roarke and Mila's. The dust rose behind him, making it difficult to see Deputy Dwyer, who'd pulled in behind him just off Main Street.

Brodie clenched his fist on the steering wheel. How had Dustin Haack discovered Londyn was at Roarke's house?

The man was relentless.

And worst of all, elusive.

That was the only bad thing about the ranch. It took forever to get there. Numerous curves and turns in the road necessitated slower travel. Tractors frequently also used the road, and livestock—and especially deer—were common and compelled all drivers, even ones in sturdy trucks with impressive grill guards, to mind their speed.

No updates came in through the radio, but Brodie was confident Juanita remained on the line with Mila or Londyn, whoever had called in. He used the hands-free feature and checked on Mom and reiterated to her to lock all the doors.

Finally, he turned on his blinker and traveled up the road first to Mom's house, then continued on to Roarke and Mila's.

Had someone called Roarke? He was assisting another rancher in the nearby town of Upton. Would he arrive before Brodie? But as Brodie reached the end of the lane, he saw no sign of Roarke's truck.

Dwyer pulled in behind him, and Brodie radioed dispatch. "Please let the reporting party know we have arrived, but will be securing the perimeter before coming to the front door."

He recognized Juanita's, "Copy that."

Brodie and Dwyer checked the area around the house, in the backyard, where it was clear Xander and his friend had been playing in the swimming pool, then on the exterior of the fence in the field. They saw nothing and no one suspicious.

As he scanned the area, Brodie looked up on a ridge on the other side of the highway and noticed a sports car. Could that be Haack? He radioed dispatch again, told them he was going to check out the sports car, gave the location, and that he would need backup, then confirmed that Dwyer would stay at Roarke and Mila's in case Haack returned.

It could be Dustin Haack in the sports car, could not be. If it was him, the guy wasn't getting away this time.

Not on Brodie's watch.

Brodie nearly lost track of the older model green sports car, but it came into sight again. He turned on his lights just as Juanita informed him that backup was on its way. The car zipped through a narrow canyon, nearly hitting a pair of antelope on the side of the road. It climbed Highway 45 toward the mountains, its erratic driver weaving all over the road.

The driver, a man with blond hair who resembled Haack,

reached over and grabbed something from the passenger side. Brodie braced for the worst. Did he have a gun? Would he attempt to shoot while driving? Success wasn't in Haack's future if so.

But it wasn't a gun Haack reached for, but a gallon of something. The man tossed it out the driver's side, causing Brodie to swerve to avoid hitting it. He radioed dispatch and instructed them to have someone check the jug for liquid—if there was any.

The solid yellow line briefly became a dotted one, allowing one to pass. Brodie kicked the truck into gear and sped beside the sports car. "Pull over!" he shouted, although it was doubtful Haack could hear him above the roar of the vehicles' engines.

Haack raised a gun and fired at Brodie's truck. The bullet pinged off the hood.

The solid yellow line re-emerged, and Brodie kept dispatch in the loop as to his location. Flat grassy ranchland gave way to pine-covered hills, and when Brodie arrived at the top of the first switchback, a semi pulled out from an overlook just at the top of the mountain, directly in front of him. Didn't say much for the truck driver's attention, or lack thereof, that he hadn't seen police lights and a truck.

Two twenty-mile-an-hour switchbacks later, Brodie arrived at the crest of the mountain. Guard rails, warnings of falling rock, and a steep grade greeted him, but no sign of the sports car. Likely, it had sped up and far surpassed anything Brodie could have achieved following the slow-moving semi, which finally pulled over at the first safe turnoff.

He touched base with dispatch. Juanita was on her lunch break, and the other dispatcher was covering. A half hour later, Brodie was still weaving around curvy mountain roads, scoping out the area for the car. Had it even come this far? Was it in the next county? He traveled a while further, then turned around and retreated back down the mountain. As he did so, he spied the sports car tucked in a grove of trees he hadn't been able to see before due to the semi.

An empty sports car.

The search was on to find Dustin Haack, but given that there was a second set of tire tracks leading out of the grove of trees, it was relatively clear someone had stopped by, picked him up, and driven him to who knew where.

The sports car had been stolen, which was no surprise, and they couldn't get a location on his latest burner phone, which had been purchased with cash in Upton. Brodie drove back to the ranch to check on Londyn and see if Dwyer needed any assistance taking Londyn's and Mila's statements.

Roarke had already arrived, and things had settled a bit.

"Uncle Brodie! Uncle Brodie!" Xander and his friend, Kit, bolted toward him. "Look what we found in Mommy's closet. We were playing a game called hider." He partially opened his hand. "I can't open my hand all the way or the moth will escape."

"Sounds like we have a detective in the house."

"Yep, that's me. My sign-ment was to find a bug, and I did."

Brodie ruffled Xander's hair, and the little boy and his friend ran off toward the backyard.

Londyn emerged from the kitchen. "Brodie." Her words escaped muffled, but he thought he detected the relief in her tone.

"Londyn. Are you all right?" What he wouldn't give to hold her. Protect her. Keep her safe from Dustin Haack and whoever else might ever wish to cause her harm.

With effort, he reined his thoughts back to reality.

Brodie took Londyn aside, and she leaned into him. Hesitantly, he wrapped an arm around her shoulder, inhaling the familiar scent of her shampoo, and resisted the urge to pull her closer. Vivid memories of how it felt once upon a time to hold her filled his thoughts.

Just as quickly as he allowed himself the memory, he reminded himself that this was because she was in danger, not because she had any feelings for him.

"Did you find him?"

"I did not." Brodie proceeded to share the updates with Londyn. "Do you know anybody in Pronghorn Falls who might be helping him?"

"I don't. We had a friend in common in Rowland, named Jasmine, but I haven't seen her anywhere around here, and while I would no longer trust her, I don't think she would aid and abet a criminal. Especially since she is my friend."

But the way Londyn looked away, Brodie figured her assessment of what Jasmine would or wouldn't do might not be all that accurate. He'd need to follow that potential lead.

A notification chimed on Londyn's phone, and she pulled away from Brodie and checked her messages. Her face turned pallid, and he saw her lips tremble.

"Londyn? What is it?"

Her hands shaking, she handed Brodie the phone.

HEY, LONDYN. WONDER IF THE KIDS WE HAVE SOMEDAY WILL BE LIKE THOSE LITTLE BOYS PLAYING OUTSIDE IN THE BACKYARD TODAY.

Chapter 17

Brodie was at his desk eating a late lunch when the call came in.

"Sheriff Brenneman."

"Brenneman, hello, this is Detective Rivas with the Rowland PD."

"What can I do for you, Detective?"

"We believe we've spotted Dustin Haack's truck at his apartment here in Rowland."

"In Rowland?" That was a relief. How nice to have a reprieve from the guy they couldn't find. Now if only the Rowland PD could nab him. Brodie detested the tedious and prolonged amount of time this case had been open and the circumstances surrounding it.

"Yes. A neighbor called in a few minutes ago on her lunch break and noticed Haack's truck parked in front of his apartment. Patrol is en route as we speak, and I'm getting ready to head over there as well."

Brodie attempted to digest the information. "Well, if that's the case, that gives us a little break here from him. Will you let me know what you find?"

"You'll be among the first to know."

"Thanks. I appreciate all your help." Brodie clicked off from the phone call with Rivas. What were the odds that Haack would leave Pronghorn Falls and return to Rowland? Was he there temporarily? Did he plan to move back? Why leave now? Not that Brodie wasn't glad that Haack left. It gave him some respite from having to worry about Londyn and Haack's next evil plan. Brodie tapped his pencil on the desk. It would be difficult to be patient waiting for the follow-up call from Rivas.

He lifted the receiver and punched in Londyn's cell number.

"Hello?"

"Hey, Londyn, it's Brodie."

Hi, Brodie." Her voice, one he would recognize anywhere and one he'd grown to love, sounded across the line.

"I have good news."

"Dustin was caught?"

"Not quite that good of news. However, his truck has been sighted at his apartment in Rowland."

Londyn exhaled a deep breath. "He returned to Rowland?"

"That's what it sounds like. Detective Rivas is on his way over to the apartment now to see if he's inside the building. He promised he'd let me know as soon as he found out anything."

"Wow. Well, I'm all for that. Maybe he gave up, and this nightmare will be over."

Londyn's shaky tone sounded about as convinced as Brodie felt. "If only. However, we don't know the details of this yet."

"I know, but you have to admit this is fantastic news, especially if they're able to catch him."

"Dustin is a slippery guy, but that's our hope."

"This is an answer to prayer. It will be so refreshing not to have to worry about him anymore."

Brodie's phone buzzed. "Look, Londyn, I have to go because there's another call coming in. This place has been crazy busy today. I'll be in touch as soon as I hear anything from Rivas."

For the first time in a while, Londyn felt freer than she had in some time. If Dustin truly was in Rowland, it obviously meant he wasn't in Pronghorn Falls. She finished loading the dishes for Aileen, who was with Mila and Xander at the homeschool co-op.

Brodie wasn't comfortable with her leaving the ranch alone, and to be truthful, Londyn had no desire to be out and about on her own anywhere but in the safe confines of the Brenneman Ranch, even if Dustin was back in Rowland. Truthfully, there was no telling when he'd decide to return to Pronghorn Falls.

But for the moment, she would revel in the freedom she'd formerly taken for granted before Dustin's obsession. She sat on the edge of the couch and folded her hands. "Lord, thank you so much that Dustin has returned to Rowland. Please let Detective Rivas and the other officers arrest him. Please let justice be served."

Deputy Huang, who'd been keeping an eye out for Dustin, sat on the front porch eating his lunch. "Deputy?"

"Londyn, hi. I just heard from Brodie that Dustin Haack is in Rowland. The sheriff gave me the go-ahead to take an hour and head into town to catch the last few minutes of my son's softball game. Are you comfortable with that?"

"I am. Thank you."

The deputy smiled, tucked the remaining food inside his cooler, and pressed the lid onto the top. "I'll be back in an hour or so. I'm sure Brodie told you that they haven't confirmed a sighting of Haack yet, so it's best to continue to take precautions."

"Yes. I agree."

"All right. I'll be back within the hour."

Londyn unloaded and folded the clothes in the dryer, then scribbled a note on a scrap of paper.

Aileen,

I went for a walk at 1:45. Will be back soon. Heading on the dirt road past Roarke and Mila's house and toward state land. I will be back within an hour.

Love, Londyn

Londyn wound her hair into a ponytail, donned a baseball cap, grabbed a bottle of water, her phone, and sunglasses, and in a move that would make both Brodie and Mr. Brenneman proud, she holstered her gun into her belly band concealed carry holster. She then locked the front door and stepped out into the brilliant sunshine. The view of the mountains from the porch was almost too much to take in, with magnificent white snow contrasting with the blue-green of the mountains and the cloudless blue sky. Londyn inhaled a deep breath of fresh air and pretended for a moment that some weirdo wasn't stalking her. At least he was in Rowland for the time being. She welcomed the modicum of peace that realization brought.

For the first time since the accident, she felt well enough to do more than a few low-impact exercises. She doubled-knotted her tennis shoes and took off on the brisk walk on the road in the direction of Roarke and Mila's. Roarke likely tended to ranch chores in one of the fields, so he would be in the vicinity.

The peaceful silence and the pleasant, but efficient, calorie-burning walk gave her time to collect her thoughts and, more importantly, pray about the recent events. It had been some time since she embarked on an invigorating power walk in the country—or outside, for that matter. While living in Rowland, the only safe exercise available was in the gym or with Jasmine through one of the safer parks in the city. How had she ever thought leaving Pronghorn Falls was a good idea?

She tilted her head toward the sky. "Thank you, Jesus, for second chances." A niggle of pain jabbed at her chest. "Lord, if it's Your will, could I please have a second chance with Brodie as well?"

Her favorite verse from Lamentations came to mind as she sped past a grove of trees filled with happy birds singing. God's mercies were new every day. She needed His mercy. Needed His grace. Needed Him to walk with her through this new beginning in her life.

Even if Dustin was still out there somewhere waiting for her.

She shivered, although not from the weather. On the contrary, the sunny seventy-five-degree day was anything but cold.

Londyn passed Roarke and Mila's house and noticed that Roarke's truck wasn't in the driveway. She shoved aside the thought that no one was around and forged ahead, pumping her arms and quickening her stride. It felt good to exercise, and the high of it infiltrated through her and shaved away the momentary stress of being somewhat isolated. She checked her fitness watch. An hour was all she needed.

Cows dotted the pasture, and the mountains beckoned Londyn toward them. She knew this road like the back of her hand. How many times had she and Brodie walked, ridden bikes, or hopped in the UTV and meandered along the route that curved and wound its way through rugged ranch land, meadows, and snow-capped peaks in the distance?

A canopy of trees weaved their branches overhead as she stepped down into a low-lying path alongside the creek before hastening back up the hill. A far distance now from Mila and Roarke's house, and even farther from Aileen's, but still on Brenneman land, Londyn continued. She paused for a minute, inclined her face to the sky, and allowed the sun to beat down on her. Summers didn't get any better than the ones in Pronghorn Falls. Warm. Low humidity. The scent of pine trees and the sound of birds chirping.

Speaking of sounds…a noise reminiscent of a woman crying interrupted the serenity. Londyn craned an ear toward the din and listened again.

"Sesame? Where are you?"

It was a female voice, and as Londyn took a few steps forward, she saw a woman through the trees patting her leg and calling to whoever Sesame was. Londyn stilled for a moment, just watching. While anyone could access this area from the main road, it wasn't common knowledge that it was here, and while the Brenneman Ranch butted up to the state land, most people didn't venture this far.

Most people.

But this woman had.

"Oh, hello." The woman turned to face her, tears in her eyes.

Londyn recognized her as someone who had disputed a bill once when Londyn worked at the hospital billing department, but she couldn't recall her name. "Did you lose someone?"

"I did. I was taking Sesame for a walk, and he disappeared. Can you help me find him?"

Londyn didn't need to see the anguish in the woman's eyes to know that Sesame was an important pet. She took a few steps closer. "Are we looking for a dog?"

"Yes. He's a Portuguese Podengo."

Londyn wasn't well-versed in dog breeds. "What color is he?"

"Yellow with white on his face, chest, and paws. He's about fifty pounds and such a sweetheart." The woman hiccupped before launching into a sob. "I don't know what I will do if I can't find him."

"I can help you. You look familiar from when I used to work at the billing department for the hospital and clinic. What is your name?"

"Renee. Renee Corker. And your name?"

"I'm Londyn."

Renee nodded. "I remember now. You were so nice to help me get my bill reduced after I hurt my back."

Scant details returned. Londyn smiled at the redhead, whose unmanageable hair had escaped from what appeared to be a former ponytail at the nape of her neck. "Where did you last see Sesame?"

"Right over there near the ravine. We decided to go on a walk after one of my friends told me it was so beautiful up here and that we could get a good glimpse of the mountains." Renee withdrew her phone from her pants pocket. "I've been trying to get some pictures to enter in the newspaper's photo of the week contest. At first, I wasn't going to take Sesame because he has a history of running off, but he was so eager to go on a walk this morning. Thank you for helping me find him." For the next several minutes, Londyn joined Renee in calling Sesame's name. She thought she heard a bark on the other side of the creek, but she couldn't be sure.

"I think I hear him down there." Renee pointed toward the road and, without waiting, started scaling the dirt path in that direction. Londyn followed her, periodically calling out to Sesame.

A truck hauling a horse trailer passed by on the road. "Maybe we should cross to the other side and see if he's over there," suggested Renee. She shoved her free hand into the pocket of her purple denim pants covered in dog hair, which did little to flatter her overt pear shape. "What do you think, Londyn?"

Londyn scanned the area across the two-lane road. The state land on that side was covered in sagebrush mingled with some rocky patches. A deer stood eyeing them. She was surprised it would be so calm if Sesame was in the vicinity.

"We can, but I doubt he's over there. Why don't we head back up the hill and see if maybe we just missed seeing him?"

Renee shrugged her narrow shoulders, and Londyn turned back around to lead the woman back to where they had come from when she heard a vehicle pull up to the side of the road.

"Oh, there's my friend. Maybe he can help us." Renee strode toward the car.

The hairs on the back of Londyn's neck stood on end, although she wasn't sure why. She didn't recognize the vehicle, and she couldn't see who was inside. Still, she'd learned long ago to listen to her gut. Maybe she should return to the ranch. She increased her speed when she heard footsteps behind her. She assumed it was Renee, but glanced back just to be sure.

That's when she noticed Dustin following her.

Londyn sped up her pace, but her foot slipped on the dry dirt of the incline. She fell and propelled herself back up again, struggling to get traction. Once on even ground, she would need to switch to a full-out run. When she reached the top, something hard hit her just behind the knees, and she fell to the ground, smacking her kneecaps and shoulder on the packed dirt. Londyn gritted her teeth and attempted once again to rise to her feet.

She was vaguely aware of Dustin's voice, "Wow, Renee, I'm impressed. I never figured you to be able to swing a tree branch."

Renee laughed as the pain radiated down the back of Londyn's leg. Adrenaline urged her off the ground just as Dustin grabbed her ponytail and wrenched her head back. "Where do you think you're going, Londyn?"

"You need to let me go. Brodie will be here any minute." Her eyes smarted as he yanked harder, and she groped for her gun. She wanted to use it at the most advantageous time possible, but with Dustin's proximity, she struggled with knowing when that time was. The last thing she needed was for him to wrestle it from her.

"I don't think he will be. He's just been called out to a disturbance on Hannon Road. Nice try, though."

With difficulty and attempting to ignore the searing pain in her knee and the awkward position Dustin had put her in while pulling her hair, Londyn twisted and elbowed him hard in the gut. Dustin faltered a second before Londyn lifted her leg and kicked him as hard as she could in the shin. He released her hair, grunted, and bent over to rub his shin.

Londyn clobbered him over the head with her water bottle and attempted to ignore the throbbing pain in her leg as she hurriedly limped away.

She heard the rush of feet and Renee's voice asking Dustin if he was all right.

But Londyn didn't wait to find out what transpired next. *Lord, please give me the ability to run.*

As much as she willed her legs to cooperate, she failed. But Londyn could walk, although she only had a few seconds' lead time.

She needed a game plan. A chance to call 911. To use her

gun.

Unfortunately, she was afforded none of the three.

Dustin gripped her shoulder and called her a few choice words.

Londyn screamed, then grabbed the underside of his arm in the delicate tricep muscle area while simultaneously aiming for his eyes. He shoved her to the ground. Londyn extracted her gun from its holster and directed it at her attackers.

"Dustin, do something!" wailed Renee.

Dustin charged her as she fired, knocking the gun from her grasp. It skidded along the ground and into a crevice.

Londyn crab walked back away from him. She needed to get her gun. Needed to get away. *Had* to get away. If he had a chance to drag her to the car, Brodie would never find her. She turned over and hoisted herself to a standing position, but Dustin had already recovered. He ran toward her, head-butting her and knocking her backward.

"That was a good one, Dustin." Renee clapped her hands. "Kinda like in the movies."

Renee's words were the last Londyn heard before everything went black.

Chapter 18

Nightmares were not an entirely foreign thing for Londyn. She'd had them a time or two in her life, especially after Dustin started stalking her. So why then would she think this was anything but a bad dream?

Blurred vision met her gaze, and she attempted to reach her bound hands toward her eyes. Londyn's head throbbed, as did her back, her legs, and just about everywhere else on her body. Speaking of legs…

Her ankles were also bound by a rope.

The stench overwhelmed her, and she gagged, thankful that she was able to draw breath at all.

As she shook her head to awaken herself, the realization set in that she was not dreaming. This was real life. She was somewhere in a small room, tucked against a wall near where a pile of dried feces was clumped in the corner. A desk was shoved to one side, and an exorbitant amount of clutter covered the floor and rose alongside the walls. A bird cage, newspapers, magazines, a hula-hoop, cardboard boxes, cassette tapes, dishes, moldy food, a dartboard, and more littered every available space except where she sat. Fecal matter was smeared in several places.

Was she alone? Could she escape? Was there a way to remove the binding on her hands and feet?

Lord, please help me.

She scooted toward a door and pressed her ear against it. Where was Dustin? Where was Renee? *Where on earth was she?* Londyn was about to attempt to somehow turn the doorknob when she heard a knock.

"Yoo-hoo."

Londyn scuttled away from the door and back against the wall. If she had the opportunity, she could kick Renee, even with bound feet.

The door opened, and Renee stood in the doorway with a cat in her arms and a large, dark brown boxer at her side. "How are you doing, Londyn?"

"Why are you doing this?"

Renee shrugged. "You should know why."

Londyn's temples throbbed. As if recovering from a concussion wasn't enough, she'd suffered further head injuries. "I don't know why."

Renee whistled, and several dogs ran toward her. Several cats roamed throughout the room. "Do you still wonder why?"

"Yes. I don't understand any of this." *Or any of Renee's involvement.* She had figured Renee to be an oddball, eccentric even, but a kidnapper? "Where's Dustin?"

"Don't worry about Dustin. He'll be back later to visit you. But for now, I want you to know that you will enjoy living here."

Londyn's chest tightened. "What do you mean *living* here?"

Renee giggled, her laugh bordering on maniacal. "You sure do ask a lot of questions." She set the cat down, and it purred and walked over and rubbed against Londyn's leg. Londyn had never been fond of cats, especially since she was allergic to them. Just as she figured, her eyes began to water, and she sneezed.

"Keep an eye on her for a minute, King." Renee patted the boxer on the head and retreated to somewhere else in the house.

Two dogs perched beside Londyn, while King growled and bared his teeth. Londyn inched as close as she could against the wall. Would the boxer attack her?

Renee returned in a few minutes with two dog dishes in her hands. "I thought you might like something to eat since it's about dinner time."

Dinner time? How long had Londyn been here?

One of the dogs rested its paws on Renee's thigh, and she swatted it away, nearly spilling the contents of one of the dishes. "This is for Londyn. You'll have your dinner soon." She ushered all the dogs, except King, from the room and balanced the dog dishes on Londyn's lap. "I hope you're flexible so that you can bend down and eat these because Dustin says I can't take the ropes off your hands or feet."

One of the dishes held several square crackers. The other appeared to be milk. A layer of pet hair floated on the surface of the milk, and Londyn retched, nausea just at the edge of her throat.

"As you know, I take in strays. Dogs others don't want, cats living outside all alone, or even sometimes I have to rescue dogs when their owners aren't looking." Renee emitted a shrill laugh. "As was the case for a couple of my newest rescues. They should never have been unleashed in the park." She hiked up her shoulder. "That's what they get for not keeping their dogs leashed. You'd be amazed at how the pets just came right to me. For treats, of course. But if a dog isn't with its owner, then it's a stray. Cats, too." Renee counted on her fingers. "I think

I'm up to twenty-three altogether, including the rabbit living in the bathtub and the goat and horse outside."

Twenty-three animals? Twenty-one in this house? Londyn had no idea how big the house was or where all the animals would even stay. Were they being cared for? Neglected? Fed? Watered? What about the horse? Was it still there? Or the goat?

"Was Sesame even lost?" she asked.

"No. He's been here all along, but it worked to get you to help me."

Londyn inwardly groaned. She knew all about situational awareness, of not falling for ploys. And yet...

A pernicious grin crossed Renee's face. "It's an important job. I've rescued them all, and one time, I even had a pet goose. But you're the first person I've rescued."

It would do no good to tell Renee she didn't need to be rescued. The woman patted Londyn on the head. "And you are a stray, Londyn. You don't have a home." She puckered her lips, blinked her eyes, and shook her head. "This will be your new home."

Her new home? Goosebumps pricked her skin.

Londyn forced herself to not only digest all that Renee was saying, but also to attempt to fit some pieces together to determine where she was. If Renee truly had rescued a horse and goat, her house wasn't within city limits.

"I would like to go home."

Renee shook her head. "Dustin says I need to keep you here for a while. But don't worry, you won't be lonely." Renee placed her hands on her wide hips. "I do have to tell you that if you do try to escape, King will have none of it."

At the mention of the dog's name, King bared his teeth.

Londyn fought the rise of panic. While she wasn't typically

afraid of dogs—and would easily consider herself a "dog person"—she wasn't fond of mean canines.

"Now, do your best to eat up, and I'll be back to check on you in a little while." Much to Londyn's relief, Renee gathered the three cats that tiptoed around the room and hauled them out before shutting the door. And at least she had taken King with her.

Londyn sneezed again and attempted to itch her eyes with her shoulder, but as she did so, milk in one of the dog dishes sloshed over the edge onto her pants.

Dare she even think about drinking the milk? What had Renee put in it? Cat dander in the liquid wouldn't do Londyn any favors. She was so thirsty, likely dehydrated if she'd been here any length of time. But no, she wouldn't chance consuming anything Renee offered.

If she thought Renee was psychotic, it would be even worse when and if Dustin arrived.

Lord, please, please help me.

She must have fallen asleep at some point. Something furry against her arm awakened her, and Londyn's eyes fluttered open. Where was she? What was that pungent odor? Why couldn't she move her arms?

A cat meowed and peered up at her as Londyn simultaneously sneezed. The cat zipped from her lap, and Londyn's eyes watered and itched. She was completely congested. Yet, she couldn't remove her hands from the restraints.

The door creaked open. "I see you're awake. How was your nap?"

Renee crouched down beside Londyn.

Oh, yes. That's where she was. Taken captive by a psychopathic animal hoarder.

"I'd be doing a lot better if you could please loosen these ropes around my wrists and ankles."

"I'm sorry—well, not really sorry—but I can't do that. Dustin is counting on me to follow his directions." Renee's eyes rolled into the back of her head, and she discharged a contented breath. "Did you know we are going to get married?"

Londyn wanted to tell Renee that whatever Dustin had promised was far from reality. He would no more marry Renee than any of the other women he'd likely proposed to. But she bit her tongue.

"He loves me, and I love him. Oh, how I *love* him." Renee swooned. "He's sweet, charming, and not to mention, hot."

Dustin was anything but sweet and "hot", although he was charming. The thought caused Londyn to recoil. He held many under his spell and had almost fooled Londyn as well.

Renee stood. "I've been so lonely until I met him." Her mouth twisted. "I'll be right back. Don't go anywhere." She emitted a high-pitched laugh and dashed from the room only to return a few seconds later with a thick magazine. "Would you like to see the wedding dress I've chosen?" Without waiting for Londyn to answer, Renee stooped beside Londyn, her back against a pile of boxes as she thumbed through the pages of the sizeable bridal magazine. "Dustin says we make such a good team, and I know we'll make a good team in marriage, too. Who would have thought someone so handsome would be interested in someone like me?"

Renee was clearly delusional.

The woman opened the magazine to a page that had been dog-eared and pointed to a picture of a model in a strapless form-fitting wedding gown with a lace bodice and a generous ruffled skirt with white flowers and pearl beads. "This is the one I have chosen. What do you think?"

Renee's expectant gaze and actual belief that she would be Dustin's bride sickened Londyn. But she would have to play along.

"It's lovely."

"Dustin told me that if I do as I'm told and hold you here until he returns, we'll set the date for our wedding. I've always thought a winter wedding would be fabulous." Renee's expression took on a dreamy state. A thought came to Londyn then. "Perhaps you and I could go wedding dress shopping. I heard that boutique downtown carries a wide selection of formal wear."

Renee slipped out of her fanciful world, her eyes enlarging and her mouth forming an "o". She blinked rapidly before answering. "Yes, that would be an awesome idea."

Londyn resisted the urge to allow a breath of relief to escape her lips. "I think so too. Maybe we could find a pearl necklace to match the beading on the flowers as well."

Renee's attention swiveled between the picture and the magazine and Londyn before a dark shadow fell across her face. "Are you kidding me?"

Londyn jolted at Renee's harsh words. The woman stood. "I think you're trying to trick me into letting you go, but that will never happen. I promised Dustin, the love of my life, that I would hold you here until he returned. Your trickery will not change that."

Renee propped up the dartboard with a man's photo on it and retrieved two darts from the top of the desk beneath a pile of papers. She threw a dart at the dartboard. "Take that," she said as the dart hit the photograph's outer edge.

"Who is that?" Londyn asked.

"Not that it's your business, but it's the man who decided it was a good idea to break my heart. We met online and were supposed to get married." She seethed the words.

"Aren't you and Dustin getting married?"

Renee whipped around and faced Londyn. Her chest rose and fell, and she tapped her foot. "Yes. Now I am." She calmed, and her pinched expression eased. "Dustin came into my life at just the right time. I realize now what true love is. That's why I would do anything for him."

The door creaked open, and Dustin entered. Renee looped her arms around his neck. "I've missed you so much," she said, planting a kiss on his lips. Dustin kissed her back, but at the same time, he focused his attention on Londyn and rolled his eyes. While Londyn couldn't see the front of Renee's face since it was Dustin who faced her, from the way the woman's head was tilted back, Londyn imagined her to be lovingly smiling at Dustin.

"Why don't you go make us some lunch?" he suggested. Without hesitation, Renee zipped from the room. Dustin kneeled beside Londyn and wrinkled his nose. "Man, this place is awful." He brushed a thumb against her cheek. "Don't worry, my love, I will get you out of here." Had he already forgotten he was part of the reason she was here? He stood just as Renee entered the room.

"I have some eggs I could make us omelets," she suggested. Londyn stared at the egg carton in Renee's hands and noted an expiration date of three months ago. She cringed. Was it because Renee had recycled the cardboard carton, or was it because the eggs were truly that old?

"Ah, that sounds perfect." Dustin stood up and put his arm around Renee. "You've always been a good cook." Renee blushed. How long had Dustin and Renee known each other?

When Renee again left the room, Dustin focused his attention on Londyn. "I want you to know that I don't really care about her the way that I care about you." Londyn's gag reflex kicked in, and nausea churned in her belly. "Now don't go anywhere," he chortled, giving her the once-over. "I'll be back in a few. Oh, and you might need this." He withdrew a filthy handkerchief from the desk drawer, twisted it, then shoved it into her mouth and tied it behind her head. "I know you, Londyn. You tend to make a commotion when things don't go your way."

Now she'd have no way of yelling or even speaking. Not that anyone but Dustin, Renee, and the animals could hear her anyway. The handkerchief tasted of a blend of cooked cabbage, moldy cheese, and liver. She gagged, the contents of food eaten that morning attempting to re-emerge. A wave of heat rippled through her, and she prayed she wouldn't hyperventilate.

Dustin left the room and closed the door behind him. The sound of crunching gravel outside drew Londyn's attention to the window. She wiggled her way toward it and attempted to prop herself up. She caught a glimpse of Brodie's service vehicle pulling into the driveway.

Londyn lost her momentum and fell back onto the floor into a pile of who knew what.

She heard a vehicle door shut, and she figured he was exiting his truck. Would Dustin try something? Londyn had to get Brodie's attention and warn him. Brodie was a sitting duck walking along without any clue that someone bent on harming him was just on the other side of the door. Londyn attempted to lift her elbow and tap on the window, but it only produced a lackluster sound she doubted Brodie could hear. On the other side of the bedroom door, she heard Dustin tell Renee, "Just be quiet. Don't answer the door, don't say anything."

"But I don't want to get in trouble for stealing that horse," whispered Renee in a panicked voice.

"Like I said, just be quiet and act like no one is home."

"Okay."

Londyn again propped herself up and watched as Brodie briefly inspected the sedan parked in front of Renee's house. She clasped a chewed-up tennis ball between her bound hands and pounded on the window again as best as she could and bemoaned the fact that she had a gag in her mouth. Brodie then turned and walked to the front door out of her sight. The doorbell must have failed because instead of hearing the classic "ding dong", there was a loud knock at the door. A brief pause, then more pounding.

Brodie stepped back from the front door and again into her view. He examined the front of the house, including the window where she stood. *Brodie!* But it came out as a muffled grunt. He looked in her direction—or at least she thought it was in her direction, and she hammered on the glass. She held her breath. Would he see her?

She released another strangled cry and thumped on the window again. *Look this way, Brodie!* But instead, he pivoted in the direction of the truck.

She had to try again. Had to get Brodie's attention. Struggling to her feet for a third time, she called to him. Instead of seeing her, Brodie climbed into his service truck and closed the door.

Londyn slid down in dejection, her back against the wall. Tears stung her eyes, and she hung her head. Rescue had been within her reach, and yet now? *Lord, please rescue me. I know that You never leave us. That nothing happens without Your knowledge. Give me the strength to survive this, the wisdom to figure a way out of this, and the ability to escape.*

Had God heard her? Would He help her?

So, so many times in her life she'd felt alone. Mom had better things to do than tend to her kids. A memory of her and Logan left in the car for hours while Mom visited the local bar flitted through her mind. It had been cold that day, and they'd huddled in the back pretending they lived in an igloo in the Arctic.

Mom emerged from the bar, a man on her arm. A man who became their first stepdad, the rebound from their father's unfaithfulness.

Jesus had been with Londyn even then. Even when she'd not known Him.

He'd been with her through the other heartaches in her life. The first time Dad promised to show up for her school recital and was nowhere to be found. His deserting his family altogether. Mom's neglect that had continued far into her teen years. The hateful words of some of the girls in junior high P.E. class about her mom's morals. The situation with Lance. Logan's estrangement after he and Londyn had been through so much together. The fearful times with Dustin in Rowland. The car accident, near strangulation, the episode in the clinic parking lot, and his visits to Aileen's and Roarke and Mila's house.

The Lord had never left her side. He never would. She was His ever since that day in youth group when she'd put her faith and trust in her Savior. Ever since she'd decided to live for Him.

Even when Londyn doubted. Even when her life was rife with trouble, even when things changed daily, Jesus remained steadfast. She couldn't lose hope.

A mangy black-and-white cat climbed onto her lap, flicked its tail in her face, and Londyn sneezed, the handkerchief impeding her, as she attempted to brush the cat aside. It hopped off and toddled through a pile of garbage.

Londyn was about to struggle to her feet when she heard the doorknob turn.

Dustin entered, and Londyn scanned the crowded, junk-filled room. An idea formed in her mind. She spied an old bird cage on the desk and the pile of remaining darts for the dartboard beneath the stack of papers.

Lord, please let this work.

"The sheriff's gone, at least," said Dustin. "I abhor it when people try to interfere with my plans."

Londyn's heart sank. She'd been so close to being rescued. Would she still have a chance to escape?

No, she refused to allow this to deter her. She could still flee. She just needed to think this out. *Lord, please guide me.*

Chapter 19

Brodie took a call about a possible missing horse being sighted in the yard at a house owned by a Renee Corker. It wasn't often he had to deal with horse thievery. He chuckled as he thought of how it was reminiscent of something out of the Wild West. Speaking of which, he'd plopped his cowboy hat on his head and climbed into his service truck.

The woman accused of stealing the horse lived three miles outside of town in a white home with mold in every crevice of the siding. He'd never been to this residence before, and based on what the outside looked like, he couldn't imagine the inside. Four inoperable junked vehicles cluttered the driveway, along with an older model sedan with current plates.

A rusty generator, a dilapidated cupboard, a moldy cardboard box that was dented on one side, and a stack of tires lined the front yard. A worn-out air conditioner missing a panel kicked on, and flies swarmed around ants beneath his feet and splatters of bird poop on the sidewalk leading to the porch. Someone had tossed a discarded spray can to the side, and an abundance of weeds grew through cracks in the porch and throughout the rain gutter overhead. He's seen hoarder places like this before, but never this bad. And he wasn't even to the front door yet. How could people even live like that? Fortunately for her, she lived outside city limits where ordinances didn't apply.

The foul odor of feces, urine, and burned food assaulted him as he stepped up on the lone step and rang the bell. Nothing happened, so he knocked, then knocked a second time. Dogs barked, and he thought he heard one scratching at the door.

Unfortunately, Renee Corker either wasn't home or she wasn't answering. It would necessitate a return visit. As he turned to leave, he thought he heard some light thudding from somewhere in the home. He investigated briefly, but neither saw nor heard anything further.

Brodie walked around to the side of the house. He cocked his ear toward a window. Was that someone talking?

Dogs barked again, drowning out whatever voices he may or may not have heard. A horse in a derelict corral caught his attention. He returned to the porch one more time, knocked, and when he heard nothing but dogs, he climbed back into his truck. If that was the stolen horse in the yard, Renee Corker wouldn't be keeping it forever.

He'd be back.

***

Dustin flicked a dog hair off his shirt. "I heard something thump in here. Was that you?"

Londyn shook her head and attempted to speak, but her words came out as warbled. Dustin untied and yanked the handkerchief from her mouth. The residual taste caused her to dry heave. "Pheh," she said, slightly pushing her tongue forward while attempting to rid her mouth of the offensive taste.

Dustin smirked. "Did you need to say something?"

"Could I please use the restroom? I've been here for several hours."

Dustin worked his jaw in a tight circle as if contemplating her request. What happened to wanting to rescue her? Would he fall for probably the oldest trick in the book?

"All right," he finally said. "You'll need to make it quick."

"Thank you."

"You won't thank me when you see the bathroom." He blanched and made a gagging noise. "Just ignore the defecation on the toilet seat, the mold in every corner, the rabbit in the bathtub, and the clothes and mile-high piles of trash, and you'll be fine."

Londyn cringed. "That bad?"

"Worse. Let's just say Renee is not the housecleaning type. You'll need a biohazard outfit." He snorted and peered around him. "Nothing like a hoarder's paradise." Dustin removed the binding from her hands and her feet. "You have two minutes to take care of business." He took a step back, and Londyn struggled to her feet. Weakness threatened from having nothing to eat for so long, and her eyes burned from the allergies. Determination and the will to survive emboldened her to achieve the goal she had in mind.

Her adversary watched her every move. How could she defer his attention from her? An idea percolated in her racing mind. "There is so much in here that Renee could sell and make good money on. Vintage items are all the rage," she said, slowly trudging over the piles of junk.

"I don't think Renee cares if she makes money or not."

"But, still, look at that old record player over there. That's like something that's even before our parents' time."

A shadow fell across Dustin's face, and Londyn wondered about the relationship between him and his family. He'd never been forthright with information about them. Not even during their "friendship" in Rowland. "I wonder if that even still has a needle in it?"

"If you're so interested in it, why don't you walk over and look?" The record player was on the way to the door, stacked on top of several boxes and right beside the desk that held the bird cage and the darts, in addition to about three feet of other garbage. She narrowly avoided stepping in fossilized dog feces as she tiptoed to the desk. She nudged the record player.

"This even has a record on it!"

"When did you become interested in old stuff?"

"I don't know, I just find it fascinating." Londyn's dry throat made it difficult to speak, and the places on her wrists and ankles where the rope had been were rubbed raw. She shoved her concerns aside. She needed her ruse to be successful.

Dustin had come to stand beside her as she inspected the record player. "I wonder if it works."

"Who cares?"

She shrugged, then, mustering all of her strength and tenacity, Londyn grabbed the old bird cage, swung it around, and connected it with Dustin's head.

"Owwwww!" He planted a hand on the desk and seethed. "You're going to pay for that, Londyn."

Dustin was quick, but Londyn was quicker. She stabbed him in the web of his hand with a dart before hitting him again with what appeared to be some sort of paperweight. She scrambled from the room. There was no easy way to rush down the hall and to the front door, not with stacks and piles of debris, cardboard boxes, garbage, and an unusable toilet sitting in the middle of the room. The dogs bounded toward her as she attempted to sidestep them.

Dustin sprinted after her. She stepped over a pile of old magazines and a bucket that had been used as a trash can. "Get back here, Londyn!"

She glanced back to see Dustin gaining on her as blood spurted from the wound on his head where she'd hit him with the paperweight.

"What's going on, Dustin?" Renee asked.

"Get her!"

"I can't really get her, Dustin. I'm in the middle of making omelets."

"King!" Dustin shouted.

Londyn dodged a broken picture frame and an archaic vacuum. Dogs barked, and she saw King behind her, growling as he ran. He nipped at her leg.

She clasped the doorknob, flung open the door, and stepped out into daylight. Brodie's truck slowly exited the driveway. "Brodie, wait!" Her legs threatened to give out beneath her. Her lungs struggled with the fresh air after spending so much time held hostage in the hoarder house. She could hear her heartbeat in her ears, thumping at a dangerous pace. "Brodie!"

The hot gravel burned her bare feet. When had she lost her shoes?

The unyielding fight within her urged her forward. Her parched throat ached from being gagged, yet she continued to yell, her voice competing with Dustin's admonishment that she stop.

King tore at her pant leg, and she stumbled. Why didn't Brodie stop?

Londyn stepped on something sharp, and the pain nearly stopped her in her tracks. Dustin grabbed for her arm, and she flung herself loose of his grasp.

"I'm coming, Dustin!" shouted Renee. "And I've got the frying pan."

Dustin's heavy breathing warned that he again drew closer. "Brodie!" Londyn's ankle wobbled as she continued traversing the uneven ground, the rocks pricking her feet. She half-limped, half-ran while waving her arms in the air. Brodie had to stop. He *had* to.

"I said, stop, Londyn!" Dustin reached for her arm again, this time his nails digging into her skin. Brodie gave no indication he'd seen her. She couldn't give up. Wouldn't. "Lord, please," she cried out. Urgency propelled her forward just as Dustin clamped a hold on her wrist.

Chapter 20

Brodie exited Renee Corker's driveway, turned on the air conditioner, and rolled up his window. He started down the dirt road to the highway when his cell rang. Detective Rivas's direct line appeared on the screen. He pulled to the side of the road and parked to take the call, hoping for good news.

"Sheriff Brenneman."

"Brenneman, this is Rivas."

"Did we catch him?"

"Unfortunately, no. He wasn't in his apartment."

Brodie knew it was too good to be true that they would have caught Haack. His stomach clenched. Every day Dustin Haack was on the loose was one day longer that Londyn's life was in jeopardy. There is no telling what a guy who would run someone off the road and try to strangle her was capable of.

Rivas continued. "We pounded on the door, and when there was no answer, we visited with the neighbor, also the reporting party. We were able to look at her cameras and check out the footage from when the truck arrived."

"Let me guess, he took off on foot?"

Brodie could hear Rivas shuffling some papers.

"No, if only it were that easy. If he had taken off on foot, we would probably have found him by now. Instead, the cameras indicated a black-haired woman emerging from Haack's truck, unlocking the door of his apartment, and stepping inside."

"A woman?"

"Yep."

"Are you guys sure you have the right truck?"

"We ran the plates. It was registered to Haack." Rivas's voice came off somewhat defensive, and Brodie regretted that he sounded like he hadn't believed the seasoned detective knew what he was doing.

"Sorry about that, sir. I didn't mean to sound disrespectful. I just...this guy's been so elusive, you can't even imagine. Every time he commits a crime, he disappears into thin air."

"No worries. I get it." Rivas cleared his throat. "Our guys knocked on the door, but there was no answer. We weren't sure if the woman who'd entered was ignoring us or if she didn't hear us. I parked across the street in my unmarked car, and within the hour, she exited the apartment with an armful of items and carried them to the truck. Her name is Dorena Mohr, and she's a nurse from Pronghorn Falls. Does the name ring a bell?"

"It does. She works at the hospital. A colleague previously interviewed her regarding this case." Brodie recalled Officer Robinson's report indicating Ms. Mohr was less than forthcoming with answers about Haack's attack on Londyn in the hospital. In a second interview, Ms. Mohr denied giving any information to Haack about Londyn's follow-up appointment at the clinic.

A denial Brodie fervently believed was a lie.

"We brought her in for questioning," Rivas continued, "and Mohr mentioned she hadn't heard us when we knocked on the door."

"What was she doing in Rowland in Haack's truck?"

"We obtained a search warrant for the apartment, but found no one else. We weren't surprised, since only Ms. Mohr entered the home, as shown on the neighbor's camera. But get this—and I'm sure it will come as no surprise to you—Haack is a lunatic. He's tacked up numerous photos of Ms. Siegler on a bulletin board inside what appeared to be his room."

Brodie clenched his fists. Dustin Haack was clearly obsessed with Londyn. What would he do if he ever caught her? "How would he get pictures of her? Were they ones he'd taken?"

"Some appeared to be, yes. Several were taken through the window in her apartment, I assume unbeknownst to her. There was one with three people—Ms. Siegler, Haack, and another woman of about their age. After some digging, we determined her to be a coworker named Jasmine Frewing. While finding this was interesting, suffice it to say, we failed to locate Haack. Dorena Mohr verified that he's still in Pronghorn Falls."

Brodie's heart pounded loudly in his ears. Did Haack intend to fool people into thinking he traveled to Rowland? Brodie put his phone on hands-free free. "Did Mohr give any details about why she drove Haack's truck and why she was in his apartment carrying things out?" The sooner he arrived at the ranch to make sure Londyn was all right, the better. He'd deal with the potential horse thief later.

"She did. Quite an interesting story. Seems Haack has a sick grandmother that he needs to see, and since he's in Pronghorn Falls on work and unable to take time off, he asked if Mohr would drive down and get a few things for him so he could fly out of Pronghorn Falls to Washington state in a couple of days, where his grandmother supposedly lives."

Did Haack even have a grandmother in Washington State? "Haack works in Rowland, not Pronghorn Falls."

"According to Mohr, he was working in Pronghorn Falls." Brodie could almost see Rivas shrug. "Haack sends Mohr down here in his truck to gather the things."

This was beginning to sound like a ploy. "This woman just believes him and drives all that way to do a favor for him?"

"When asked about her relationship to Haack, Mohr said they recently started dating after Haack had a traumatic breakup with his former girlfriend."

Haack had a former girlfriend? That was news to Brodie. He'd have to ask Londyn for details.

Rivas continued. "According to Mohr, the former girlfriend broke Haack's heart, and he was struggling with some depression after the breakup. Mohr, herself, recently went through a difficult divorce, so she said when they found each other, it was just meant to be. She mentioned, and I quote, 'Dustin is sweet, charming, thoughtful, and my dream guy'. It was about the only time she spoke in a tone that was anything but annoyed and exasperated. The woman doesn't know the meaning of respect."

"I doubt Dustin Haack is anyone's dream guy. More like a nightmare. If he's so sweet, why would he have all those photos of Londyn Siegler tacked up on his bulletin board? Didn't Ms. Mohr find that bizarre at the very least?"

"One would think. He's obviously someone able to deceive those who are naïve, as I believe Ms. Mohr is."

"True. We may be able to find out more information from her. Hopefully, between both of our agencies, we will be able to track this guy down. My question is why would any woman want to date him when he's wanted by the police?"

Rivas was silent for a moment. "Not sure other than maybe

she didn't realize he's wanted."

"It's been in the newspaper, the local TV station, and on online news outlets. She would have to live in a cave not to know."

"As we are both aware, there are several reasons women are drawn to criminals. One being maybe she believes he's innocent of any wrongdoing. Two, of course, is the rebound from her divorce, although I'm far from a psychologist."

Brodie knew they could discuss the topic for hours and fail to understand why women like Ms. Mohr would desire anything to do with a man who was wanted by local law enforcement.

"Apparently, Haack gave Ms. Mohr food and gas money. He said she could stay at his place overnight and then return to Pronghorn Falls with the list of items he asked her to gather."

The latest scenario brought about more questions than it answered. "All right, thank you. I appreciate the update."

"We'll still be on the lookout for him here just in case he returns," said Rivas. "No doubt about it, the guy is cagey and has thought out this most recent ruse."

Brodie made a mental note to contact the small airport and apprise them of the APB. Airport personnel would need to keep watch if a man matching Dustin's description attempted to fly out of Pronghorn Falls. Although he strongly believed the grandmother in Washington State thing was nothing more than a scheme.

"Thanks for all your help, Rivas. Here's hoping our agencies can nab this guy."

He'd barely hung up when Mom's number and image flashed across the screen.

"Hey, Mom."

"Brodie, Londyn left a note that she went for a walk. That

was several hours ago, and I can't find her."

"What?"

"She said she'd be walking on the dirt road past Roarke and Mila's house toward the state land. Neither Roarke, Deputy Huang, nor I have seen her.

His panic lurched him into overdrive. What had Londyn been thinking?

"All right, Mom, I'm on my way. Tell Roarke and Huang to keep looking. You stay at the house until she returns."

He contacted dispatch, flipped on his blinker, and glanced in his rearview mirror. And that's when he saw her.

Brodie leaped from the truck. "Londyn!" He scrambled toward her, his boots slipping on the loose gravel. He met her halfway and lifted her into his arms, and set her in the truck. "Wait here and lock the door."

He sprinted to the house, weapon drawn. "Police! Come out now."

An engine's roar and squealing tires drew his attention to the sedan. Haack careened toward him, and Brodie slid out of the road and into the weeds adjacent to the driveway just as the car raced past him. Brodie stumbled to his feet, service pistol at the ready when he had a clear shot. The sedan weaseled its way through on the left side of the truck and down the road to the highway.

Londyn unlocked the door, and Brodie slid into the truck. He contacted dispatch as he began his pursuit. He tossed a glance at Londyn. Her appearance horrified him. Her eyes were swollen, bloodshot, and watery. Her hair was matted to her forehead. "I'm so glad you're all right."

"Thank you for seeing me."

He almost hadn't. Had almost driven to the ranch to find her. If he'd continued on that course…

No. He wouldn't consider that outcome for Londyn. She was safe now, and he intended to keep her that way.

The truck careened to one side over a pothole he hit a little too hard. "Hold on."

Haack swerved around a corner on the country road ahead of them. Brodie gritted his teeth and gripped the steering wheel while informing dispatch of his location and the need for backup.

A school bus stopped ahead, its lights flashing. Brodie hit the brakes as Haack flew past the bus extension arm. The thought of a kid getting mowed over sickened him, and his blood froze in his veins. He stopped behind the bus, grateful that the first student had just now exited.

When the bus continued driving, Brodie safely passed it, noting the bus number. He'd need the footage from the on-board camera.

He surveilled the road ahead. There was no sign of Haack.

A driveway ahead prompted him to stop. He cut the engine. "Londyn?"

Tears fell silently down her cheeks. He unlatched his seatbelt and moved closer. He wanted to hold her. To reassure her. To never let any harm come to her again. "What happened at Corker's house?" He feared the answer.

"They kidnapped me when I was on a walk. I-I had my gun, but it was knocked from my hand, and they tied me up and held me there." Her lip trembled.

He climbed out of the driver's side and walked to her door, opening it. She fell into his arms. He ran a gentle hand over her hair and rested his chin on her head. What if he hadn't been there? The smell of animal urine emanated from her, and clumps of dog hair covered her shirt and pants. He observed some blood on her dirty bare feet. "You're safe now," he whispered.

Londyn clung to him. He closed his eyes and thanked the Lord for keeping her safe until he could reach her. "Did he harm you in any—" He choked on the words, fearing what Haack may have done.

She shook her head, and Brodie released a tight breath. A spine-shuddering sob escaped her, and he gathered her closer. Her pain tore at him, and he yearned to erase all she'd been through in the recent and distant past.

How long had he wanted to hold her again? To feel her in his arms? But not this way. Not because someone wanted to harm her.

Londyn withdrew, and he instinctively gently framed her face with his hands. "I'm going to take you to the clinic."

"I just want to go to the ranch."

"Are you sure?"

"Yes. Please."

"Can we at least call Mila and have her check over you?"

Londyn nodded. He should step back. Get back in the truck and drive her to the ranch, but something kept him there, his hands resting on her upper arms, and his eyes searching hers before she again collapsed against him.

He would comfort her for as long as she needed.

Chapter 21

Renee Corker slouched at the table in the conference room four hours after Brodie rescued Londyn and delivered her to the ranch. He'd visited the kidnapping site and had located Londyn's gun and returned it to her. Then he'd driven into town after he and Huang took Londyn's statement. Dwyer stepped in and traded places with Huang at the ranch.

He flipped the on switch of the video recorder and grabbed a notepad, pen, and a bottle of water. Irritation seeped through him and settled in his throat. He probably shouldn't be the one questioning Renee, and he was grateful his undersheriff, Deputy Huang, was there to assist.

Brodie had numerous questions to ask Renee Corker about the kidnapping and confining Londyn, not to mention questions about the horse theft and his suspicions of animal cruelty. He was still awaiting the emergency search warrant.

Corker had already been Mirandized, and Brodie added, "Just to let you know, this will be recorded."

"Yes. All right. Sure, that's fine." Corker chewed on a dirty fingernail. "I know I shouldn't have taken that horse, but I found it wandering around all by itself, and I was worried it was hungry and thirsty. I'm just that kind of person. Really concerned about animals, you know?"

They'd discuss the theft later. "The horse is in the process of being returned. I want to talk to you about keeping Ms. Siegler hostage in your house."

"Hostage? She wasn't a hostage." Corker reached up and twirled a piece of matted red hair around her finger. "I don't know why you're calling her a hostage."

Brodie slammed his hand on the table. "I'm calling her a hostage because you restrained her at your house and wouldn't let her go."

Huang gripped Brodie's shoulder. "Sheriff, could you step outside with me for a minute?"

Brodie reluctantly followed Huang out onto the hall. He knew he'd been out of line for losing his temper that way, especially so early in the interrogation, but the thought of what could have happened to Londyn, not necessarily by Renee Corker's hand, but by Haack, infuriated him.

"Look, man, I know this is personal for you, but if you can't separate yourself from the case, you're not going to be able to be in there."

While Brodie was Huang's superior, he was also Huang's coworker and friend, and Brodie valued and respected him. "Sorry. I just—I thought of what could have happened to Londyn and then knowing she was kidnapped, bound, and held there against her will with all those animals, and she's allergic to cats and this woman..."

"I know. I get it. I do. But let's go back in there and get some answers. If you want, I can lead the questioning. Ms. Corker is flighty, and I don't think she's going to be forthcoming if we don't handle this in a certain manner."

"You're right. I'm sorry."

"No worries. You all right?"

"I'm good."

They again entered the room, and this time, Corker was leaning back in her chair. "How long do I have to stay here?"

"Until we're done, ma'am," said Huang.

Brodie stroked his chin, noting the need to shave. "Is Dustin Haack your boyfriend?"

"Dustin Haack? I don't know who he is. My boyfriend's name is Dustin, but his last name isn't Haack. It's Cays."

Brodie scribbled the alias on his notepad. Made sense that Haack lied to some of his pawns about his real name.

Renee Corker, who had suddenly decided to become a voracious conversationalist, continued. "And he's really not even my boyfriend. He's my fiancé because we're going to be getting married soon." Corker folded her arms across her chest and jutted her chin. "That is why I can't go to jail because of that horse. I did take care of it when it was at my house. I fed and watered it, and gave it a yard to play in."

He thought of the other animals he suspected were behind the doors of that house. The warrant couldn't come soon enough.

"Tell me how Ms. Siegler came to be at your house."

"She helped me with a bill I had when I hurt my back. I appreciated all her help."

Huang jumped in and asked the next question. "So you knew Ms. Siegler—Londyn—from the billing office?"

"Yes."

"When did you invite her to your house?" asked Brodie.

"Oh, I didn't invite her. Dustin said it would be a great idea and a way to repay her for her kindness for helping me with that bill, you know, by letting her live at my house since she's homeless right now." Corker chewed again on her fingernail. "Besides, I'm going to be moving in with Dustin after we get married, so I thought Londyn could stay there temporarily. I can't stand the thought of someone not having a home." She gestured with her hands. "She lost her home, you know."

"Dustin told you it was a good idea to bring Londyn to your house and offer her the opportunity to stay there until you sold the place after getting married to Dustin?"

Corker clapped her hands. "Yes. And after we're all done here, if you give me your addresses, I can mail you both a wedding invitation."

"That won't be necessary." It was doubtful Haack truly wanted to marry Ms. Corker, especially with his obsession with Londyn. Brodie pressed on with his line of questioning. "Please tell me how you knew Ms. Siegler was going to be out for a walk."

"That's easy. Dustin told me. He's always trying to do nice things for people. Have you met him? He's one of the sweetest guys." Renee Corker swooned. "So good-looking too."

Neither sweet nor good-looking were words Brodie would use to describe Haack. "How did Dustin know about Ms. Siegler's walk?"

Corker shrugged. "Said he'd been watching her."

"And you don't think that's strange?"

"No. He's always caring for the less fortunate and trying to help them. He also said that Londyn is prideful and would be embarrassed to have to stay with someone since she's home-less. He said we would have to convince her. He was right. She didn't come willingly. But I did appreciate that she thought I lost Sesame." Corker jutted her lower lip. "Come to think of it, she was rather rude when Dustin was trying to get her into my car. I understand being prideful, but being outright snotty when someone is trying to help you?"

"How did you get her into the car?"

"First, I have to tell you it was just like some action movie. Dustin clocked her over the head to try to knock some sense into her."

Brodie's annoyance flared. "And you didn't see anything wrong with that? With him hurting her?"

"I don't think he meant to hurt her. She was extremely stubborn and was putting up a fierce fight. He warned me that she was one of those kinds of people who didn't easily accept help and that she also…" Corker lowered her voice. "That she also had—you know—issues." She glanced up at the ceiling. "But she's just like all my cats and dogs. She needs a good home. So, I decided I was the one to help her, or rather, Dustin decided I was the one to help." A large smile lit her face, revealing a few empty spaces in her mouth where teeth had once been. "He has the best ideas!"

Brodie hoped that one of these days, one of Dustin Haack's brilliant ideas would lead law enforcement right to him. "What happened next?"

"We finally got her into the car and drove her to my house."

"Where was Dustin at this point?"

"He had to get back to work."

"Where is he employed?"

A dreamy expression covered Ms. Corker's face. "He's going to school to become a lawyer, just like those ones you see on TV. He's so smart, and I know he'll be an amazing attorney after he graduates. Sadly, he's also super busy and has a ton of coursework." She picked at a scab on her arm. "Doesn't matter, though. He said once he lands his first job, he's going to buy us a brand-new house in that fancy subdivision just past the tree farm."

It always surprised Brodie how gullible some people were. And how convincing Haack was. He was about to ask the next question when Corker continued.

"I was rather disappointed that she wasn't very grateful. And then Dustin told me he was going to be coming over for dinner. I could hardly wait. And then you showed up about that horse, but Dustin said not to open the door."

He bet that Ms. Corker did everything Haack told her to. "Do you know where Dustin is now?"

"Probably at his house."

"Do you know where that is?"

"No, I don't."

Frustration simmered through Brodie. "You were dating this guy, and you don't know where he lives?"

"Yeah, that's right. We never went to his house. We always came to mine." Corker lowered her voice. "I honestly think he's embarrassed because it's not the kind of house he wishes he had, and he wants to impress me. But I'm okay with that. I know that once he gets his important lawyer job, he'll be able to afford the house that we both deserve."

It was obvious Renee Corker did not have all of her faculties. "What is the name of the college he's attending?"

"Some online university. I don't recall the name of it right off hand."

Brodie's gaze connected with Huang's, and Huang raised his eyebrows.

"We are going to have to arrest you, ma'am." Brodie pushed back his chair and stood.

"I told you I was sorry about that horse. That's the problem with people these days. You make a tiny mistake and nobody even cares if you're sorry." Corker folded her arms around her chubby self.

Brodie listed off the charges.

"I did *not* kidnap anyone. I told you the story behind that, and it is not my fault if you can't understand. What is it with people? You try to do something nice, like take a homeless person off the street, and look what happens."

It was a moot cause to try to explain anything to Renee Corker. Brodie nodded at Huang. "If you wouldn't mind finishing up here, I would appreciate it."

"No problem at all, sheriff."

Brodie left the interview room. He paused and peeked in the window one last time, where Ms. Corker was animatedly telling Huang something, her hands flying as she spoke. If only they'd been able to catch Haack at Renee Corker's house. That would have been the icing on the cake, as the saying went. But at least, most importantly, Londyn was safe, and while it may be the optimist in him, Brodie figured they were one step closer to finding Dustin Haack.

Chapter 22

Brodie didn't particularly like having to visit people at their places of employment, but the sooner he spoke to Dorena Mohr, the better. He caught up with her just as she was leaving for the day.

"Ms. Mohr?"

"Maybe."

Brodie was always amazed at the nerve of some when they interacted with law enforcement. Where was the respect? "Ms. Mohr, I'm Sheriff Brodie Brenneman."

"I know who you are."

"I need you to come down to the Sheriff's Office and answer a few questions about visiting Dustin Haack's house in Rowland."

"I don't know what you're talking about."

"Did you speak with Detective Rivas in Rowland the other day?"

Ms. Mohr's head jerked up. "Maybe."

"I have a few follow-up questions. It won't take long. Are you available to meet at the station?"

She sighed an exaggerated breath. "I suppose."

Of all the women Dustin Haack had trapped with his manipulative ways, Dorena Mohr, in some ways, was the worst. Probably even worse than Renee Corker. Dorena's defiance, disrespect, and evasion of the questions didn't make it easy.

Ms. Mohr arrived at the station seconds after he did. She skidded into the parking lot in her expensive vehicle, tossed him a disparaging glance, then followed him up the stairs and inside. Brodie led her into the interview room, read her her Miranda rights, and set a bottled water in front of her. "Would you care for coffee?"

"Nope."

Brodie informed her he would be recording. "It is my understanding you went to Rowland to retrieve some items for Dustin Haack."

"I don't know why you're calling him Dustin Haack. That's not his name."

"Then what is his name?"

Mohr rolled her eyes. "His name is Dustin Cays."

Brodie made a note on his notepad. "What is your relationship with Haack, as I'll refer to him by for the duration of the interview?"

"We're dating."

"Did you find it strange, then, when you saw all of those pictures of another woman on his apartment wall?"

Dorena Mohr muttered a few curses beneath her breath. "Not really. Londyn was his ex-girlfriend, and she did him wrong. I wasn't worried or jealous or whatever because I know he hasn't been back to his place since he's been here on business. He'll remove her photos once he returns to Rowland."

"What kind of business?"

"He's a consultant for a large company out of New York."

Haack certainly was a slick one. "Do you know the name of the company?"

"He told me, but I don't remember. If you want to know what it is, maybe you should ask him."

"Did you ever loan him a vehicle?"

"Yes. He's borrowed my car before."

"Tell me more about his relationship with Londyn Siegler."

"After what Londyn did, I don't blame him one minute for being upset with her." Dorena Mohr folded her arms across her chest. "Are we finished?

"What did Ms. Siegler do?"

"They were engaged, and then she broke it off because she was seeing his colleague. She was also stealing money from him, and now she wants him back. Too bad, I say. Dustin is a great catch, but she doesn't deserve a second chance with him."

"Where is Haack staying?"

Mohr flipped her auburn hair over her shoulder. "The hotel, not that that's any of your business."

"Actually, Dustin Haack, aka Dustin Cays, is wanted for a slew of crimes, so that makes it my business."

"Yeah, whatever."

"What hotel?"

Dorena Mohr stared at him, her gaze unwavering. She narrowed her eyes. "Pronghorn Falls Hotel out there at the edge of town by the first exit."

"Where else has he stayed?"

"How should I know?"

"You mentioned you were dating him, so you would know where he was staying."

"That's the only place I know."

"Has he stayed with you?"

Mohr ground her teeth, and her nostrils flared. "That has absolutely nothing to do with anything."

Brodie repeated his question. "Has Dustin Haack stayed with you?"

"He has, but he's not now. There. Satisfied?"

"What is your address?

"You mean you don't have that accessible to you?" Mohr waited a handful of seconds before rattling off her address.

He considered Dorena Mohr. She was a woman in an honorable profession and seemed somewhat intelligent. What drew her to someone like Dustin Haack? Of course, as Rivas had mentioned, Mohr had recently gone through a painful and difficult divorce. Likely, Haack found her at a vulnerable moment.

"You're acting like Dustin is a criminal. He's not. The one you need to go to and talk to about this is Londyn. She has been doing her best to get him into trouble just because he wouldn't take her back. How's that for revenge?"

"How long have you known Ms. Seigler?"

"I only met her that time she was in the hospital. She's not the smartest bulb in the chandelier, driving off the road in a rainstorm. The humorous part? She thought she could win Dustin back by purposely injuring herself. That he would come crawling back because she was hurt. Not the case. He doesn't want anything to do with her, but she won't leave him alone. She's been harassing him and doing all she can to cause trouble for him. Want to arrest someone? Arrest her."

Brodie wanted to enlighten Ms. Mohr that the reason Londyn went off the road in the rainstorm was because Dustin Haack *ran* her off the road, but he knew it was fruitless to try to explain that. "When is the next time you'll see Haack?"

Mohr shrugged, her shoulders staying by her ears longer than necessary. She pressed her red-lipsticked lips together in a tight line, and for the first time, her frosty gaze darted from

Brodie to the video camera in the corner of the room. Sweat beads glistened on her upper lip.

"I don't really think it's the sheriff's department's business to know about my dating schedule."

"It is when it involves a crime. The way I see it, you can either cooperate or I can arrest you right now on suspicion of aiding and abetting."

"I have not aided, abetted, or assisted with any crimes. I'm a nurse at the hospital, and I am well-respected with ties to the community. I am in no way a criminal or hoping to be a criminal." She punctuated each word slowly and thoughtfully for emphasis. "Furthermore, as I mentioned, Dustin. Is. Not. A. Criminal. You have the wrong guy. And he should sue you for harassment."

Sadly, the world had become a sue-happy place, but Brodie doubted any judge would find in Dustin Haack's favor on this one. Interviewing Mohr had wasted his time. "I will let you know if you need to return for more questioning. In the meantime, please don't leave town."

"If I'm not being charged with something, can I go now?"

Before he could answer, she rose and shoved in the chair, causing it to smack into the table.

Chapter 23

The time for the fundraiser had come. Brodie stepped inside Mom's house, anticipating a reprieve from work and from protecting Londyn from Dustin Haack.

Londyn.

The thought of her caused his heart to gun into overdrive. He looked forward to spending time with her tonight at the adoption fundraiser at Jimmy's, even if part of him remained wary. Holding her after Haack and Corker kidnapped her reminded him again how much he loved her.

And how he had no desire to be rejected again.

Mom reclined on the couch with a book. "Londyn should be ready soon."

"Thanks." He plopped on the couch beside her. "Are Roarke and Mila on their way?"

"As we speak."

His knee jiggled as a flicker of apprehension flowed through him.

Mom honed in on it right away. "Brodie, there's something I've been meaning to talk to you about."

"Oh? Are you all right?" Mom experienced another flare-up recently, causing everyone to be more alert about her health.

"I'm fine. It's about Londyn."

Brodie scanned the stairs, sensing an oncoming lecture. "Londyn?"

"You two really need to talk."

"I know."

Mom was giving him that look. The look that said, *no, really.* The look that said she was serious, with her lips pursed and her head tilted to one side.

"It's not that easy," he muttered.

"Of course, it's not. Nothing worthwhile ever is."

They hadn't discussed what he referred to as "the situation" since she'd returned. Truth be told, they'd both been avoiding it. To be fair, she'd been too busy running from Haack, and Brodie had been too busy protecting her. "I'm not good at this talk stuff, Mom." Emotional stuff gave him hives.

"It's necessary. You've almost lost her to this crazy lunatic. You two need to clear the air, and I'm sure you're wondering about why she left."

"I am."

Mom leaned toward him. "Talk to her, Brodie."

"But what if..."

Mom shook her head in tandem with her index finger. "No what ifs. She's worth whatever inconvenience you might feel at clearing the air between you two. Pray about it first, of course, but it needs to happen soon."

Londyn walked up the stairs then, and as usual, the sight of her stole his breath. Today, she'd curled her hair and tucked it beneath a cowboy hat. She'd dressed in cowgirl attire—a fringed skirt, white boots, and a colorful western shirt. "Whoa."

Mom smirked at him before turning her attention to Londyn. "You look lovely, dear. You two have a great time, and don't worry about anything here. I see that Roarke, Mila, and Xander just pulled into the driveway."

They bid Mom goodbye, and seconds later, Brodie opened the truck door and Londyn climbed in. "You look beautiful."

"Thank you. You don't look too bad yourself." She punctuated her sentence with a smile, and Brodie attempted to return his focus on getting them to the fundraiser.

"Are you planning on entering the pizza-eating contest?"

"Probably not. There's no doubt in my mind I could potentially win, but there is something more desirable about enjoying the supreme with extra cheese instead of devouring it. Chief says he's going to enter for sure, but probably won't be line dancing afterwards."

Londyn laughed, reminding Brodie how much he had missed her. When they arrived at Jimmy's, they parked in one of the last available spots. "And here I thought arriving a half hour early would be a good idea," said Brodie.

"I think it would be if the entire town wasn't here. But this turnout is impressive. It will raise a lot of money for the adoptive families."

That was Brodie's prayer. If they could help even a couple of families give a child a forever home, it would be worth it. That and the fact that the place was crawling with law enforcement, so Dustin Haack wouldn't be an issue tonight. Roarke, Mila, and Xander were at Mom's house, along with a deputy, just in case Haack made an appearance there.

Several people played pool while others ate dinner, and still others bid on the silent auction items. The Pronghorns, a well-known popular band that played an assortment of Christian music as well as secular rock and country music from the 60s, 70s, and 80s, drew an exuberant crowd, some of whom had perched in front of the stage and were clapping. Would

Londyn be willing to dance with him during the line dancing portion of the evening? Brodie glanced her way. It wouldn't be too difficult to forget the past months and believe everything was as it had been before he proposed. Would he ever gather the courage to address the proverbial elephant in the room—to ask why she'd rejected his proposal?

During a break from the music, Jimmy stood at the front of the stage. "Welcome to our very special fundraiser. Here to give us more information are Sheriff Brenneman and Chief Neeley."

Londyn admired Brodie. Not only did he take his role as sheriff seriously, but he also took every advantage to participate in important community events. His dad would be proud.

Brodie looked exceptionally handsome tonight in his snug t-shirt, jeans, and cowboy boots. He dwarfed Chief Neeley, who, while broad-shouldered and with a little girth around the middle, was much shorter than Brodie.

"Thank you all for coming. Our goal this year is $20,000, and we are hoping to assist families seeking to adopt locally, nationally, or internationally. As I'm sure is the case with all of us here, adoption is close to my heart. Please don't be shy when bidding on the numerous items in our silent auction." He listed off the items, including an Alaskan cruise, rifle, gift certificates, and a brand-new cowboy hat. "Thank you to Jimmy, who is donating 100% of the cover charge, and for being willing to loan us the space in his fantastic alcohol-free business." The crowd again clapped, and Jimmy bowed.

Chief Neeley said a few words before the band began to play. Londyn and Brodie joined several others at a booth for pizza and pop. It was just like in the olden days when they would meet with friends on a Friday or Saturday night.

After the pizza-eating contest, which Chief Neeley won, the band played some classic 80s rock, along with upbeat Christian tunes, before hitting the first notes of modern country music.

As if no time had passed between the last time they were there and now, Londyn and Brodie slipped right into dancing with the Overtons, Huangs, and several others. Those on the sidelines clapped in time with the music as the singer crooned. The two-step came next, followed by country swing, country waltz, and the cowboy cha cha. Brodie held her hand and swung her, her skirt swishing as she moved in time to the music.

Other couples intermittently left the dance floor until only Londyn and Brodie were left. The crowd that had lined up on the sidelines began to clap and chant their names. The sounds grew louder, and Londyn glanced up at the TV screen and nudged Brodie. Their names flashed across the screen in perfect time to the music, as he watched for any sign that she needed to take it slow due to still recovering.

Brodie's eyes twinkled, and a smirk shone on his handsome face. "Should we take them up on this?"

They had won a dancing contest a few years before, and while this wasn't a contest, it would be just like old times.

"I thought you'd never ask," she teased.

The band performed a song that was perfect with a two-step mixed with a little country swing combination.

They moved in perfect time with the music. Brodie spun her around and dipped her. Londyn came back up, her face so close to his. She inhaled the scent of his aftershave, a pleasing smell she'd memorized. Their gazes connected, and for a moment, time stood still.

Her heart pinched. What she wouldn't give for another chance with him.

Brodie parked outside Mom's house. The lights were on inside, and he was glad Roarke and Mila were still there and that a deputy was keeping an eye on things. Brodie killed the engine, and he and Londyn sat in silence for several seconds.

Finally, Londyn spoke. "Thank you for the great time tonight."

Brodie rested his arm on the steering wheel and faced her. The porch light, combined with the bright moon, cast a glow on her beautiful face. Was it possible to love someone the way he loved her? To continually wish for and hope for a future, even when it wasn't possible? There was so much they needed to discuss. So much left unsaid. "It was fun. Remember when we won the dance competition a few years ago?" They shared such a vast amount of memories.

"I do. We won a gift card to Jody's Restaurant and movie theater tickets. I'm grateful we didn't have to worry about Dustin tonight." Her face clouded. "I hope we catch him soon."

"We *will* catch him. It hasn't been for lack of trying, but the guy has slipped through our fingers numerous times."

"I wish I hadn't been so foolish to believe he was upstanding."

Brodie tapped his thumb on the steering wheel. "Unfortunately, Haack is cunning and experienced at charming people."

"Charming is right. Everyone where I worked, including my boss and coworkers, believed him to be something he wasn't. He, Jasmine, and I hit it off right away. I think it helped because our cubicles were right next to each other. Unfortunately, through all this, Jasmine took Dustin's side." Londyn blinked rapidly, and the pain in her voice told of her former friend's rejection.

Brodie recalled that Detective Rivas had interviewed Jasmine and hadn't been impressed, but there was nothing criminal to pin on her. He thought of all of those who had rejected Londyn in her life. Her mom, in a way, when she put her desire to marry and divorce in rapid succession above her children. Her dad, who left when Londyn was little and never looked back. Her brother, who had estranged himself from his family. And now Jasmine. No wonder she was standoffish and afraid when it came to permanent relationships. "I'm sorry about Jasmine."

"Thank you. I should have wised up sooner when I realized she'd told Dustin other things I'd told her in confidence."

"As far as Dustin goes, while I'm no psychiatrist, I do suspect some narcissistic and sociopathic tendencies."

An owl hooted, a coyote howled, and the porch light flickered before continuing its shiny glow. He and Londyn had always been able to enjoy each other's company, even when no words were spoken. Tonight was no exception. As a matter of fact, dancing with her at Jimmy's brought back a slew of memories of how close they'd been. Of how he'd eagerly wanted to take the next step in their relationship.

And how she'd wanted just the opposite.

With effort, Brodie shoved the thoughts aside. If friendship was all Londyn desired, he'd do his best to acquiesce.

"Do you remember when your dad would take us to the range?" asked Londyn, interrupting Brodie's thoughts. "He was so patient, teaching us everything that we would need to know about gun safety. He would set up those empty water bottles and pop cans, and then later that snazzy target we got him for his birthday."

"I remember like it was yesterday." Brodie missed his dad every day. What he wouldn't give to be able to bounce questions off of him, seek his advice on not only matters of law enforcement, but his godly wisdom regarding the challenges of life. God had taken Dad home far too soon. "The only consolation—and it's a big consolation—is that we'll see him again someday."

"I'm sorry I brought him up, but he was just such a remarkable man and a dad not only to his own kids, but to kids like me who needed a father.

"And he loved you like a daughter."

Brodie detected movement inside the house. A little hand pushed aside the curtain, and a round face pressed against the window.

Brodie was surprised Xander was still up. They should probably get inside so Roarke and Mila could get home. But Brodie found it a struggle to leave Londyn's company.

She rested her head against the seat. "Brodie, I know I hurt you badly when I left. I know I hurt Aileen, too. I have so many regrets."

In the dim light, he thought he saw a tear trail down her cheek. "I don't understand why you left. All you had to do was say you weren't interested in marrying me, and we could have gone our separate ways or even continued to date. But you just said no, and then you took off and moved to an entirely different town." So much inside of him needed to know her reasoning for leaving. He had questions he'd wanted to ask since that day, and now, as the words wanted to surge to the forefront, Brodie knew he should pray first before uttering even one of them. But the thoughts on his mind formed the words that spilled from his mouth before he could seek the Lord's wisdom. "I guess I just don't understand. I love you, and you didn't feel the same, which is obvious. All you had to do was say so."

"And break your heart even more?" Londyn's abrupt words caught him off guard, but they were true. If she did love him and did care about him the way he loved and cared about her, she wouldn't have moved to Rowland. "I apologize, too, for not staying in touch as well as I should have. I started well with Aileen, and I could have done better with you."

"I am glad you periodically texted Mom."

"I love her, and she is more like a mom than my mom ever was."

Mom had mentioned that she and Londyn had sat down one evening since Londyn's return and talked at length. Mom possessed a forgiving heart, so it was no surprise that she and Londyn resolved the issues between them, and Mom had forgiven Londyn's brash actions. As for Brodie, it wasn't so much that he struggled with forgiveness—even though he did—but far more that he struggled with the pain of the realization that he cared for someone who could never return those same feelings.

The garbled thoughts rammed through his mind. He didn't know what to say to Londyn or where their future would lead. Would he be content with always just being friends, or were they *even* still friends? After tonight, the way he held her with his arms around her when they danced and the way she'd smiled as he'd spun her around, how they'd shared pizza and talked as though there was nothing between them, he knew without a doubt he still loved her. Probably now, even more than ever. But he would let her go. With God's help, he would let her go.

"I hope that you can forgive me, Brodie." Londyn's voice wavered. Brodie focused his attention out the front window and across the driveway.

"I do forgive you."

Search my heart, Lord. I do forgive her, right?

"Thank you." Her words came in gasps, and he longed to pull her into his arms and comfort her. Tell her all would be all right. But he couldn't, *wouldn't* risk that type of rejection again.

"Can we reestablish our friendship?" she asked.

"Sure." His voice sounded flat in his own ears. But wisdom dictated that with Dustin Haack on the loose, and how he had come so close to losing Londyn, he shouldn't waste even a second of time holding a grudge. He cleared his throat. "Did you like living in this city?"

"It was all right, but I'm a small-town girl. I missed Pronghorn Falls, especially during rush hour traffic." She offered a wistful smile. "Here, people know each other, and they talk and smile and they have each other's backs. Rowland's a huge city. Yes, I made friends there, and I liked my job, but it's not the same atmosphere as Pronghorn Falls."

"Do you plan to stay here then?"

"I've been praying about it, but I hope so. I feel like this is my home. I reapplied for my former job and hope to hear back from them soon. Once we catch Dustin, I'll find an apartment."

"You know Mom will allow you to stay at the ranch for as long as you need."

"I know, but I never want to take advantage of her generosity."

"Did you know I was going to ask you that night?" Brodie had been told he was predictable. Had Londyn suspected when he showed up that night and suggested that they go to the park that he was going to ask her something as monumental as marrying him?

"I thought you were acting strangely. But I honestly didn't think anything about it, and a marriage proposal wasn't on my radar." She clasped her hands together. "I had a lot on my mind that night because of what happened with Mom and Lance."

Brodie hadn't known anything had happened between her mom and her mom's most recent boyfriend on that night. Although he did know that Londyn's mom was now remarried to someone other than Lance.

"Mom decided earlier that day that she no longer wanted to be married to Lance, so she left him for a guy she met at work. Of course, she called me all excited about it." Londyn sniffled, and Brodie rummaged around in the glove box for a pack of tissues and handed her one.

She dabbed at her nose. "I immediately called Lance and expressed my condolences. He told me that because he and my mom were no longer married, I was no longer welcome in his life either."

Brodie hadn't known these details. He'd met Lance a few times and knew he worked at a local construction company, but that was the extent of his dealings with Londyn's former stepdad. Brodie suspected Londyn's mom wouldn't stay with Lance—the man Londyn was closest to out of all of her mom's husbands—but he'd had no idea her mom had broken up with him the same day Brodie proposed. "I'm sorry about Lance. I know he filled the role of father more so than the others."

"He did. At first, I thought maybe because he was hurting so badly, he took out that pain on me. I know we're all guilty of doing similar things." She glanced at Brodie before returning her attention to her folded hands. "I seem to have a knack for not keeping the important men in my life.

"I'm still in your life, Londyn."

"I know," she whispered. "And I'm grateful for that."

"Londyn…" The pain pinched his chest. But he had to know. "Why did you leave?"

Londyn wiped a tear away with the back of her hand. "Ironically, I hurt you more than I ever could have imagined that night. I will always regret that for as long as I live." She blinked rapidly even as the tears welled in her eyes. "But honestly, I was so afraid of being just like my mom.

"Your mom? You're nothing like your mom." He nearly spat the words.

"What if I had married you and couldn't maintain our relationship and broke your heart?" A cry escaped. "I couldn't have lived with myself if I had hurt you in that way, yet I did hurt you." Her shoulders shook. Should he wrap his arms around her? Comfort her? The mass of conflicting emotions inside him was relentless. Anger, frustration, hope, and love for her all tied into one. So he remained on his side of the truck, feeling cold and numb while she cried.

I just—" she extracted a wad of tissues from the pack and dabbed her eyes. "I'm sorry, I'm just a mess."

"We had a great night tonight at Jimmy's. We can talk about this later, as I don't want anything to ruin that."

"We did have a great time. It was almost as if…"

He waited for her to continue.

"If I were in your life permanently and turned out like my mom and—"

"First of all, you're nothing like your mom. At all. Secondly, I know that every man who was ever supposed to love you has walked out of your life. Your dad, Logan, Lance, and your grandpa when he died. But I'm not like that. I'm loyal and steadfast, or at least I'd like to think I am."

Makeup smeared across her cheeks, and a stray hair stuck to her face. "You are loyal and steadfast. You're an amazing man, Brodie Brenneman. That's why I thought you deserved so much better than the daughter of a woman who can't stay married and is a lousy mom as well."

"I think I'm old enough to be able to determine who I would like to spend the rest of my life with."

"I wasn't saying that. I know you're wise and—I'm sure you prayed before proposing. Despite my ridiculous actions, I care about you greatly, Brodie."

"As a friend."

"Yes, as a friend."

A slam of anger pitted itself in Brodie's stomach. This conversation wasn't going anywhere. At least they were still friends. Was he hoping she'd change her mind after their time at Jimmy's? After the harrowing experiences she'd faced? After he reassured her, he was there for her? Cared for her? "I wanted more than friendship, Londyn, and I can't force you to love me."

She straightened in the seat and pointed at him. "Well, for one, you know how strong-willed I am, so I don't think anyone can force me to love them or to do anything. And two, I pretty much do love you."

"Like a brother? Like you love Roarke, Grayson, and Danny when he was alive?"

"No, not like that."

She sobbed, and without another second of hesitation, he stretched his arms around the console and pulled her close. She rested her head on his shoulder. "I'm just so sorry, Brodie. If I could take back that day, I would."

Her words now were so muffled in his mind because he was thinking about how she said her love for him was not like the brotherly love that she felt for Roarke, Grayson, and Danny. But he'd probably heard her wrong. Heard what he *wanted* to hear. Or maybe he had heard her correctly. Maybe there was hope. He reached over and swiped a tear from her face.

Londyn had never been one to share her innermost thoughts. It had served her better to keep her feelings inside, but in this moment of transparency with Brodie, the words had fallen from her mouth before she could stop them. How she wished multiple times over that she had not left Pronghorn Falls that day the way she had. If only she had handled things differently.

Sure, if she'd stayed, she would never have met Dustin and had to worry about nearly losing her life at his hands, but it was so much more than that. If she'd made a better choice, she wouldn't have hurt the only man she had ever loved—whom she would only *ever* love.

Londyn denied her feelings for him for far too long, worried that she would hurt him the way Mom had hurt so many of her husbands, including Lance. She allowed pride to cloud her vision and stupidity to replace wisdom. And now she might never—and rightfully so—have the chance with Brodie that her heart deeply sought and yearned for.

She rested in his arms, inhaling the familiar scent of him. She knew every contour of his handsome face. The mole on his neck and the tiny scar behind his ear. The way the corners of his eyes crinkled when he laughed. She knew his favorite food, his favorite pastimes, and the things that bothered him most in his job. She knew all about his future dreams and goals and how deeply the love for his family ran through him. He knew just as much about her. He knew all about her past, what she wrestled with when it came to her mom, and the rejection she'd so often felt. Had a slice of that fear of rejection wormed its way into her heart when it came to Brodie?

No. He was not like the men who had left Mom, including Dad, who'd been unfaithful. He wasn't like Logan. Brodie wasn't like Lance, who, because Londyn was her mom's daughter, now wanted nothing to do with her. Lance reminded her of that during her subsequent calls.

Brodie was a good, kind, honest, and gracious man who cared for others and sought to do what was right. Who did his best to follow the Lord and commit his ways to Jesus. The tears burned her eyes and blurred her vision. She appreciated his forgiveness. Appreciated that he still wanted to spend time with her. Appreciated perhaps most of all the way he put his life on the line to protect her from a narcissistic sociopath.

A glimpse at the window indicated Xander again waving at them. Mila gently took him aside and closed the curtain. This entire family was at risk because of Londyn. This entire family had put their lives on hold because of a madman. If something happened to them because of Dustin, it would be Londyn's fault. She would never forgive herself.

She loved Brodie so much more than just as friends. She loved Aileen like a mom, loved Roarke and Grayson as brothers. Was so grateful for the new friendship she'd found with Mila, and how Xander had readily adopted Londyn as his aunt.

Londyn wanted to be around to share a life with the Brennemans. How could she have resisted their kindness and their love in pursuit of her own selfishness and fear? She'd spent a few hours with Aileen discussing her error in leaving. Had rested in the comfort of the woman who was her surrogate mom. The one who'd forgiven her and encouraged her to discuss this with Brodie, no matter how difficult it would be.

The one who prayed with and for her.

A full range of emotions settled in her heart. "Brodie, I do care about you, and I do love you, and not just like a brother."

With her head resting on his chest, she could hear the rapid beat of his heart, but he said no words. Instead, he was silent just as she predicted he would be. Did he believe her? Believe her sincerity?

"I take full responsibility for what happened." She'd spent more time in prayer these last few months than she ever had throughout all of the trials—some of her own doing—and some at the hands of others.

All that had happened in the past and all that now happened, especially with Dustin's stalking, cemented hers and Brodie's relationship. She relied on him more now than ever. But that wasn't why she loved him. It was so much more than that.

"Londyn..."

"I know, I've just been rambling, but I do have feelings for you."

"I don't want you to feel like I'm pressuring you."

"I don't." She stared into his eyes. "I don't feel like you're pressuring me."

"Well, in that case. This changes a lot of things."

She put a hand on his chest. "Am I too late?" Londyn bit her lip and prayed she hadn't blown it completely. That God's will would be done in this situation.

Twin creases marred his forehead. "You're not too late, Londyn. You could never be too late."

Hesitant relief and joy billowed within her. "I'm not too late?"

"No. You're not too late."

The lights flickered on and off, and Brodie jerked away,

ever ready to react to any danger. But when he pointed at the window, Londyn laughed.

Xander stood in the window, giggling. Londyn could almost hear his little boy laughter.

"I somehow don't think it's anything nefarious or even an electrical or a burned-out lightbulb issue," said Brodie.

"I agree. I think we have our culprit for the flickering lights."

Brodie deepened his voice. "Young boy, approximately four feet tall, fifty pounds, in footy pajamas decorated with bugs. He was seen with two accomplices, a live dog named Yukon, and a stuffed one named Spider."

"Spoken like a true member of law enforcement."

They both laughed, a welcome reprieve from the heavy emotions of the past half hour.

"I suppose we should probably go inside," said Brodie. "I'm sure Roarke and Mila would probably like to get Xander home for bed."

"Thank you for forgiving me and for the second chance."

"We needed to have this conversation."

"We did."

"Xander cracks me up. He's going to be one tired boy tomorrow with this lack of sleep. You ready to go inside?"

She wasn't, but she knew that was the best course of action, especially where rambunctious little boys were involved. Xander bounced around in the window. Londyn already loved Xander and wanted to be a part of both his and the new baby's lives.

This family *was* her family.

Chapter 24

Brodie returned from serving papers and sat down to check his messages when there was a knock at the door.

"Sheriff?" Juanita Andrade, the new dispatcher, stood in the doorway.

He motioned her in. "Hello, Juanita, what can I do for you?"

Her shoulders drooped as if she carried the weight of the world on them. In a voice barely above a whisper, she asked, "Can I speak to you?"

"Sure."

Juanita thumbed in the direction of the door. "Can I close that?"

Brodie nodded, and Juanita shut the door before taking a seat in the chair across from him. Deputy Dwyer peered through the window, his brow furrowed. Brodie gave him the thumbs up and returned his attention to Juanita. "Is there something wrong?" Clearly, she was not her usual bubbly self.

Her chin quivered. "Oh, yes, Sheriff, very wrong."

Brodie's mind could go to a million places, and he hoped he would be able to help his new employee with whatever ailed her. Brodie pushed the box of tissues in her direction. Her cheeks were dotted in red splotches, and her black hair hung limp to her shoulders, so uncharacteristic of the usually put-together dispatcher. He didn't have the schedule memorized, but he hoped Juanita had some time before she had to report to duty. Brodie waited for a few seconds for her to gather herself.

"Everything is so wrong. Have you ever been disappointed in someone and in yourself?" Her voice cracked, and she averted her gaze to something on the wall behind Brodie.

"I have." Brodie could be hard on himself when he made a mistake. He'd never liked failure. He thought of Londyn. She'd disappointed him, but he'd also disappointed himself when he hadn't done everything he could to stay in touch with her. To maybe have convinced her to return to Pronghorn Falls *before* Dustin Haack decided to put her life in jeopardy.

With effort, Brodie returned his attention to Juanita. "Do you want to tell me what's wrong? Maybe I can help." He was next to clueless when it came to women's emotions. Having grown up with three brothers, tears were not an everyday occurrence. On the rare occasion Mom had been upset, everyone took notice.

"I had no idea about...no idea he was how he is. And then I just—I really—I thought he was the one." Juanita wrapped her arms around herself. "All of my sisters are married, and here I am." She plucked another tissue and slumped in her chair.

Brodie wasn't sure he was the best person with whom she should discuss her relationship woes. "Maybe you could talk to Deputy Overton about this." He wasn't trying to pass her off, but this was awkward.

Juanita shook her head. "No, I have to talk to you about it."

"All right." Brodie assumed that the guy she had spoken about nonstop and was so enamored with had broken up with her. He searched for the words to say and asked God for wisdom. He lowered his head and attempted to catch Juanita's eye, but she kept her focus on her hands. Hands now folded so tightly her knuckles turned white. "Juanita…"

She finally looked up at him as a tear slid down her cheek.

"You'll find the man God has planned for you, but don't waste your time on ones who don't appreciate you."

"I know. I do know that. And thank you, but there's more." Brodie's phone rang, and he flicked a glance at the receiver before choosing to allow it to go to voicemail.

Juanita hiccupped. "Do you need to answer that? Because I don't want to take you away from important things."

"It's fine. It can go to voicemail." Brodie felt ill-equipped to deal with this issue. "Juanita, you know that I care about my employees and that I have an open-door policy. I am here to help if I can."

"Thank you." Juanita craned her neck toward the door. Her gaze then darted from Brodie to the desk, then back to Brodie again. "As you know, I met him at the bar, and we went out five times in two weeks. We seemed to hit it off. Now, looking back, he probably just said all the right things."

"What is his name?" Call it the investigator in him, but Brodie felt he'd be better able to assist Juanita if he knew the heartbreaker's name. Had he ever met the guy? Did he have a prior record?

"Linder. But I don't think that's his real name."

The latter part of Juanita's statement took Brodie aback. He knew guys lied in the dating world sometimes, but if Juanita suspected he was lying, why had she…

"Anyway, we were hanging out a lot, and he told me he was thinking about a future together. So here I am, thinking all about marriage and family and children." Juanita blew her nose, and her next words choked out between mournful whimpering. "I'd already told my family I'd met the one, but then I saw him with someone else."

Brodie shifted in his chair. "I am sorry to hear that. Are you sure you don't want to discuss this with another woman?"

"No, Sheriff, I have to speak with you." Juanita wrung her hands. "I confronted him when I saw him with the other woman, who is a nurse at the hospital. I had the unfortunate instance of meeting her when I had to go there to visit a friend of mine who'd recently had an operation. Linder apologized and told me she meant nothing to him. He went out of his way to reconcile with me and bought me this beautiful backpack purse I had my eye on at a store downtown."

"Well, maybe nothing is going on with the nurse."

"That could be the case, but Dorena later told me they were exclusive and had been dating for some time."

"Did you say Dorena?" Brodie's spidey antennae went into overdrive.

"Yes, she's the nurse."

Brodie was about to inquire further when Juanita continued, her words tumbling from her mouth in a rush. "It's not so much that he apologized. I could probably forgive him and move on if that were the case. But it's what I discovered and what I've done that are the issue."

"What did you discover?"

"I discovered that I—"Juanita bit her lip. "I discovered that I was dating a man who also had another name and is the one you have been searching for."

Pronghorn Falls law enforcement was currently only searching for one individual. "Do you mean Dustin Haack?"

"Yes. But at first, I talked myself out of it because he told me his name was Linder. But when I saw that flyer we distri buted..."

Brodie spun in his chair and reached for a paper from the other side of his desk. "This flyer?"

Juanita nodded. "Yes. Things started fitting together. His name might be Linder, but it's also Dustin Haack. It began to make sense why he kept asking me to do things for him. Things I did at first. Information I shared," She palmed her face with both hands, and her breathing shuddered.

Brodie attempted to wait patiently, but the questions filled his mind in rapid-fire fashion.

Juanita removed her hands from her face. "He told me the reason he was asking all these questions was because his dad was a cop, and he'd always been interested in law enforcement. I'm such an idiot for falling for this." She started to sob again.

Pieces of the Haack puzzle were slowly beginning to fit together. "Dustin Haack, who told you his name is Linder, asked you for information that you, as a dispatcher, were privy to and not allowed to share?" Brodie's toes curled in his cowboy boots. It was obvious Juanita had been duped, and he was grateful she'd come forward, but if Brodie had known earlier, he might have caught Haack by now.

Juanita sniffled. "Yes. All kinds of information, especially about when law enforcement answered certain calls, and other things, too. And I didn't realize he and Dustin Haack were one and the same, and then when I did realize, I didn't want to believe it. Not when he told me he cared about me, and I'd fallen in love with him." She picked at her purple-painted nail. "I'm in a lot of trouble, aren't I?"

A mixture of anger, irritation, and pity for Juanita rose within Brodie. Juanita had been feeding Haack an impressive amount of information, making it more of a challenge to apprehend him. Putting Londyn in further danger. Brodie ran a hand through his hair. "I'm going to record this, and I will also need a signed statement from you."

"Okay," Juanita muttered. "Whatever you need, I will cooperate."

Brodie Mirandized Juanita before pressing record and videotaping her as she repeated everything they'd discussed so far. After she had done so, he continued with further questioning.

"He was buying me all kinds of presents and treating me like a princess, and I thought he was so charming and handsome, and I told him about when the police were going to be arriving in certain situations."

"Did it not occur to you that he was committing crimes?"

"Not at first. Then I went through this thought process that you guys had the wrong guy. No way could it be Linder. He could never hurt anyone, and you have no idea how convincing he is. Then I asked him about it."

Brodie scribbled down the notes. "When you asked him about it, what did he say?"

"He told me about an ex-girlfriend named Londyn, who was out to get him and would do anything to destroy his name. He said she'd done it before in another town and that she had followed him to Pronghorn Falls. He was so persuasive. He even got tears in his eyes. I've never seen a guy with tears in his eyes unless someone died."

"Go on."

"He told me some things that Londyn had done to him, and it didn't sound far-fetched to me at all. But now I can't believe I fell for it." Juanita began to sob uncontrollably then.

It made sense that this was the way Dustin was continuing to elude police—since Juanita fed him information and warned him of law enforcement's location and ETA after he'd committed a crime. Brodie had to hand it to Haack. It was well planned, and Brodie hazarded a guess that his crimes were committed only when Juanita was working her shift. While Brodie couldn't believe someone could be as naïve as Juanita had been, he also knew Haack had fooled Londyn as well, and she was anything but foolish and naïve. "What kind of information did you give him?"

She lifted her head and swiped the tears with her hand. "I told him whenever I received a call about a crime in progress. Any crime. Do you remember that time when you had to follow him up into the mountains and he was in a sports car?"

"Yes."

"I told him when you pursued the perpetrator and where law enforcement was. And other times too, like the time after there was that issue at the animal hoarder lady's house." Perspiration shone on her brow. "And other information."

"Can you elaborate?" Brodie waited for Juanita to offer clarification.

She wouldn't meet his eye, and instead stared again at that space on the wall behind him.

"He asked me a lot of questions about your family's ranch, and I think he already knew some things, like where the ranch was, but he also asked about your brother's house. I found some information in the database and gave it to him."

Brodie closed his eyes and prayed that God would help him contain his frustration. He already knew how Haack found Mom's house due to the tracker on Londyn's SUV. No wonder Haack knew where to go the day he showed up at Roarke and Mila's. No wonder he knew where to send Ms. Corker when they kidnapped Londyn.

"He asked me things like your brother's name and your brother's wife's name and if there were any children, and he disguised it in a pleasant conversational tone when we were talking. It wasn't like he was interrogating me about these questions. He sounded genuinely interested."

"Why did he say he needed to know this information?"

"He's the CEO of this huge development corporation that is interested in offering your family a high dollar amount for the ranch because they have been wanting to find some property to develop into a dude ranch. He said he hoped your family would take his company's offer, seeing as how you had a family member who was dying of cancer, and you needed the money."

"A family member dying of cancer?"

Juanita bobbed her head. "Yes. That's what he said. I felt sorry for you, and I knew your dad had been killed a few years back, so I wanted to be helpful." She tugged at the sleeve of her shirt. "You don't really have someone in your family dying of cancer, do you?"

"Thank the Lord, we do not."

"I've been so stupid. I know I shouldn't have given out any information, and I look like a dummy, but honestly, he was so convincing. You have to understand how he is."

"What made you decide to stop helping him?"

"After I saw him with the nurse, I reevaluated. I stayed up all night thinking he's not who he said he was if he has someone else on the side, so what else is he lying to me about?" Juanita wrung her hands. "I saw the flyer with Linder on it before, and I was thinking about it, and I thought maybe I should tell you about him. I know I am so fired."

Brodie didn't elaborate that being fired was probably the least of her worries. Misuse of computer information came to mind, as well as other charges. "I do appreciate you coming in and talking to me."

Juanita nodded slowly. "I couldn't live with myself if something happened, and I could have prevented it. I know I'm gullible, but I didn't do this on purpose. Please believe me."

Brodie withdrew a bottled water from the case to the left of his desk and offered it to her. He did believe Juanita, but needed to do his best to appear unbiased. "Did Linder, aka Haack, ever tell you where he was staying?"

"No. His work is headquartered in Indianapolis. Because that's so far from here, he was staying in a hotel for a couple of weeks while he was looking at ranches to purchase."

Haack certainly excelled at lying, manipulating, and fabricating false identities.

"Whenever we would go out, we would always meet at my place or at the restaurant, never at the hotel, so I'm not even sure if that's true."

"Is there anything else you need to tell me?"

Juanita shook her head. "I don't think so, other than I really am sorry."

"You did the right thing coming to me." After a few more minutes of talking with Juania, Brodie stopped recording and encouraged her to write down and sign her confession.

So much more made sense now.

Chapter 25

Londyn was putting dishes away and turned, just as Xander ran up to her, Spider in his arms and Yukon at his side. Yukon rose up on his hind legs and pressed his paws on Londyn's leg, begging for a pat.

"Guess what, Aunt Londyn?"

She loved it that Xander considered her his aunt. She ruffled his hair. "What's that?"

"Do you think we could go outside and search for some bugs to look at under the new microscope Mommy and Daddy bought me?"

"I think that sounds like a fantastic idea, and after that, why don't we make a batch of chocolate chip cookies?" Londyn patted Yukon on the head, and he offered a multitude of doggy kisses on her hand.

"Yum." Xander rubbed his stomach. "I could prob'ly have cookies for breakfast, lunch, and dinner if Mommy let me."

Londyn highly doubted chocolate chip cookies would become Xander's only meal, and she laughed.

Roarke came to the doorway. "It looks as though I've left Xander in good hands. Deputy Huang is out front keeping an eye on things, and I'll be back at the house doing some yard work."

"How is Mila feeling?" Londyn asked.

"Puny. I think she's ready for this little girl to make her appearance, although it'll be a while yet." Roarke's face lit up, and Londyn knew he was excited to be a dad again.

"Well, don't worry about us here. We'll be eating cookies and finding bugs." Xander jumped up and down. "Dad, this is why I told you I wanted to come and visit. Aunt Londyn is my favorite aunt."

Xander's words warmed her heart, and the boy hugged his dad while Yukon wagged his tail and ran around in circles.

"Want me to show you the tricks I've been teaching Yukon?" Xander withdrew a snack from his pocket. The dog's toenails tapped on the wood floor as he pranced around in excitement, anticipating the treats that were to come.

He held a treat above Yukon's head. "Sit, boy." Yukon sat on his haunches, and Xander tossed him a treat. "Now beg." The dog obeyed and was rewarded.

"Dance, Yukon, dance."

This time, Yukon stood on his back legs and teetered around in a circle.

"That one will get you two treats."

"Wow, it looks like you've been busy."

Xander bobbed his head. "Yes, I have, ma'am. And he's good about obeying."

Londyn laughed at the little gentleman before her. "You are doing a great job."

"Did you know that pretty soon I'm going to have a baby sister?"

"I did know that. Are you excited?" Last time, Xander had been disappointed the baby wasn't going to be a boy.

"Yeah, kind of. Although girls are weird. But I am going to

help Mommy take good care of her."

"I remember when you were born." It seemed like yesterday that Danny's wife, Drea, brought Xander home from the hospital.

"You do? What was I like?"

"You were tiny and so precious."

Xander scrunched his nose. "Precious?"

A few minutes later, they embarked on a bug hunt in the front yard where Deputy Huang was stationed.

"Look! I found my favorite bug—a pill bug. Uncle Brodie calls them roly-polies." He allowed the crustacean to inch its way across his palm. "I'm going to see what he looks like under the microscope."

The bug sat still for less than a second before wandering to the edge of the slide and onto the picnic table.

"I think we should probably stick to finding dead bugs," suggested Londyn.

"Yeah, you're probably right. How did you become so smart about bugs?"

"I've studied them some."

Xander eyed her suspiciously. "I'm really surprised because you're a girl."

"Some girls like bugs, and since I grew up with your daddy, Uncle Brodie, and Uncle Grayson, I was around bugs quite a bit." She wouldn't mention how she'd been terrorized with a grasshopper a time or two and how she wasn't fond of worms.

"I miss Uncle Grayson. I haven't seen him in a lot of years." Xander's brow furrowed. "I was just a little boy last time he was here."

"I know, I miss him too." Londyn knew it had been difficult for the Brenneman family after Mr. Brenneman had died and Grayson had subsequently left for a job out of state. While the rest of the family leaned on each other, Grayson retreated. In Londyn's opinion, he hadn't handled it correctly. Not that she was one to talk.

"When I have a baby sister, I'm gonna teach her all about bugs." Xander positioned the dead bug on the slide. "God did a really good job on this one." He moved to the side, and Londyn peered through the microscope as well. It was amazing, all the detail on one tiny insect.

The sound of crunching gravel averted Londyn's attention to the driveway. For a split second, fear funneled through her until she noticed it was Brodie's truck, and her pulse quickened. Would Brodie believe her promise that she loved him, not as a brother, but as something more?

"Oh, look, it's Uncle Brodie!" Xander jumped from the picnic table. "Uncle Brodie, we've been 'specting things underneath the microscope. Wanna come see?"

Brodie lifted Xander and swung him around before depositing him on his shoulders. "I sure would like to come see, and guess what I brought?"

"What?

"How about some burgers from Jody's Restaurant?"

"Oh, yes, I like burgers, 'specially from that place." Xander held on with one hand and rubbed his tummy with the other. Brodie carefully opened the passenger side of his truck and claimed two white food bags. He greeted Londyn with a handsome grin as he walked toward her.

"I hear you and Xander are spending some time together today."

"We are."

"Sounds like the perfect day." His gaze connected with hers, and her heart did a little flip-flop. Then, in an unexpected—but not unwelcome move, he leaned over and brushed her lips with a kiss.

"That kind of stuff is gross," Xander announced.

Londyn and Brodie laughed, and Brodie whispered to Londyn, "Wait until he gets older."

She gestured for both of them to join her at the picnic table, where she pushed aside the microscope. "Let's wash our hands before we eat."

Brodie lifted Xander off his shoulders. "I already washed my hands, Aunt Londyn."

"When was this?" asked Brodie.

"Yesterday," he said, completely serious.

Londyn attempted to hide her amusement and planted her hands on her hips. "I think you need to wash them again."

Minutes later, Brodie led the prayer before they ate the hamburgers and fries. Deputy Huang joined them, and the deputy recounted tales of the days when he would get paid a nickel for every grasshopper he caught.

Xander took an oversized bite of his hamburger. "I'm going to ask Daddy if I can do that."

"What would you buy with all those nickels?" asked Londyn.

Xander finished chewing and tilted back his head to contemplate her question. "I would buy some doggy treats for Yukon, and then I would buy one of those butterfly farms I saw in the store."

"Sounds like a worthwhile purchase," said Brodie, "but why does that not surprise me?" He reached out, eyes searching hers as he tentatively took her hand in his. An electric current zipped through her, and she offered a breathless smile. He inclined toward her and captured her lips in a quick kiss.

"Eww," whined Xander.

But Londyn wasn't paying attention to Xander's response.

She was relishing the warmth of Brodie's kiss.

The day didn't get any better than this.

Brodie admired the way Londyn had taken Xander under her wing, not that the kid wasn't easy to love, because he was. Although Brodie was more than biased. He recalled the days when he and his brothers teased Londyn by chasing her with grasshoppers and how she enjoyed fishing, but not putting the worms on the hook. For as much as she loved being outside, there were some things she wasn't fond of, like worms. And she loved plenty of girly things like her special porcelain dolls, flowers, and the color lavender.

The benefits of knowing someone for years.

Brodie was thankful he'd been able to spend his lunch with her since the day was slower. The kiss was an added bonus. And now, as he sat there watching Londyn and Xander examine fries and sesame seeds through the microscope, a warm feeling wormed its way through him. He wanted to someday share a life with her. But he would tread slowly. So much had changed since their discussion after the adoption fundraiser at Jimmy's. After church yesterday, Londyn had packed a lunch and they'd shared a picnic at an out-of-the-way park in nearby Upton. While they'd only discussed benign, lighter topics, Brodie hoped this latest turn of events was the beginning of a new chance with Londyn.

Things had changed between them for the better. He would take it slow as he never wanted to scare her away again. And if he could apprehend Haack, all would be right with the world.

Chapter 26

A week later, Londyn and Brodie loaded the canoe and hopped into Brodie's truck. It had been some time since Londyn had canoed, and she'd always enjoyed being up in the mountains and out on the lake. When Brodie suggested this, she eagerly agreed. While they'd seen no sign of Dustin during the past week, it would give her a break from having to be constantly vigilant. They left town and started up the winding road to the Pronghorn Mountains.

She cast a glance in his direction. He wore a gray athletic-wear tank top that accentuated his toned build, along with swim trunks revealing white, muscular legs. His arms were tanned from time in the sun assisting Roarke at the ranch. The wind ruffled his short dark hair, adding to his clean-shaven, rugged appearance.

Lush green surrounded them with millions of pines and aspen groves dotting the landscape. The slow-paced speed limits allowed extra time to take in the beauty of God's Creation. The cool air from the air conditioner blew through the vents, and Londyn watched the temperature go from 86 degrees in Pronghorn Falls to a comfortable 75 degrees once they started to climb. Brodie reached over and clasped his fingers around hers while keeping one hand on the steering wheel. Her heart pounded frantically in her chest. Now all she had to do was keep from messing up this second chance.

A familiar song sounded on the radio. "Wow," she said. "I haven't heard this song in forever."

"It brings back memories, doesn't it?" Brodie temporarily released her hand and turned up the volume. "This takes me back a few years."

"I think the last time we sang this song was when we were having a campfire at your parents' house a couple of years ago, and Grayson decided to bring his portable speaker."

"That sounds like Grayson. He always has to have his music."

Londyn nodded. "Well, he does have a great voice."

"He does. I think we were all singing, and Dad, of course, was ad-libbing."

Londyn noticed the faraway look in Brodie's eyes, and she squeezed his hand. She hated how life could be so unfair.

She and Brodie lifted their voices together, harmonizing with the original singer's voice. Londyn loved the Christian song that spoke of fully relying on the Lord, no matter what the circumstances.

The song ended, and a grin crossed Brodie's face. "I have to admit we do sound good together."

Pronghorn Lake came into view, with its clear waters splashing against the rocky and sandy shore. Brodie took a left and drove down the winding road to the parking lot. A mama duck and her ducklings swam across the lake, reminding Londyn of all the times she and the Brenneman family would feed the ducks oatmeal.

With the exception of a family loading up their kayaks and paddleboards, no one else was around, which would make for a nice, peaceful time out on the water. Londyn could hardly wait. They planned to eat lunch while floating peacefully along the water.

A moose in the distance caught her eye, and an eagle soared overhead. Brodie backed down the road parallel to the dock, which was often used to unload watercraft, to fish, or even to lounge on while watching the ducks.

Pronghorn Lake did not allow motorized boats, and the launching area was somewhat primitive, but Londyn wouldn't have it any other way.

When she was in junior high and high school, Londyn spent the majority of her summers camping with the Brennemans. Mom was just happy to get her out of her hair. Looking back, Londyn wished she had invited Logan. Perhaps that would have drawn them closer and given him a surrogate family as well.

Brodie stopped the truck and leaned toward her. He brushed a wisp of hair behind her ear. "I'm really glad you agreed to go canoeing."

"I'm glad you asked. I've missed being out on the water."

Brodie cupped her face in his hands, and the nearness of him caused a peculiar flutter in her belly. She closed her eyes as his lips met hers. It was a kiss with longing and tenderness all wound together in a pleasing moment that ended all too soon.

She and Brodie had been given a second chance—one she vowed to do right by.

"Guess we should go. The lake is calling us." Mixed antic-ipation swirled within her. She could easily kiss Brodie again, but she also looked forward to some time on the water. Brodie unstrapped the canoe, and in tandem, with her on one side and him on the other, they lifted the canoe off the rack and set it at the edge of the lake. Brodie grabbed the paddle and the life jackets from the truck bed and stuck them inside the canoe. Visiting on a weekday proved a perfect idea. On the weekends, Pronghorn Lake was overly crowded.

"I'm going to use the restroom," Londyn said after she withdrew the ice chest with their lunch from the back seat.

It was a short walk uphill to the vault bathroom, and she could see Brodie from its location. He was leaning over the canoe and ensuring everything was properly stowed before their excursion. He would then move the truck out of the way and to the upper parking lot so others could launch their own canoes and kayaks if desired.

A few minutes later, Londyn emerged from the outhouse. She perused the lake area, looking for Brodie and wondering why his truck was still in the launch area instead of in the upper parking area near the restrooms. She stood on tiptoe and peered around a line of trees, but still couldn't see him. The canoe was where they'd left it. Had he needed to use the restroom as well? She turned the corner to the men's outhouse. The door, as always, was shut, and she didn't hear any noise inside, but she decided to wait for him, and they could walk back to the lake together.

In the distance, a rabbit scampered across a trail that wound around to a warming hut. Years ago, she, Brodie, Roarke, Grayson, Danny, and Drea had snowshoed several miles to the hut where they drank an abundance of hot chocolate and ate a barrage of snacks. Such fond memories.

Londyn moved back around to the other side of the outhouse and spied a mama deer with her two speckled fawns, but there was no sign of Brodie.

She rapped again on the outhouse door. "Brodie?"

No answer.

He was probably wandering through the woods as he often enjoyed doing, and she walked down the hill to his truck. The windows were down as they had left them, but Brodie was nowhere in sight. The warm sun beat down on her while a chill simultaneously ran through her. Brodie wouldn't wander off too far without telling her.

She cast a glance back at the outhouse. Hopefully, he hadn't gotten sick. Usually, the winding roads weren't a problem for him. She hiked once more back up to the men's outhouse and tapped on the door and called his name. She repeated it when there was no answer, then returned to the truck and decided to wait for him. A short hike without telling her seemed out of character, but maybe he got sidetracked by a moose or fawn he wanted to get a picture of.

Londyn kneeled and removed her life vest from the canoe. That's when she noticed the truck tires had been slashed. She stilled, unable to move as worry clouded her thoughts.

A sudden yank on her hair jerked her neck back.

A voice hissed in her ear. "Get on your feet."

She would recognize that voice anywhere.

Bile rose in her throat, and her heart raced so fast it caused her chest to hurt. She slowly stood, her legs shaking beneath her as Dustin held the metal barrel of a gun to her temple.

"Walk this way," he growled.

Thoughts of ways to escape from someone with a gun ran through her mind from the situational awareness training. But her mind drew a blank. Dizziness nearly tottered her off her feet.

Dustin shoved her forward a short distance through several pines immediately past the edge of the lake. On the ground lay Brodie. "Too bad your boyfriend has to suffer for your stupidity."

"Brodie!" she screamed, emotion clogging her throat.

Dustin laughed. "Go ahead, check on him. Make sure he's still alive." He shoved her again. Londyn fell to her knees beside Brodie. He was unconscious, a bloody wound on the back of his head where he'd likely been hit by a gun.

She felt for a pulse. He was alive.

Thank You, Jesus!

Londyn wasn't a nurse, but she *did* know that concussions, which was what Brodie likely had, could be dangerous. "Brodie, it's Londyn. Can you hear me?"

Brodie stirred slightly, and his back rose and fell with his breath.

A snore waffled through his nose, and Londyn experienced an unexpected release of some of the tension. No one would ever say they were thankful Brodie snored.

Until now.

She bent over him once again, feeling the brush of his hair against her cheek as she placed a kiss on the side of his forehead. "It's going to be all right," she whispered in his ear, for his benefit, but also hers.

"All right, that's enough." Dustin grabbed her arm and thrust her backward. She slipped and fell onto the ground before he grasped her upper forearm, his nails digging into her flesh and causing her to cry out in pain.

"You're coming with me. Don't think of trying anything. If you do, I'll finish him off."

As if to prove his words, Dustin raised his gun and aimed it in Brodie's direction.

"No!"

"Very good. You're learning." He swiveled and pointed the gun again at her, determination in his dark eyes. The hair lifted on the nape of her neck as sweat simultaneously trickled down her back.

"Walk along."

Could she turn around abruptly, catch him off guard, and kick, hit, punch, or knee him—whatever it took to immobilize him? She thought of her gun tucked inside her belly band holster. Could she quickly reach for and use it? While the thought of shooting someone disturbed her, she would do whatever it took to save Brodie and to escape from Dustin.

"Where are we going?"

He shoved her in the shoulder with his palm. "Get going."

While she never would have thought Dustin to be a wimp, his hatefulness and obvious mental disorders would render him far more dangerous despite his slim stature. With one hand, he gripped her neck hard, and with the other, kept the gun on her. He guided her to the shore.

What was Dustin thinking of doing? Drowning her? Her mind went a million places. Londyn thought she heard Brodie stir again, but resisted the urge to turn her head. Dustin's volatile temperament wouldn't mesh well with his trigger finger.

They stopped at the lake's edge, and he removed his hand from her neck. He reached inside his pocket and extricated a clump of keys Londyn recognized as Brodie's and tossed them into the lake, dashing her hopes again. Brodie needed medical help, and driving was the only way to transport him to town. With slashed tires and no keys, his chances of survival if his wounds were life-threatening now became slimmer.

Did Brodie still have his gun?

Dustin whipped Londyn around and thrust her forward once again, this time toward the canoe.

"You know, I never realized how easy it was to incapacitate someone." A faraway stare shadowed his face. "All those times in school when I had to deal with all the jocks thinking they were better than me. Well, I just took out someone larger and more athletic with a whack of a gun." He chortled, his sardonic laugh echoing through the trees. "I've never really been a gun guy, so I had a choice to make when I snatched his gun from his holster. His, or the one I'd *borrowed* from an unlocked vehicle?"

Dustin angled his head close to hers. He was so close she could feel his breath on her cheek. "Guess which gun I chose?"

When she said nothing, he raised his voice and yelled, the veins in his neck protruding as his face reddened. "Guess. Which. Gun. I. Chose?" he repeated, punctuating every word, his tone nearly deafening her.

"I'm not sure," she stuttered.

"I chose the one I stole. No one knows I took it. But they sure can't accuse me of stealing Brenneman's and using it. And no one will ever be able to find it since it's now at the bottom of the lake along with his keys."

Londyn's lungs constricted.

Please, Lord, give me wisdom and strength to circumvent this situation. She cast a glance at the bright blue sky. She knew God heard every single prayer she'd ever uttered. He would hear her. He would help her. Her throat tightened as the tears threatened.

"Get in the canoe," Dustin growled.

"Can I put on the life jacket first?"

Dustin regarded her for a brief moment, shooting daggers at her before he pasted on his venomous smile. "To show you that I'm a nice guy, go ahead and put on your life jacket. Although it won't do you much good for where we're going. And don't even think of trying anything. If you do, your sheriff won't make it to see tomorrow." He pointed at the boat. "Go ahead and grab your life jacket."

Dizziness caused the area around her to swirl, and she unsteadily bent over and fished her life jacket from the canoe, careful not to allow the pressing of the gun in her belly band to become more prominent through her shirt.

Lord, could this maybe be a way out?

She couldn't extract her pistol without Dustin noticing, but she could use other methods at her disposal. She remained stooped over the canoe for a few seconds, attempting to catch her breath, pray, and methodically plan.

"Hurry up. I don't have all day." He focused on a sluggish older-model motorhome struggling up an incline on the highway above the lake.

She threaded one arm, then the other, through the life jacket and snapped it in front. Then, in a move that would make Mr. Brenneman proud, she kicked Dustin hard in the shin before kneeing him in the groin. The next plan of attack was to go for his eyes, but when she did, he backhanded her, his hand connecting hard with her face.

She reeled, seeing stars in her vision as she teetered. She fell backward on the hard earth below. Dustin raised his right hand and aimed the gun at Brodie.

"No!" she screamed, staggering to her feet and tackling Dustin as the bullet rang through the air.

She dared to look to see if it hit Dustin's intended mark.

Dustin seized her by the hair and held the gun near her cheek. "I told you if you tried anything, I would finish off your sheriff. What about that did you not understand?"

She held her breath, afraid to breathe, and without moving her head, scanned in Brodie's direction. There was no blood or any other sign that the bullet had hit him, but there was a skiff in the dirt where the bullet landed.

"Get into the canoe."

It would be game over if he removed her from the area, but she couldn't risk Dustin shooting Brodie. She fiddled with the clasps on the front of the lifejacket.

Dustin urged her forward, stopping her in front of the boat. He collected a roll of string sitting on a horizontal log. "Put your hands behind your back," he demanded.

He was going to tie her up?

"I promise you, Londyn Siegler, if you give me any trouble—even the slightest bit—I will shoot the sheriff, and this time I won't miss." A spark of wrath ignited in his eyes, and his poison-tipped gaze seared right through her.

If she could get away, then she could use her own gun. An idea percolated through her mind.

"Put your arms behind you."

Londyn reluctantly did as she was told, and Dustin moved behind her and pulled the rope tightly around her wrists. She lifted her right leg and kicked him hard, donkey-kick style, in the shin.

Dustin groaned and released a stream of oaths, his words singeing her ears. He rammed her from behind, shoving her to the ground. She hit hard with no way to catch her fall.

Londyn's eyes smarted.

"Was that worth it?" he jeered.

There was still hope.

There was always hope.

She squirmed, attempting to break free. Dustin put a knee on her shoulder blade and pressed hard into her skin, hard enough to feel it even through the lifejacket. He bound her ankles.

"Now, my love, if you will behave yourself, this will all go well. We're meant to be together. Quit fighting it. Quit fighting *me*." Dark frost lit his eyes, and she bemoaned the fact that she hadn't realized what kind of person he was before. He hurled her into the canoe. "Sit down."

She did so and attempted to wiggle her ankles, but the binding was too tight. She could already see where the rope was digging into her tender flesh. "I know you wouldn't want me to be uncomfortable," she said in a tone she wished sounded more confident. "Can you please loosen the rope a little bit?

Indecision captured his gaze. He grabbed the paddle and started rowing. When they were in the middle of the lake, he stopped the canoe, put the paddle in the notches, and marginally loosened the binding on her ankles.

"And my hands, too?

"Nope. You've already given me too much trouble. I'm not going to have you get any ideas about escaping."

She scanned the area and saw no one else in the vicinity. A verse from Psalm 50:15 reminded her that the Lord was never far away. *Lord, I call upon you in the day of trouble, and you will rescue me.*

He would rescue her, wouldn't He?

The jackhammering sound of a semi's Jake brake on the highway broke the silence, but Londyn doubted the driver could see her from the road, and even if he could, he would have no idea she was in danger.

Dustin paddled further from the shore. Further from Brodie. Tears strained at her eyes. Brodie remained in a heap near the pines, and there was nothing she could do.

Nothing she could do to help him.

That was the worst part of it all. He may lose his life because of her. Because of her foolish decision to leave Pronghorn Falls and seek employment at a place where a man named Dustin Haack had first befriended her, then showed his true colors.

It was a peculiar thing knowing the man whose heart she had broken might not survive. That she might not truly have another chance with him, not because he didn't want to give her that second chance, but because his life had been stripped from him by a ruthless lunatic. A man Londyn once trusted.

She started shaking, fear rooted deep within her. The pastor last week had spoken about fear. Of how it wasn't of the Lord. Of how God gave us peace amid troubling times.

Lord, please. Let someone find Brodie. Don't let it be too late. Help me escape from Dustin.

Her leg muscles cramped, and her arms fell asleep. Dustin whistled as if it were just another day at the lake. Would screaming do any good? There was no one to hear her.

"Why are you doing this?" Her words wavered, and she regretted that she didn't sound strong and capable.

"Why am I doing this? You had a chance, Londyn."

"What do you mean?" She needed to keep him talking.

A sneer crossed his face. "What do I mean? It was always supposed to be you and me. I gave you every chance to realize we were meant for each other."

How should she play this? Pretend to agree with him that she had made a mistake in not accepting his overtures? Tell him she'd never like someone like him? Offer a fake apology? It was obvious Dustin was mentally unstable. His nostrils flared, and his gaze contained even more animosity than before.

"I gave you every chance to realize I'm the only one who will ever love you."

"Why did you send me texts, call me, and break into my apartment?

"How else was I supposed to prove to you that you needed my protection? A woman new to the city who's receiving texts and phone calls from someone who is watching her is a little unnerving, right?” Dustin threw his head back, his laugh maniacal. “You needed someone to keep you safe, someone like me. Someone to keep you safe *from* me.” Dustin’s pupils dilated, and he launched into a story from the third person. “How could he make her see that it was fate that brought them together? That he was there to help her when she received texts or visits outside her window and door? That when someone was peering at her through binoculars as she perused the Internet, that he was there. There to save her. Be her hero. It was the only way he could prove his love to her.”

Dustin cracked his knuckles. “Of course, she didn’t make things easy. He told her time and again he had feelings for her.” He grinned, his breath heaving in rapid spurts. He then glowered. “But she wouldn’t agree to date him.” He spat into the water. “This is all your fault, Londyn. If only you had cooperated.”

Fear caught her in its jaws. Dustin was a lunatic. “Where are you taking me?”

“You’ll find out soon enough.”

Would he kill her? Allow her to live or hold her hostage? Tremors filled her words. “How are you able to miss so much work?

“My grandmother in Washington is very, very sick. Sonja is an understanding boss. I have to take care of my grandmother and will be back when I can. Besides, you worry too much about things. Someone who’s an employee of the quarter twice in a row pretty much has the boss in his pocket. And my poor, poor ailing grandma. I never cared much for her, but a grandson always takes care of his family. And as far as anyone knows, that’s where I am right now.”

Dustin tapped the paddle that rested across the width of

the canoe. "What matters is that we're together. If only you had realized sooner, if only you had told me you would be interested in dating me rather than that sheriff, I wouldn't have had to kill him. And it's all your fault, Londyn."

A strangled sob escaped her throat. Surely Brodie was still alive. Surely. He'd been breathing when she'd checked on him. She hadn't seen any signs of him being shot.

The if onlys ran through her mind again, and she peered up at the bright sky above. If Brodie had succumbed to his injuries and she didn't make it out alive, they would both be in the presence of their Savior. And while that would be a glorious day, she wasn't ready to go yet. She wasn't ready for Brodie to go either. Londyn must do all she could to see that they both survived.

"No one will think to look for us on the water," said Dustin. Londyn didn't counter his statement with the fact that they actually *would* look for them on the water since Brodie's canoe was missing.

Dustin steered them from the lake and toward the river. If it had been the day she'd planned, Londyn would be riding in the canoe, enjoying Brodie's company and beholding the amazing beauty of God's Creation.

"Not too much farther now." Dustin lifted the paddle and maneuvered the boat skillfully through the calm water.

"Are we going to stay in the mountains?" she asked.

"I didn't realize I needed to give you my itinerary, but yes, we are staying in the mountains in a pleasant little cabin that I think you'll like. I've been crashing there periodically during my visit to Pronghorn Falls." He shrugged. "No one would ever think to find me there. Brilliant, wouldn't you say?"

Londyn could think of other words to describe Dustin's wicked intentions. Words like crazed, deranged, demented, or unbalanced. Brilliant, no.

This time, Dustin flashed her a broad smile, and his gaze roved over her. "Just you and me, passing the time away together. Sounds perfect, doesn't it?"

More like the next scene of the nightmare she'd been thrust into. "I didn't know there was a cabin here."

"It's Dorena's parents' cabin. They're only here a week out of the year. It was easy to convince Dorena to hand over the keys to me when I told her I was mourning my grandma and needed some time away in nature." Perspiration shone on Dustin's brow. "But, hey, all I had to do was promise her a few things, sweet-talk her, and lie about caring for her, and I pretty much got what I wanted."

"Dorena?"

"Yeah, you know Dorena Mohr, a nurse at the hospital? We hit it off right away that day you decided to drive off the road and land yourself in the ER." Dustin shook his head. "She's almost as foolish as that dippy dispatcher, Juanita."

Londyn's jaw dropped. "Juanita?"

"She's been a big help. Amazing what can happen when you schmooze someone lonely."

Londyn had known about Renee, obviously, but not Dorena or Juanita. How many women had Dustin fooled in his effort to succeed at his loathsome crimes?

Chapter 27

Brodie's head ached in a way it never had before. He moaned and attempted to roll over. The first time, he failed and fell back onto his chest. He persevered, gathering what momentum he could, and finally rolled onto his back. His eyes fluttered open. What had happened? Where was Londyn? With effort, he propped himself up on his elbow and glanced at his truck in the area near the lake. Hadn't he unloaded the canoe? Where was it? He reached a hand to his holster. His gun was gone.

He moved a little too quickly, and the stabbing pain in the back of his neck added to the pounding in his head. If Londyn was gone, the canoe was gone, and his gun was gone, it could only mean one thing.

Slowly, with extreme effort, Brodie recalled a few details. They had unloaded the canoe, Londyn had walked up the hill to the vault restroom, and then everything had gone black.

He reached a hand to the back of his head. Something crusty greeted his fingertips, and the touch exacerbated the pain.

There wasn't time to lounge beneath the pines and contemplate the details. If Londyn had returned yet from the restroom and he'd been whacked over the head, Brodie could only deduce one thing.

Londyn was in trouble.

A sizable granite boulder beside him offered the perfect crutch. He slowly sat up and rested first an arm, then a hand on the boulder, and, with his legs wobbling, struggled to his feet. Where had Dustin taken her?

Brodie took a step forward, and he fought the dizziness and blinked several times before holding a hand to shield his eyes as he scanned the entire area around the lake as far as he could see.

On the second glance, he spotted the canoe in the distance at the very edge of where the lake detoured into the river. He squinted, noticing two figures in the canoe.

Adrenaline pumped through him. He scanned the road, the lake, and the many hiking trails leading up the hill. The entire area was a ghost town. His legs arguing the entire way, he stumbled to his truck, opened the door, and retrieved his phone.

No signal.

Lord, please give me the ability to find Londyn, and please keep her safe.

Woozy throbbing added to his splitting headache, the pulsating causing Brodie to grip his head and scrunch his shoulders upward.

He had no time for this.

But how would he get to the canoe? How would he rescue Londyn?

He forced himself through the pines that ran adjacent to the lake, attempting to again catch sight of the boat. He limped, wondering why his legs felt so weak when it had been his head that had been whacked.

He claimed a better view of the canoe, and Haack pivoted. Could he see Brodie?

Brodie ducked and hid to the side of the tree, wishing for the first time in his life that he had sloping shoulders. There was no shouting, yelling, or any other indication that Haack had seen him.

Brodie breathed a prayer of gratitude.

As a law enforcement officer, Brodie had found himself in many volatile situations. As his dad always said, a sheriff's main duties were, of course, to uphold the Constitution, but also to serve papers and tend to the jail. Dad's final comment on the matter rang through Brodie's ears. Catching the criminals was a bonus.

Only this time, he wasn't only trying to *catch* the bad guy. He was endeavoring to save the life of the woman he loved.

A downed tree in his path cost him precious seconds as Brodie veered around it. There was no way he could keep up with as fast as Haack rowed down the river, a river whose waters were flowing in just the perfect direction to accelerate the stalker's travel.

But Brodie would give it his all.

He tripped over a hole and crashed to the ground. The pain reverberated through his head, reminding him of his likely concussion.

Stunned, Brodie attempted to gather his wits before again checking his phone to see if he had service yet. He didn't. He knew that getting a signal in the Pronghorn Mountains was nearly impossible, but there were spots where one bar occasionally occurred.

He could still see the canoe, and if he hurried, he could bridge the distance between himself and Londyn.

If he hurried. Who was he kidding?

But he'd never been the type to quit. Using a nearby tree stump, Brodie pulled himself to his feet and did the best to ignore the pain in nearly every part of his body. He'd been in worse scrapes in his time in law enforcement, not to mention when he was a kid and he and his brothers would manage to engage in all sorts of shenanigans.

He hobbled along much slower than he'd like. A tree branch slapped him hard in the face as he slithered through a tight area. The landscape turned hilly with an incline toward the river. He wished he knew where Haack was taking Londyn, and he wished he had service to call for backup. Brodie refused to give thought to Dustin Haack's endgame motive. The man was as depraved as they came. A charmer. A manipulator. Unpredictable. Tactical. Vindictive. Devious. Cruel. Obsessed. Lacking a conscience.

The list could go on, and Brodie was far from a psychiatrist, but the character traits of this dangerous man urged Brodie to persevere no matter what it took or how much the pain in his head argued.

Surely at some point, Haack would be stopped.

The pines thickened, and swarms of bugs buzzed in front of him. The occasional chipmunk or squirrel crossed his path, and he'd already spotted several deer, an elk, and a moose in the distant meadow. One would think Brodie was out of shape with the way his breath came in gasps as he climbed up one side of the hill, then nearly slid down the other. The boat stopped, and Brodie hid behind a thick-trunked tree.

Haack dragged the canoe to the shore. Brodie stayed hidden as he watched Haack roughly pull Londyn to her feet and shove her out of the canoe. She nearly tripped, and he grabbed her arm to right her. It was obvious her hands and feet were bound.

Brodie fisted his hands at his sides, and his body tensed. The sooner he extricated Londyn from Haack's grasp, the better. He weaved in and out of the trees as he attempted to draw closer. Fortunately, with her feet bound, Londyn was taking small, deliberate steps. Haack held a gun on her, which would be the biggest deterrent to overcome.

He detested hostage situations.

Stopping periodically and maintaining his cover, Brodie continued along through the web of trees. Thankfully, he was on the same side of the river as Londyn and Dustin. If he hadn't been, there would be no way he would have been able to swim over to the other side without extreme difficulty. The rushing spring waters and his own injuries would have precluded him from being successful at that endeavor.

A pinecone Brodie hadn't noticed crunched beneath his shoe.

Haack swiveled in Brodie's direction. His head jerked up, and he aimed the gun at Brodie. The bullet ricocheted off a nearby tree. Brodie ducked and sought cover as more shots were fired.

"Don't come any closer," Haack yelled.

Brodie's heart pounded in his chest. He needed a weapon, but more importantly, he needed a plan. Terror stabbed at his heart. He needed to devise a strategy to rescue Londyn with no interference.

Please, God.

Dustin Haack continued to haphazardly waste bullets. Brodie sat with his back to the rocks, allowing him better cover and protection.

He fished his phone from his back pocket. There were no bars, but there *was* a possibility he could still call 911 even without service because his phone would search for the nearest cell tower and send the signal there. And he knew there were cell towers nearby. Except, he'd be unable to speak with Haack so close.

Haack paused his target practice. Good. Maybe he depleted his bullets. But that wouldn't stop him from hunting down Brodie's location. Brodie peered around the corner, keeping himself as compressed against the mound of rocks as possible. Haack walked in the opposite direction, checking behind trees.

Brodie pressed the SOS emergency feature on his phone just as the boom of another gunshot echoed. He then texted a message as well, doubling his efforts. Sheriff Brenneman, emergency situation, Pronghorn Lake. Send help asap.

Haack's thundering voice boomed. "I will find you. You can't hide forever." Haack stomped, his actions more befitting of a toddler than a man in his thirties.

Brodie muted his phone's volume and stuffed his device into his pocket. A peek through a crevice between two rocks indicated Haack was now stationary and standing beside a bound Londyn, his gun aimed in Brodie's direction. How many bullets would the man squander on him? Would he turn the weapon on Londyn? Haack shouted again, his words laced with anger and profanity. Brodie would buy his time until Haack finished and had either spent all the bullets or had given up, figuring he'd already hit Brodie. In which case...

When the next bullet whizzed past him, Brodie released a muffled yell and pounded the ground as if he'd toppled over.

"I told you to stay away! You finally got what you deserved," Haack shouted. Brodie tarried behind the rock formation. It was a win-win situation for him. Either Haack would figure he was mortally wounded and go about his business while Brodie watched from a distance. Or, if Haack instead decided to investigate whether Brodie had been fatally shot, he would leave Londyn where she was and come searching for Brodie. In which instance, Brodie would launch a surprise attack on his adversary.

Haack shoved Londyn to the side, causing her to trip and fall to the ground with no way to catch herself. Brodie gritted his teeth, barely catching himself in time before protesting. It took all of his control not to react—to not leap to his feet and bolt toward—and pay back Haack for what he had done and was doing to Londyn. But to let Haack know his position at this point would set Brodie's plan up for instant failure.

With God's help, Brodie resisted that urge. Instead, he remained as still as possible, keeping his ears fine-tuned to the sounds around him, including Haack's pounding footsteps as the man grew closer. Haack shuffled on the pine needles in Brodie's direction, then stopped. Londyn had maneuvered her way back into the canoe. Haack must have realized it, because he turned around and started again toward her, his gun raised. This was Brodie's chance.

And if he failed...no, he wouldn't fail. He couldn't fail. Failure was not an option.

Ignoring the stabbing pain in his head, Brodie pushed forward through the trees in pursuit of Haack. The man pivoted and scanned the area behind him as Brodie again slimmed himself behind a cluster of tree trunks. Silence, except for the cry of a red-tailed hawk.

Finally, he heard the sound of footsteps again. Brodie's heart pounded wildly in his chest. He would never become accustomed to the adrenaline rush that tore through him when pursuing a perpetrator.

Londyn made a sound, distracting Haack from Brodie.

This was Brodie's chance.

Brodie launched from his location and sprinted toward Haack, tackling him from behind. Haack's gun flew from his hand and landed a few feet away. Brodie slithered along the ground, reaching for it. Haack did the same. Brodie reached up and punched Haack in the face. The man reeled backward before grabbing a rock and attempting to clobber Brodie with it, his aim striking Brodie slightly above the ear. The combination of pain from that and his first head injury caused Brodie to momentarily freeze. If he were in his top form, neutralizing Haack would be no problem, but at this moment, his being in tip-top condition was negligible.

In the canoe, Londyn attempted to remove the bindings from her ankles.

Brodie and Haack wrestled perilously close to the cliff's edge. Brodie wasn't afraid of heights, but being so close to tumbling down into a ravine, he would do all he could to avoid meeting his demise.

The gun lay beyond Brodie's reach, resting in the prickles of a shrub. If he could just reach it...

Haack leapt on him, shoving them both closer to the edge. Brodie flipped Haack over, causing the man's head to dangle perilously over the edge. Brodie palmed him in the face. "We can do this the easy way or the hard way."

Haack muttered something unintelligible before spitting in Brodie's face. Of all the things he was expecting, Brodie wasn't expecting that. He flinched, and in that split second, Haack pummeled him hard in the side of the head. Totally unprepared, Brodie slid partially down the embankment before he again climbed to the top and wrestled Haack for the upper hand before Haack could grab the gun. This time, Brodie shoved Haack, and the man tripped and plummeted down the side. Brodie released a stout exhale. The man lay at the bottom of the incline in a heap. Brodie scrambled to his feet and limped toward Londyn.

"Stay in the canoe!" he shouted. There was no time to locate Haack's gun. Londyn's feet remained bound, but her hands were free. Brodie staggered to the boat, clutched the paddle, and dipped the end into the water, propelling them away from the bank and down the river.

If only he had his gun. Haack still had his, but if Brodie got a good enough head start, even if Haack did recover from his unconsciousness, they would be far enough ahead and out of range.

"I'm so glad you're all right," Londyn breathed.

He stared at her pretty face. Bruising marred her cheek-bones, and blood crusted near the corner of her forehead. Whatever revenge he could think of wouldn't be enough to compensate Haack for what he had done. The reminder that revenge was the Lord's stirred in Brodie's subconscious, and he struggled to remind himself of God's Truth on that subject.

Paddling against the current when he was in less-than-stellar condition was not an easy task. Every muscle ached, and his biceps groaned against his demands. "I thought I'd lost you." His voice cracked. He couldn't lose her again.

A gunshot rang through the air. "Get down!" Brodie craned his neck to see Haack running alongside the river's edge. How had he recovered so quickly? But in Brodie's line of work, he found that unhinged people most often had more tenacity. Perhaps because they had more to lose, especially in eternity.

"I have my gun." Londyn's words surprised him.

"You do?"

"Yes, it's in my concealed carry." Londyn fumbled around briefly, hoisting her life jacket up so she could access the belly band around her waist. She withdrew her pistol. At that moment, Haack took another shot.

Londyn jerked, her eyes going wide as her gun clattered to the bottom of the canoe.

Brodie followed her gaze to the now bleeding wound staining her sleeve. "*Londyn!*" Brodie's voice reverberated through the remote area. He tucked the paddle in the notches and, in one swift motion, reached for her gun. He aimed it at Dustin Haack and shot twice, both times hitting the intended target in the body mass area.

Haack toppled to the ground. If the man survived that, he was truly invincible. Brodie knelt beside Londyn, careful not to tip the canoe as he applied pressure to the wound in her arm. "Stay with me." Tears smarted his eyes.

"Brodie?"

"Don't try to talk. Save your energy." After tending to her wound as best as he could, he took advantage of an unexpected second wind pumping through him and navigated the canoe back to the lake. A helicopter droned overhead, and he shifted the paddle to one hand and waved furiously, then continued on the route back to the lake. The current had increased due to the winds picking up, and the canoe rocked back and forth. The last thing they needed was to overturn. The waves lapped at the shore, but at least the shore was in sight.

Brodie stopped a few feet from the docking area, the tumultuous water sloshing on the sides of the boat and tossing the canoe to and fro. A Pronghorn Falls County Sheriff's truck peeled around the corner. He'd never been so happy to see a co-worker. He lifted Londyn and battled the current to get her to the shore. The turbulent water battered his legs and nearly caused him to lose his footing, especially since the throbbing in his head increased tenfold, but he forged ahead.

The sound of ambulance sirens wailed in the distance.

"Brodie?" He stepped onto the rocky shore and struggled in the direction of the deputy's truck and stared down into the eyes of the woman he loved.

"It's going to be all right, Londyn. The ambulance is almost here." So much could have happened. How many times had he praised God in just the past five minutes?

"Brodie?" she whispered.

"Yes?"

"I will marry you."

Those were her last words before she lost consciousness.

Epilogue

There couldn't have been a more perfect day for a wedding. The July temperatures were in the mid-70s, accompanied by clear blue skies. It had been a minor miracle that they'd so efficiently thrown together a wedding, and Londyn praised the Lord for second chances, especially with Brodie.

She wasn't willing to allow anything to come between them ever again.

Londyn nursed her arm, which was healing from the superficial gunshot wound. Brodie's injuries improved as well, and Dustin succumbed to the bullets Brodie aimed his way. She'd never have to worry about him again.

Behind her, an intricately carved wooden cross stood beside the altar. Londyn stared out over the "sanctuary" of the outdoor chapel. There were seven rows of wood-hewn benches on each side. They'd been filled immediately, and rows of plastic chairs expanded the sitting area.

Brodie had jokingly teased that it had become a bring-your-own-chair event. Roarke added that it might be the wedding of the century. Londyn would have been fine if no one except close friends and family had shown up to their event, as long as she was marrying the man she loved.

The expansive mountain range surrounding them on three sides provided an unparalleled view. Birds chirped happily as if celebrating the occasion. In the distance, two speckled fawns leaped and played as their mother protectively watched over them. But Londyn's attention wasn't on the mountains, chairs, birds, or fawns. It was on her soon-to-be handsome husband.

And now she stood facing her groom as the pastor recited the words that would bind them together forever in matrimony. Brodie sported a white tux that looked stunning against his dark hair and tanned skin. And in typical Brodie fashion, he wore his favorite cowboy boots. Of course, not to be outdone, Londyn has slipped on her own cowboy boots beneath the elegant and beautiful dress with its ornate pearl buttons and lace bodice. It still choked her up to think that she was wearing Aileen's wedding dress. While cut far too short, if Londyn could have the kind of godly marriage with Brodie that Aileen shared with Mr. Brenneman, it would be the ultimate.

Xander made a dashing appearance as the ring bearer wearing his miniature white tux, complete with his brand-new bug watch and a kid's gold sheriff's badge. Even the last-minute addition of Grayson's appearance was a surprise.

"And do you, Londyn Seigler, take Brodie Brenneman to be your lawfully wedded husband to have and to hold from this day forward, for better, for worse, for richer, for poorer, in sickness and in health, to love and to cherish, 'til death do you part?"

"I do."

The pastor flicked a glance in Brodie's direction. "I now pronounce you husband and wife. You may kiss the bride."

Brodie gently pulled her to him. She needed no encouragement, for she knew she belonged in his arms. His mouth found hers, and shivers of excitement ran through her. For a few seconds, she forgot they were standing at an altar in the mountains in front of two hundred people. For a few seconds, it was just her and the man she vowed to love no matter what came their way.

The caress of his kiss sent her stomach into a wild swirl. She was vaguely aware of Roarke's voice. "I think that's probably good for now," he said.

It was only then that Londyn realized they had been kissing for quite a while. They reluctantly ceased, and Brodie stepped back, their gazes still fixed on each other. Finally, he grabbed her hand, and they ran down the aisle, her boots pounding the freshly cut weeds of the rustic venue. Birdseed came at them from all directions as their guests cheered.

Brodie opened the door of the UTV's passenger side, and she climbed in, tucking the dress beneath her. He sprinted to the other side, but not before being bombarded again by birdseed. Brodie started the engine, and they trailed down the road toward the lodge where they would stay for their honeymoon.

They traversed along the narrow dirt road, dust kicking up behind them. Londyn squeezed her eyes shut, then reopened them, just to be sure what she'd experienced was reality and not a dream.

Brodie pulled to the side a mile later.

"I love you, Londyn Brenneman."

"I love you, Brodie Brenneman. Thank you for waiting for me."

"I would wait forever for you." His lips found hers again, and Londyn thanked the Lord for His grace and marveled at His ability to take a lost little girl and place her in a loving surrogate family, and when she grew up, give her a Godly husband who would love and cherish her.

God was so good.

DON'T MISS THIS SNEAK PEEK

MOUNTAIN JUSTICE - 3

SOMETIMES EVIL LURKS IN PLAIN SIGHT.

Don't Miss This Sneak Peek

Someone had been in her house.

And not an invited guest.

Oaklee Newbold was pulling her car into the garage when she noticed the single side door that led into the house stood slightly ajar. She'd closed it before she left. Hadn't she?

Yes, of course she had.

She'd never leave it open.

And she'd never leave it unlocked. So, how then...

Oaklee put the SUV in reverse and backed out of the garage, her vehicle thudding off the curb once she reached the end of the driveway. It was then that she noticed the shades were drawn in the upstairs bedroom.

Another clue that something wasn't right.

Her heart thrummed in her chest, and her imagination created all sorts of variables that she conjured up from reading suspense novels. What was the intent of the intruder? Was she a victim of a robbery? What if she'd been in the house at the time? What would anyone want with the contents of her humble townhouse?

Were they still in the house?

She clicked the lock on the SUV door a couple of times just to be sure.

Moose, her yellow retriever, jumped from his place in the

backseat into the front seat and began to bark. "It's all right," she said, but her own words did nothing to calm her.

Driving to the end of the street, Oaklee pulled to the curb in front of Mrs. Meriweather's house and dialed the number that would solicit help.

Who is he really?
And why is someone after him?

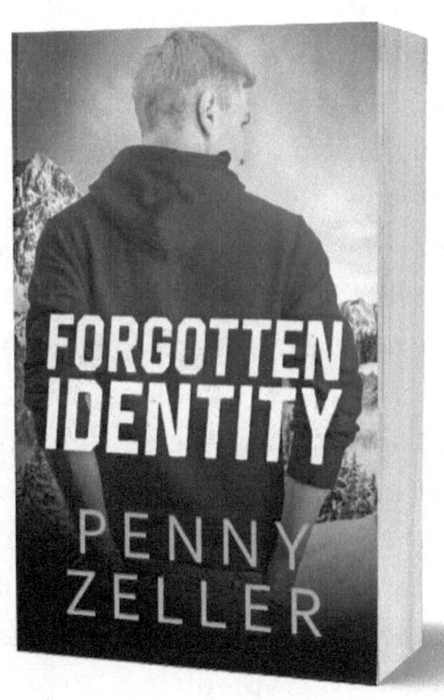

Forgotten Identity

Of all the days for the dog to run off.

Mariah Holzman plodded after the family border collie, who continued barking even as he looked back to ensure someone noticed his most recent escape antic. The cold bit her face, and her jacket did little to protect her from the falling temperatures. The weather service had predicted a storm for the area, warning that any travel could be dangerous, but apparently, Nosy refused to heed that advice.

Instead of coming at Mariah's call, Nosy had stopped in a deep thicket of trees with large boulders next to the ravine, his tail wagging. He barked once, then twice, content to ignore the dark clouds forming in the sky.

"Probably another dead rabbit," Mariah muttered. Nosy's shenanigans usually wouldn't be a problem, but the eerie calm that had befallen the forest sent shivers up her spine.

She really needed to stop editing suspense novels right before bedtime. Just because the storm would hit earlier than anticipated and the forest stood too still didn't mean anything was amiss.

"Come back, Nosy!" Seven-year-old Jordan zipped after the dog. His waddle, caused by his bulky snowsuit, would be amusing if not for the lingering sense of unease settling in Mariah's middle.

She shook her head to clear the irrational dread. The events of suspense novels didn't happen in real life, and even if they did, they wouldn't happen in the safe and small town of Mountain Springs.

"Jordan, wait up."

Her son slowed to a deliberate plod. "We can't leave him out here."

"He'll come back in a few minutes."

"What if he doesn't?"

"We can't stay out here long. A storm is blowing in."

Tall lodgepole pines silently swayed in the breeze, their calm movement in direct opposition to what was to come. While she loved the trees, Mariah knew that soon the cabin would no longer be in sight due to the thick mass of pines intermingled with a smattering of aspens.

The wind gusted, causing an aspen's branch to snap.

Mariah took a deep breath. There was nothing wrong. Nothing would happen except the storm hitting sooner than predicted.

Another gust brought a smattering of snowflakes.

If the snowfall increased in intensity, the trees wouldn't be the only things blocking the cabin from view.

Of all the days, you silly dog.

A flock of tiny black-and-white birds zipped past overhead, presumably to get to a safe place before the storm unleashed its fury.

Thankfully, Nosy plopped his hindquarters in the snow and continued to bark.

"No." Mariah grabbed Jordan's shoulder when he prepared to again run to the dog. "It's too slippery that close to the ravine."

"But Nosy's okay."

"Nosy is a dog who sometimes has very little common sense." *Hence his name.*

Mariah bit back a sigh as they neared. While grateful Nosy stopped when he did, couldn't the dog have chosen another place to investigate besides the ravine that could be deadly if someone misstepped and fell into it? At least the handful of boulders near its edge warned of the ravine's proximity.

Nosy's barking turned to a whine as he pawed at the snow.

No, not just the snow.

The snow *covering* a shoe protruding from behind a large boulder.

If you want to be among the first to hear about
Penny's latest book projects, sign up for her newsletter
at www.pennyzeller.com. You will receive book and writing
updates, encouragement, notification of current
giveaways, occasional freebies, and special offers.

If you enjoyed this glimpse into the lives of Londyn and
Brodie, please consider leaving a review on your social media,
Amazon, Goodreads, Barnes and Noble, or BookBub. Reviews
are critical to authors, and those stars you give us are such an
encouragement.

Author's Note

Dear Reader,

Thank you for taking this trip with me to Pronghorn Falls for Londyn and Brodie's story. For some of you, this may be your first visit to the mountain town, while for others, it's a return trip. Either way, I appreciate you taking the time to join Londyn and Brodie as they contend with the evil Dustin.

When this story first percolated in my mind, I knew I wanted to give Londyn and Brodie a second chance at love. After the close friendship they shared throughout most of their lives, I knew they were meant to be together. We couldn't just leave them at the park that night, Brodie wearing his heart on his sleeve as he proposed, and Londyn so fearful to be like her mom that she rejected Brodie and withdrew from their relationship almost entirely.

It was good to revisit with Mila, Roarke, Xander, and Aileen. They've become like family, and who wouldn't want to spend time at Aileen's house, a refuge several miles from town nestled between prime ranch land and the Pronghorn Mountains?

One of the best parts of being an author is creating characters. Giving them personalities, accomplishments, struggles, and difficult decisions. We authors are avid people watchers and research extraordinaires. In the case of Dustin, I spent time researching narcissism and sociopathic tendencies, as well as visiting with those who had experienced life with a narcissist.

During the penning of this novel, prominent stories in the news about elusive criminals inspired me to create the slippery Dustin Haack. Could someone really be that elusive? Turns out, they can be. Story after story told of criminals evading the law for determined amounts of time, some for years or decades.

Juanita's character was inspired by some cases I stumbled across, where the dispatchers shared privileged information with the public.

As a former homeschool mom (we've since graduated our daughters from the Zeller Academy), creating little Xander and his homeschool co-op was an added layer of fun. He provided comedic relief, and his love for bugs was inspired by my youngest daughter, who was an avid bug collector in her youth. Did I mention we still have all those bug collections stored here at the house?

The main male character is always a delight to write. Who doesn't love a handsome cowboy who risks his life to rescue the main female character? One who is justice-oriented? A man of faith who loves his family? Creating a strong main female character is important as well. Not one who can wrestle a gang of men to the ground with one hand behind her back, as Hollywood would lead you to believe, but a strong woman in both faith and ability, who also stands for what is right. She may not be able to karate chop the bad guy, but she's not going to be a victim either.

A funny blooper in this story was an error found in the first round of edits. *A helicopter drowned overhead instead of droned.* Oops!

As always, I am so grateful for you, my reader. Out of all the book choices available, you chose *Unexpected Danger*. Thank you for your loyalty. One last visit to Pronghorn Falls is on tap, this next time in the case of Grayson's story, which will feature newcomer Oaklee. Stay tuned!

Until next time, happy reading!

Blessings,

Penny

Acknowledgments

To my family. Thank you for all of your patience during the late nights for the deadlines and for your continued encouragement. I couldn't do this without you.

To my oldest daughter for assisting me in acting out scenes for the story. Thank you, particularly, for practicing with me the scene where Londyn shut Dustin's hand in the door. I know the neighbors were a bit concerned when we repeatedly tried that one out with a glove. I appreciate your willingness to come alongside me in my strange requests to ensure the escape scenes are feasible. A heads up: I do have something I'll need your help with for *Deadly Secrets* that involves the main female character's attempts at escaping from a scary situation.

To my Penny's Peeps Street Team. Thank you for spreading the word about my books, for always being so willing to read and review my stories, and for your steadfast encouragement and support.

To my beta readers. You are the ones who see my project at its beginning stages. Thank you for all of your wonderful suggestions.

To Gary Ellis, retired law enforcement, for ensuring my police procedures were accurate. I am so appreciative of all the time you spend poring over my manuscripts and providing me with detailed information. I couldn't have written this without your valuable insight.

To Josh Wageman, PhD, DPT, MPAS, who assisted me with Londyn's injuries from the accident. It is such a blessing to have you on speed dial!

To Cathy and Rick Worman for your assistance on some scenes in this book. Rick, your expertise as a retired sheriff was invaluable. Thank you for inspiring the horse theft scene.

To JJ and the others in my Crime Scene Writers group. I appreciate your patience in answering my numerous questions about laws, police procedure, and scenarios. JJ, you are a wealth of knowledge!

To my developmental editor at Mountain Peak Edits & Design. What would I do without your guidance on ensuring plots, characters, and settings are the very best they can be?

To Julie, who allowed me to corner her while we were getting our hair done at the salon. Your insight as a psychologist was so helpful in creating Dustin's narcissism and sociopathic tendencies.

To my readers, may God bless you and guide you as you grow in your walk with Him.

And, most importantly, thank you to my Lord and Savior, Jesus Christ. It is my deepest desire to glorify You with my writing and help bring others to a knowledge of Your saving grace.

About the Author

Penny Zeller is known for her heartfelt stories of faith-filled happily ever afters and her passion to impact lives for Christ through fiction. Her books feature tender romance, steady doses of humor, and memorable characters that stay with you long after the last page.

While she has had a love for writing since childhood, Penny began her adult writing career penning articles for national and regional publications on a wide variety of topics. Today Penny is a multi-published author of over two dozen books and is also a fitness instructor, loves the outdoors, and is a flower gardening addict. In her spare time, she enjoys camping, hiking, kayaking, biking, birdwatching, reading, running, and playing volleyball.

Penny resides with her husband and two daughters in small-town America and loves to connect with her readers at her website at www.pennyzeller.com, her blog, www.pennyzeller.wordpress.com, and her Facebook page at www.facebook.com/pennyzellerbooks where she posts faith, funnies, writing updates, and encouragement. All of her socials can be found at https://linktr.ee/pennyzeller.

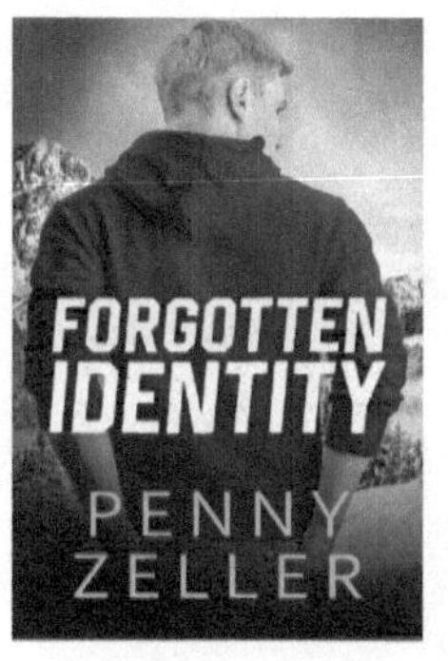

FORGOTTEN
IDENTITY
PENNY
ZELLER

DEADLY
SECRETS
PENNY ZELLER

UNEXPECTED
WITNESS
PENNY ZELLER

UNEXPECTED
DANGER
PENNY ZELLER

UNEXPECTED
TARGET
PENNY ZELLER

PENNY ZELLER
Love in the Headlines

PENNY ZELLER
recipe for love
a christian small town romance

PENNY ZELLER
under the mistletoe
a christian small town romance

PENNY ZELLER
Henry and Evaline

PENNY ZELLER
Love Under Construction

HORIZON SERIES

WYOMING SUNRISE

HOLLOW CREEK

HILLTOP SERIES

PENNY ZELLER
Love
FROM AFAR

PENNY ZELLER
Love
UNFORESEEN

PENNY ZELLER
Love
MOST CERTAIN